little
· IT ·

Dear Little Black Dress Reader,

Thanks for picking up this Little Black Dress book, one of the great new titles from our series of fun, page-turning romance novels. Lucky you — you're about to have a fantastic romantic read that we know you won't be able to put down!

Why don't you make your Little Black Dress experience even better by logging on to

www.littleblackdressbooks.com

where you can:

- ⚥ Enter our **monthly competitions** to win **gorgeous** prizes
- ⚥ Get **hot-off-the-press** news about our latest titles
- ⚥ Read **exclusive** preview chapters both from your **favourite** authors and from brilliant new writing talent
- ⚥ Buy **up-and-coming** books online
- ⚥ Sign up for an essential slice of romance via our **fortnightly email** newsletter

We love nothing more than to curl up and indulge in an addictive romance, and so we're delighted to welcome you into the Little Black Dress club!

With love from,

The *little black dress* team

Five interesting things about Jules Stanbridge:

1. I hold on to the dream that when I find the perfect pair of jeans/shoes and a dog called Bob, my life will be perfect.

2. Three o'clock in the afternoon is hot buttered crumpet, toasted teacake or a slice of cake time. This is non-negotiable.

3. I don't like KitKats, Creme Eggs, vanilla ice cream or the Beatles. This, according to many, means I am a freak and something that should never be revealed on a first date.

4. When I am happy, or thinking about something I shouldn't be, I sing a couple of la, la, la's out loud. It's a dead giveaway to my internal workings and can also, depending on who I am with, act as a warning.

5. I am pretty sure I suffer from a combination of attention deficit disorder and low boredom threshold. This means I am prone to daydreaming, not listening (and then wondering why I don't understand), and falling in and out of love at an alarming rate.

Sugar and Spice

Jules Stanbridge

little
black
dress

Copyright © 2009 Jules Stanbridge

The right of Jules Stanbridge to be identified as the Author of
the Work has been asserted by her in accordance with the
Copyright, Designs and Patents Act 1988.

First published in 2009
by LITTLE BLACK DRESS
An imprint of HEADLINE PUBLISHING GROUP

A LITTLE BLACK DRESS paperback

1

Apart from any use permitted under UK copyright law,
this publication may only be reproduced, stored, or transmitted,
in any form, or by any means, with prior permission in writing
of the publishers or, in the case of reprographic production,
in accordance with the terms of licences issued by the
Copyright Licensing Agency.

All characters in this publication are fictitious and any resemblance
to real persons, living or dead, is purely coincidental.

ISBN 978 0 7553 4712 4

Typeset in Transit511BT by Avon DataSet Ltd,
Bidford-on-Avon, Warwickshire

Printed and bound in Great Britain by
Clays Ltd, St Ives plc

Headline's policy is to use papers that are natural, renewable and
recyclable products and made from wood grown in sustainable forests.
The logging and manufacturing processes are expected to conform to the
environmental regulations of the country of origin.

HEADLINE PUBLISHING GROUP
An Hachette Livre UK Company
338 Euston Road
London NW1 3BH

www.littleblackdressbooks.com
www.headline.co.uk
www.hachettelivre.co.uk

For my family: my inspiration;
every day, in every way

Acknowledgements

Thank you to Jane at Gregory and Co. for taking me on and sticking with me; if she regrets the decision she has been too nice to say so. To the rest of the G & Co. team and LBD for their support. To Anna for picking me up from the horrors of the slush pile. To Emma, for her enthusiasm and editing skills at the beginning. To my mum for her love and for turning me into a domestic goddess (with a little help from Nigella and Delia). To my sister, who despite the demands of three gorgeous blue-eyed boys still manages to find time to make me laugh and mop up my tears. To her husband Rob for putting up with my visits. To my brother and his wife Jane for equal measures of support, wine and food. To TB for everything and more. To Abs, Josie, Ivy, Debs, Vicky, Jon, Kevin, Glenn and Rob for telling me more than once, and believing that I could and should. Ta XXXX (sweet and delicious ones).

Epigraph

'Approach love and cooking with reckless abandonment'
(quote stuck on my fridge – the Dalai Lama said this
and who am I to argue? Although some would say this
has been my downfall!)

'Follow your dreams. Live the life you've imagined'
Henry David Thoreau
(another quote stuck on my fridge)

A photograph of The Princess and The Bear
(also stuck on my fridge)

Recipe

Take one single thirty-one-year-old female
Add one teaspoon of uncertainty and whisk
Add two tablespoons of bad news
One big decision
300 fairy cakes
One smile and a couple of blushes
A handful of memories
One kiss – add more if desired
A sprinkling of jealousy
Gently fold in some hope
Five heaped teaspoons of tears
865 mince pies and two Christmas wishes

Mix all the ingredients together. Bake for 365 days.

Take one single thirty-one-year-old female, add one teaspoon of uncertainty and whisk

It is the afternoon of Friday 9 June and I am making scones. Usually I find baking therapeutic and soothing but today an inner feeling tells me something is wrong. I have nagging pains and although I do not feel ill, I have the feeling that all is not well. I wait for the scones to cook: fifteen minutes go by and the feeling remains. I remove the scones from the oven and put them to cool on a wire rack knowing they will go uneaten because I know, before I go to the toilet, before I go to the hospital, before the doctor confirms it, I am losing my baby.

Two months later, Moo had given birth to The Bear, Freya had given birth to The Princess, and I had fallen apart.

My sister Moo knows this more than anyone. As she feeds her six-month-old son, The Bear, I put the finishing touches to our sister-in-law Freya's birthday cake. It is a Victoria sandwich with a buttercream and jam filling.

Hopefully, the pale pink icing will be expertly drizzled on top and the sugar-frosted rose petals will be applied without mishap. Icing is not my strong point. Give me a wooden spoon and I can beat the hell out of some butter and sugar, but anything that requires long-term concentration and a delicate hand just highlights the point at which the God of all creation got distracted by Reese Witherspoon and left me wanting.

'Are you really okay?' Moo asks.

'I'm okay,' I answer, smiling at her.

'I just worry that Christmas may have been hard for you . . . with the babies and everything.'

'It was fine, stop worrying.'

Her concern weighs heavily. I wish everyone would believe me. It happened, it was horrid, but now it has to be fine.

'It's all good,' I say, and smile.

'Mmmmm . . . So, when do you go back to work?'

'Monday. God, another year just fills me with dread.'

Actually, if I'm truthful, it makes me feel sick to the stomach. My shiny career doesn't quite hold the sparkle it once did and unless I do something about it, I will spend the rest of my days working for people like Jessica North, Vampire Queen of the Home Counties. My January issue of *Red* didn't help. There they are, the women who walked away from the rat race and now make millions from making chilli jam or vintage tablecloths. They are smiling and telling me how they gave it all up and found happiness. Look at my beautiful house with its quirky accessories brought back from trips abroad (style tips over the page), my gorgeous children and stylish friends who are laughing whilst eating balsamic-drenched vegetables from my organic garden (recipes overleaf). God, I hate them! Every New Year I look at these women and I want what they have; except the irritatingly smugly beautiful friends. Every New Year I get the feeling that I have been living someone else's life and some bastard has hijacked mine. Would the real Maddy Brown please step forward? Please! Preferably before she reaches her thirty-second birthday.

'Wouldn't it be lovely to do this for a living?' I muse, adjusting a rose petal.

'What, make cakes?'

'We could have a little bakery like the one in *Sex and the City*, selling fairy cakes and big slices of Victoria sandwich, like Mum used to make,' I say. I am transported back again to Mum's kitchen, flour gently falling on my head like snow while I wait to lick the spoon.

It was the first cake that Mum taught me how to make: soft, fluffy, golden sponge oozing with raspberry jam, the indents of the cooling rack forming lines of caster sugar that would stick to our lips and fingers. She helped me whisk the sugar and butter when my arm got tired, and taught me to be gentle when folding in the flour. Afterwards, Moo and my younger brother Ben would miraculously appear and we would all sit on the kitchen floor with the mixing bowl and argue over the leftover mixture. I soon graduated to the complicated procedure of weighing the ingredients and, by the age of twelve, baking the cake for Sunday tea was my responsibility.

Moo responds with a mmmmm . . .

This is a different mmmmm from the rest. This is a mmmmm based on a delicious memory. Our other mmmmms are frequently used when we are thinking, playing for time or unwilling to say something that will offend or commit to an opinion. Mmmmm is a very useful device, especially when dealing with a sensitive family.

'None of that heavily iced rubbish. Nobody likes the icing anyway.'

'God, no. Anyway, neither of us know how . . . so no icing and all of our cakes would be made to traditional recipes, like marmalade cake or lemon drizzle cake.'

'Banana cake . . .'

'Organic ingredients, no preservatives and handmade. None of this mass-produced rubbish. What was it Mum used to say? The secret ingredient for the perfect cake is a teaspoon of love and kisses.'

'Made with a teaspoon of love and kisses! That could be our tag line; our what do you call it, UPS?'

'USP.'

'We could call ourselves The Three o'clock Bakery.'

'Or Teatime Treats.'

'Sisters are Baking it for Themselves?'

We both dissolve into peals of laughter. Well, when I say peals, I don't mean the delicate Jane Austen kind that our gender would suggest. It's the loud, raucous kind that's frowned upon in restaurants. It's the one thing we have in common; other than that we couldn't be more opposite. Moo has thick, dark brown hair like Mum, but her pale skin, personality and, much to her disappointment, a set of sausage fingers, all come from our father. I got his freckles and the reddish hair, so I think she got off lightly. Moo is exactly like her favourite cake, raspberry, blueberry and lime cake, light and golden, interspersed with jewel-like colours and a zest that kicks ass. She is vivacious, gorgeous and funny with eyes that sparkle with life, a large, expressive mouth, and an honesty that can sometimes appear quite brutal to the uninitiated. Some people are born to shine and my sister is one of them. She lights up the room with her larger-than-life personality and wardrobe to match of vibrant colours, bold, one-off pieces of jewellery and her signature deep-plum lipstick. I, on the other hand, am the quiet one, the one who is always in the kitchen at parties usually wearing something simple and anonymous like a pair of jeans. (I have twelve pairs and profess to being a bit of an aficionado on what makes a good boot cut.) I would like to be more Sienna Miller but whenever I attempt to be, with a colourful scarf thrown nonchalantly around my neck or wearing an embroidered peasant top, it always ends in disaster and I look like a fifty-year-old eccentric let out from the institution for the day.

I have never been good in the life-and-soul-of-the-party department, preferring instead to bask in the glow of those that are. Throughout my life, I have always been drawn to the brilliant stars, probably with the hope that some of their glitter and sparkle would settle on me like fairy dust, and they perversely have been drawn to me, perhaps in the knowledge that I will never outshine them. Moo tells me this is no bad thing. Some people, she says, feel sick after a cream slice, wishing instead they had gone for the marble cake with its mixture of vanilla and chocolate sponge. Why marble cake? You tell me. And why haven't I met a man who likes marble cake? Anyway, as much as I would have liked a little more of my sister's sparkle and confidence, being me hasn't really been a problem. Until now, that is! Now I have a curious yearning to shine like Kylie and shake my arse to the camera. Well, maybe not, but you know what I mean.

The Bear, a big boy with an even bigger appetite, senses a shift in concentration. He is a soft, squidgy doughnut that makes you lick your fingers every time.

From behind he resembles a rugby-playing Pooh Bear, hence the name. He sits there with orange gloopy stuff all around his mouth, up his nose and in his hair, just like a plump baby owl, with white fluffydown on his head and mouth wide open. Moo resumes shovelling. Her top is covered in the remnants of The Bear's lunch and she looks like she needs a good hose down. This is not the sister I am used to. Even her lipstick is missing, which is a little disconcerting; I could have sworn she had it tattooed on. Without it, she looks pale and not like Moo at all. I have a horrid feeling that aliens have robbed me of my sister and replaced her with someone I'm not sure of any more; someone who doesn't wash her hair every day.

'Bringing old-fashioned baking back into people's lives!' Moo declares.

'Perfect for when relatives come round for tea, a gift for a friend . . . delivered to the door; like flowers?' I suggest.

'Wrapped in cellophane with a ribbon and a gift message?'

'In a gift box. You open the box and there it is.'

'Sugar and Spice?'

'I like it!'

'We would have to have a website.'

'In pale pinks, creams and browns.'

'Classy, romantic, with great photos of the cakes.'

'And maybe some recipes?'

We visualise it and sigh.

Interview in *Red* magazine

'So, Maddy, how did you come up with the idea of Sugar and Spice?'

'Well, we commissioned a huge amount of

market research; there was an analysis of current trends, demographics and lots of brainstorming sessions. We really left nothing to chance.'

'You've had quite a year: been voted business-woman of the year, become Chairman of the National Cake Council, the new face of Chanel, and celebrated the opening of your fifth cake shop in New York.'

'Well, it's been hard but I was committed to our vision from the start.'

'You've recently written a book based on your experiences?'

'Yes, and I couldn't believe it when my agent phoned to say it knocked Harry Potter off the best-seller lists this week. It's all very exciting.'

'What an inspiration you are to women every-where.'

'There would have to be a chocolate cake in the range,' I announce, placing Freya's cake carefully in my pastel-blue cake tin.

'Naturally.'

'But what kind?'

The perfect chocolate cake recipe is as elusive as the perfect man. If I could find it, then I am pretty sure the other would follow. It is the holy grail of cakes and my sister and I have been searching for it for years. Not that she needs to. She seems to have done perfectly well without it and has been happily married to Bob for six years.

'Talking of men, we need to find you one.'

'I don't need a man!'

'I don't need chocolate cake, but it doesn't stop me

from wanting another piece. It's been too long, Maddy. You need a big slice of something in your life.'

'Dark, strong, bitter-sweet . . . not too sweet . . . the taste of seduction and comfort . . . of being loved.'

'See, talking like that you definitely need a shag!'

World domination by cake and a double spread in *Red* magazine are forgotten as we make our way to Ben and Freya's. Ben is the baby of the family. He wants to be the eldest but I won't let him and I am hanging on to the position by the skin of my teeth. As time goes by though, I think he may be better qualified for the job. We arrive to find Mum already there. Dad and his second wife, Susan, are thankfully on holiday. The other person missing isBob, Moo's husband, who has remained at home to look after their three dogs, Hamlet, Ophelia and Macbeth, and the six white rabbits that form part of his magic act. That's his excuse, anyway, but we all know it has more to do with a rare opportunity to attend one of his Magic Circle meetings. By day Bob is a maths teacher but every weekend he dons his black suit and silver bow tie to become The Magic Man; available for parties, weddings and bar mitzvahs.

'I've told him, he is not to have any of those people in the house while I'm away,' Moo tells us, shovelling a mushroom vol-au-vent down in one go.

'Why, what's wrong with them?' I ask.

'I don't want middle-aged men who insist on being called The Big Kahuna and who get their wives to dress up in sequinned leotards to be role models for The Bear as he grows up.'

I think of Moo and her Tuesday-night spirit circle but decide not to mention this. It's another thing we don't have in common; talking to dead people.

Ben wanders over carrying his daughter and places a glass of champagne in my hand. Since putting on a few extra pounds, he has become the spitting image of Dad, with thickset features, a wide nose that looks as if it has been fashioned from putty, and broad shoulders. His hair, cut close to his rather large head, is dark, almost black in colour like Mum's and Moo's. He has always maintained that I am adopted.

'Great cake,' he says.

'Thanks,' I reply and kiss the tiny fingers of The Princess. Three weeks younger than The Bear, she is the spitting image of Ben when he was her age, with Pink Lady apple cheeks, a mop of wayward black hair, long eyelashes, and a pretty red rosebud mouth. Today she is dressed in striped pink and lilac leggings, like a fairy cake covered in pink icing and multicoloured sprinkles. A cheeky smile rarely leaves her face, promising a lifetime of mischievousness and a trail of broken hearts. Just like her father.

The talk flows easily as we recount our festive and New Year experiences. Mum seems to hover in the background, playing with the babies and not saying much. Well, she does say one thing, but we all choose to ignore it. Moo was telling Freya how hard she was finding it keeping up with The Bear's demands and Mum piped up with 'He's a man, and the need for food and clearing up after him will never end – then, you take your eyes off him for a minute, and he disappears to find someone who gives him more attention.'

As I said, we ignored it because sometimes it's just not worth getting into. Mum is a lemon cake. The light, fluffy sponge is the caring, nurturing part of her that administers hugs and kind words, but the woman who swears in

French and wants to stick a knife through my father's heart is the tartness of the lemon.

Before she met him, Mum studied and then worked as a hat designer in Paris. Her subsequent fondness for all things French meant that as children we were subjected to subtitled films we didn't understand and croissants for breakfast at the weekend. This particularly annoyed my father who wanted bacon and eggs like any 'normal bloody person'. We were also named accordingly; Ben's real name is Pierre but we have always called him by his middle name, Moo was christened Michelle and I am Madeleine after the shell-shaped cakes the French dip into their tea. Everyone calls me Maddy, although, with a surname like Brown, it was only a matter of time before I was called Muddy Brown at school.

After swapping Yves Saint Laurent and tiny pastries for a Barnsley lad and eating fish fingers, my father left her for Susan, a sales rep who was twenty years his junior. We didn't see him again until six months later. There were no explanations as to his disappearance from Mum, who resolutely refused to discuss it, and when he did eventually reappear with his future new wife in tow, I had convinced myself that he was either dead, or worse: he had left because he didn't love me. He has never contradicted me otherwise.

A bullish self-made man, he has high expectations of us all despite never having attended a parents' evening in his life. Moo and Ben seemed to have satisfied those expectations: Ben as a city financier, now working for the family business, and Moo as founder and artistic director of the youth theatre company, Real Time Theatre. Moo always knew what she wanted to do. Me? I drifted for ages until finally ending up in the marketing department of an international pharmaceutical company. Pedalling drugs, Dad calls it. He thinks he's being funny.

I look at Mum and smile. Maybe that's why Dad and I don't get on: because I serve as a reminder.

I always thought Mum and I were complete opposites, although more and more these days, when I hear myself or catch sight of my reflection in the mirror, I find that the similarities become more obvious as I get older. I share her average-for-a-woman height of five feet four inches, greenish, hazel eyes that, according to one ex-boyfriend, resembled the colour of a muddy river (he was surprised when I got the hump), and those funny arched eyebrows that make me look as if I am constantly surprised. I have also inherited her lack of confidence, quick temper and the need to be reassured that everyone loves me every day. A few years ago, I would have been mortified at such a thought, but now I think it could be worse. She doesn't have a moustache, which is good, but she is shrinking at an alarming rate, which is not so good. But let's face it, in the grand scheme of things, short is always preferable to facial hair. I heard somewhere that after a certain age women lose their pubic hair. Perhaps it just jumps up to their top lip and chin. I make a mental note to ask Mum about it later.

Ben has a vol-au-vent case on his nose and is pretending to be a moose with The Princess and The Bear. He is the picture of contentment with his young family. Freya says that he and Dad clash; so alike physically, but so dissimilar in nature, their two big heads locked together like the stags you see in the mountains. Freya pops another vol-au-vent with the middle scooped out into his mouth. It provides us with the first opportunity to tease him.

The size of his head (he was born with the head he has now) and his weird hang-ups with food have always provided us with a great source of amusement, and both are subjects that do not deserve any mercy. Aside from a long list of no-no's which includes green food, noisy food and garlic within a fifty-mile radius, the most mystifying for me is his love of quiches and the like with the fillings removed, oh, and fried eggs, without the yolk. Freya has worked wonders over the last few years, transforming him from someone who lived on a diet of custard creams, Jammie Dodgers and alcohol, his skin permanently tinged yellow as his liver cried out for something nutritious, to someone who can even eat vegetables. Well, peas anyway, although they are green so I am not quite sure how that works. Freya thinks it's an endearing aspect of his personality. Aaah, the blindness of love. Personally, I think he needs a good slap!

Moo and I dissolve into laughter at Ben's expense as we remember a childhood of finding brussel sprouts in sleeves, pockets and plant pots. We laugh even louder when we are three. Our laughter comes from a shared sense of humour and, usually, at the expense of each other. Those around us become excluded and look on bemused as we tell stories, recall the past and tease each other mercilessly. We are members of the exclusive Sibling Comedy Club where there is a strict door policy (my attempts to impose a dress code have so far been unsuccessful) and a regular happy hour when we laugh at things other people just don't find funny, bouncing off one another until our sides ache.

My brother is very funny with his sharp, droll, sometimes cruel observations on life, especially those that involve us. My sister is funny in a different way; her sense of humour comes from an intrinsic part of her character. Her bubbly nature, her laugh, her quick wit, all combine into a Victoria Wood of sorts. Me? I'm sometimes funny when I'm with them but only because they make me feel funny. Funny by default, I suppose. They are the ones who make me laugh the loudest and it feels good. It feels like me.

The afternoon is a pleasant one and the perfect way to end my extended festive holiday. Time to go home is signalled by another round of nappy changing, tears, bottle sterilising and milk making, which means we all have to be quiet so that Moo and Freya don't lose count of the scoops they need. I stay on the periphery, suddenly feeling awkward with no part to play in this daily ritual. Sensing my unhappiness, Moo hands me The Bear to look after. This is her way of making me feel included, but sometimes it just makes me feel worse. Nuzzle in, close your eyes, and drown in summer pink peonies, soft ripe peaches, cherry blossom, and tiny cupcakes of rose-water sponge with the lightest vanilla buttercream, topped with delicate pale pink rose petals and sprinkled with caster sugar. I feel the familiar constriction in my throat and my eyes fill up with tears. Mum, always sensitive, walks over and squeezes my arm before taking The Bear. I make my goodbyes and find a quiet space where I cannot smell the soft, sweet fragrance of babies.

With a return to work looming, I decide to clear my head and make another Victoria sandwich for the girls in the office. Baking is good for soothing the soul. To say I am dreading going back is an understatement. I turn the mixer to full blast. The thought of returning to the treadmill of a multimillion-pound corporation that barely registers my existence, and dealing with my control freak of a boss brings me back to the question I have been asking myself for the last few months. There must be more to life . . . ? Okay, there is the expense account, my Audi with sports interior in the driveway, the international travel and the salary to buy not one, but two pairs of Manolos; there is that . . . But does it make me happy? Really happy? As I lick the spoon of cake mixture I ponder this question, but I already know the answer. Once upon a time, it did, but that was before the miscarriage, that was before what I am now calling my epiphany. Could I do something else? Could I bake cakes instead of marketing drugs that have had millions of pounds spent on their research and further millions spent on ruthlessly persuading doctors to prescribe them? No, because that would be stupid and my Manolos would look ridiculous with an apron. There must be a health and safety clause about not wearing them in the kitchen anyway, and those hair nets . . . urgh. I turn my attention back to the cake slowly rising in the oven. I love this part: the waiting, the expectation that something beautiful and delicious is about to happen. It is like giving birth every time except without the pain and the prospect of pooing in front of your loved one.

With the cake cooling I plump up the cream fluffy cushions that complement my beige sofa, light some co-ordinating candles and settle down to the *Strictly Come Dancing* results with a glass of wine. I have developed a little crush on the *Blue Peter* presenter and he looks particularly good in lycra and sequins, which is not something you can say that often about a man. When I moved in I had a trendy New York loft/*Sex and the City*-type interior in mind, but in reality, I suspect it looks more like an IKEA showroom. No matter, it's mine and it looks good through a wine-induced glow.

The usual forty-minute journey to the outskirts of Oxford takes longer than normal and I panic as I run in nearly twenty minutes late. Thankfully, my boss Jessica is nowhere to be seen and I slip into the Primary Care Sales and Marketing department of Pharmagenica International almost unnoticed. Everyone is finding it hard to get back into the swing of things after the Christmas break. Nursing double-shot Americanos, the talk is of Christmas, exploits over the New Year and resolutions of losing twenty pounds in three months by eating two bowls of cereal a day. As project manager for a new arthritic drug that will soon be launched on to the market, I should find it an exciting time, but, with my files in front of me and a screen full of emails, I cannot summon up the passion and drive I once felt. The adrenalin high that once upon a time accompanied the sign-off deadlines, the training of the sales reps and the presentations to the board (although that is more akin to terror than adrenalin) has gone. As everyone orders another coffee, I nervously produce my cake tin. The oohs, aahs and general surprise that I have been responsible for making something so melt-in-the-mouth, so delicious and so wonderful causes me to blush and my heart fills ready to burst with pride.

The chatter and laughter is short-lived as Jessica emerges from her office. It is as if the oxygen has been cut off from the room. Everyone holds their breath and looks down for fear of eye contact, praying that today they are not the target of her impossible deadlines. She is like a vampire, sucking the life-blood of everyone who encounters her and using it as her own.

'Maddy, I need those projections by eleven,' she barks at me.

'Did you have a nice Christmas?' I ask and she is momentarily taken aback.

'Yes . . . thank you,' she replies suspiciously. With her expertly layered, shoulder-length black hair, the whitest skin I have ever seen, razor-sharp cheekbones and narrow black slits that pass for eyes, I always feel the urge to put my hands over my neck when she comes close.

'I'm still waiting for the data from the Medical team to come through, so eleven might be a bit ambitious,' I reply as non-confrontationally as I can.

'Have you spoken to them today?'

'Er, no.' I have been here barely twenty minutes after the festive break! What is the matter with the woman?

'By eleven.' She looks at me for a moment, daring me to answer and my coffee freezes over. Suddenly her mouth breaks into a smile and I look around feeling a little unnerved. The reason appears at my desk: tall, dark and smelling of expensive cologne.

'Morning, ladies,' Don Truro, the head of Communication, says, beaming.

'Don. What a lovely surprise,' Jessica gushes.

Liar, Liar, pants on fire! Jessica hates surprises.

'Good Christmas?' she simpers and I want to vomit.

'Good, good. Always nice to be back, though? Aah, Maddy, just the girl I want to speak to. I need your feedback on the results of the Phase Four that came in before Christmas.' Don is his usual energetic self, barely taking a breath between each thought process. I open my mouth to speak, but Jessica is there like a terrier down a rabbit hole.

'Don, I can fill you in. The results are in my office.' She indicates for him to follow her and I am left gaping as they walk off. I spent hours on that! I worked until six on Christmas Eve on that sodding feedback! Bitch! As I look at everyone with their heads down and brows furrowed, I get an urge to swipe all my paperwork to one side, stand up on my desk and shout out: 'Bollocks to this!'

I don't, because the worry that Jessica would push me off without a backward glance is a real one, so instead I click through the mountain of emails that all seem to have that annoying little red priority exclamation mark next to them.

The week doesn't get any better and by the weekend I am as stressed as I was before the Christmas break. With tea and toast I ponder alternatives as I sit at the desk in my spare bedroom-cum-office. Spurred on by the thought of chocolate cake, or as Moo so eloquently put it, a shag, I flick through my recipe books and vast collection of saved magazine cut-outs for a recipe to try. I am obsessive about ripping pages out of magazines: articles about travel, recipes, gift ideas; I have files for them all. I just know that one day I will need that important information regarding the hottest hotel in Barcelona or those chocolate shoes that will make the perfect gift for someone.

Not only do I have a perfect view of my own tiny garden but also the garden of the house across the road. And there he is, Edmund. I don't know what his real name is but he reminds me of Blackadder, with his spindly thin, pale body, rather large head and prominent features. Every morning Edmund chops wood in his underpants. I don't know why, but he does. He chops away, sometimes stopping to hike up the underpants that match his body – grey and slightly baggy – until his four-foot-nothing and at least sixteen-stone wife comes out in her floor-length quilted dressing gown and drags him back in.

The doorbell rings and I drag myself away from Edmund – he must be freezing! I answer the door and James, my soon-to-be-ex-husband, walks in, followed obediently by our dog, Frog. James is going away with six friends on a stag weekend somewhere in Manchester and Frog is staying with me. Heaven help Manchester. Heaven help me! Frog is a Staffordshire bull terrier and so named because he looks like a frog when he lies down with his back legs splayed out behind him. Brindle coloured with a little white-bibbed chest and an increasing amount of grey around his whiskers, Frog is one of the links that bind James and me, despite having been separated for what seems an eternity. We met at a mutual friend's twenty-first birthday party. He was the only one who wasn't in fancy dress and I remember thinking that I had to have him and knowing I would. Oh the certainty of youth! James is a farmhouse fruit cake, light and golden in colour, with a smattering of plump sultanas, raisins and cherries and a delicious crunchy sugar topping. The sort of cake that is perfect for a cup of tea with your grandma and, like all good fruit cakes, James has got better with age. With hair the colour of demerara sugar and skin the colour of caramel from working outside, the extra weight and muscle he has gained over the years suits him. I honestly thought we would stay together for ever, but somewhere along the way we changed and evolved into friends. Like my parents, I had failed to make my marriage work and that pissed me off more than anything; it also meant starting all over again without someone holding my hand. Now, in between a succession of blondes that appear in his life, James comes round for something to eat, sometimes we go out for a meal or settle down to watch a DVD. Like friends and family, we have stopped trying to understand our relationship and have just accepted that this is the way it is. Perhaps it will always be this way and at ninety we will be sharing puréed food and saving each other a seat in front of the TV in the old people's home. There has only been one little glitch in this otherwise perfect separation and the following morning we agreed it was a one-off and best forgotten, not knowing that the forces of nature had other plans for us.

'You be good for your mum.' James strokes the top of Frog's head and Frog replies that he will in a voice that sounds remarkably like James but a little more high pitched.

With a perfunctory kiss, James heads off, leaving me and the Frog alone to begin our usual battle of wills. Despite now being ninety-one years of age in dog years, deaf, almost blind and with rheumatism in his back legs, which means he sways rather than walks, the urge to stick two fingers up at me while doing something I have told him not to has unfortunately never left him. He sniffs around, whines for twenty minutes, pees in the kitchen and then, bored, insists on dragging various knickers from the dirty washing bag around the house. I win the fight to get them back, although some of my prettiest, tiniest knickers are now ripped. Round one to Frog. A long drawn-out walk uses up his energy and I leave him snuggled up on a blanket by the radiator, snoring loudly. I, on the other hand, have some therapeutic shopping to do with my friend Lou. I have found that buying something I don't need makes me feel better about wasting my life away working for someone like Jessica.

I stare into my cappucino and listen to Lou's plans for 'getting me out there'. Urgh, just the phrase makes my blood run cold.

'You can't wait for someone to just turn up, Maddy,' she says, and I wonder why not.

'I am actually quite happy without a man.' Which is one of those truth/lie things that anyone who knows me well enough chooses to ignore. I believe it most of the time, but sometimes, yes, I admit, I do have a little fantasy about falling in love with someone kind, funny, tall and delicious ... my perfect chocolate cake. If I'm honest, though, I don't know what I would do if someone came along. I can't remember the last time I went on a date. No, that's a lie. I can, but I would rather forget it, so it doesn't count. I certainly can't imagine ever falling in love again. My success in the romance department leaves a lot to be desired, and as much as I hold on to the belief that the fairy-tale happy ending I cry over in films really does exist, it seems to have eluded me so far. At some point in the past year I have filed the L word away in a file marked 'Archive' and the S word is in a dust-covered file marked 'Forgotten what it's like'.

Lou has been my friend for nearly twenty years, which, when I think about it, is a miracle, because we have absolutely nothing in common. Don't they say opposites attract? I don't know what it is, but I do know that my life would be dull without the bling effect she brings to it. She is glamour personified, our very own local Posh: always immaculately dressed in up-to-the-minute trends, beautifully French-manicured nails, with a diamond the size of Asia on her finger. Unlike Posh, though, her long glossy brunette locks, with carefully added golden highlights, are her own and not some Russian peasant's, and she doesn't mind admitting that her magnificent breasts are a miracle of modern cosmetic surgery. She is a real Black Forest Gateau of a girl: rich, gorgeously extravagant and absolutely delicious.

When I first met Lou, I was more than a little in awe of her. She seemed so confident and grown up compared to anyone else I knew at university, and as I tried to blend into the background she walked around as if she owned the place. Everyone was in love with her, including the tutors, but a mutual passion for Blondie meant we became the most unlikely of friends. A marketing manager for a national brewery company that specialises in trendy bars, Lou is still a force to be reckoned with and not one to mince her words.

'I have to be brutal though, sweetie, we really need to improve the packaging. You need to get your nails done, buy a push up bra and get some cleavage on show.' She demonstrates by pushing her own lovelies up. The chap next to us cannot believe his luck and nearly chokes on his coffee. The thought of getting my non-existent cleavage out on show fills me with horror.

'Okay, let's not waste any time. I'm having a little dinner party on the fourteenth of next month and I think you should come.'

'I think I have something on then,' I respond in a panic, wondering what she has up her sleeve.

'What are you doing?' Lou immediately fires back at me because we both know I'm not doing anything.

'Oh, I don't know, Lou; I have a thousand things to do.'

'Like what?' Her mind is already working overtime and she taps into her phone. 'Look, it will be a group of nice, harmless, friendly people, and there is someone I want you to meet. He is single, friendly, quite good-looking. In fact, he is just your type.' Lou bites into the almond croissant we are sharing. She is the only person I know who doesn't get a flake of pastry or icing sugar stuck on her lip. I inwardly groan, the words 'he is just your type' ringing in my ears. This is always a recipe for disaster and, although my experience is limited, I have always found that friends and family are not to be trusted with this kind of decision, because in reality their idea of what my type should be is very different to mine.

'Darling, can you phone Dave and make sure he is definitely coming on the fourteenth, and we need an extra chair, and remember to order those white lilies. Not the ones with the pink bits, the trumpet ones.' Lou snaps her phone shut and turns to me, smiling.

'So that's settled then,' she confirms more to herself than me, and I find myself nodding.

Friday Night with Jonathan Ross

'So, Maddy, why is a gorgeous successful woman like you single?'

'Ah, that's a good question. I guess I'm just too busy right now. I never have time to go out on dates.'

'But you have been linked with a number of eligible men including Robert Downey Jnr, Robbie Williams and George Clooney?'

'Oh, Jonathan, you should know better than to believe everything you read in the papers,' I tell him, but as always he is not to be swayed.

'So what of the latest rumours of you and George? Come on, you can tell me,' he laughs.

'George and I are just very good friends.' I smile enigmatically.

With a Benefit Hollywood Glo to give me a bit of colour, a new pair of jeans (I know!) and a black wraparound dress Lou persuaded me to buy, and not wear over my jeans (spoilsport), I head back home to a Saturday evening spent with a smelly dog.

The next day I try the first of my perfect chocolate cake recipes. Chocolate loaf cake is a recipe that uses boiling water, which seems a bit strange, but I go with it anyway. Me and the Frog are soon waiting in anticipation of its loveliness as it bakes away in the oven.

Waiting for a cake to cool down has to be one of the hardest things to do and I'm not sure who is dribbling the most. It's the moment when delicious aromas of still-warm ingredients fill the air. After twenty minutes I'm so hungry I want to eat my own arm and I cut the first slice. Still warm, it falls away in my hand. Not bad; it's nice and moist, which is always good for a chocolate cake but, disappointingly, it's not that chocolatey and just a little too dense for my liking. Nope, this is not the one and I cross it off my list.

'Sorry, Mr Loaf, but the panel have decided that it's not you that will go through to the next round.'

'But I can also be a great alternative to sponge fingers in a trifle.'

'Sorry, no.'

'But, but—'

'Security, would you kindly remove this loaf.'

Frog, however, has no such reservations and doesn't

even notice when James arrives back. He is looking a little worse for wear. I make some restorative pasta to soak some of the alcohol up and we spend the evening watching a DVD. After we both cry at the ending he takes Frog home and I get ready for work tomorrow. The familiar dread returns even before I have gone to bed.

After an early morning meeting at an ad agency, I arrive back at the office mid morning to a room full of miserable people. I wonder what path of destruction the Vampire Queen has taken today. I ask Donna what the problem is and it seems the rumours of redundancies that have plagued the offices of Pharmagenica for the last six months have finally turned into reality. I hadn't really taken any notice; talk of takeovers and redundancies are all par for the course of working in the pharmaceutical industry.

'But our department is okay,' I tell her.

'Apparently not. Chris has already been told he is going.' Donna looks as if she is about to cry. I attempt to reassure her that with the product launch only weeks away we will be safe.

'They can't get rid of us now,' I tell her as I check my emails. There is one from Jessica asking me to see her in her office at 3.30 p.m. Oh God, what does she want now? A change of strap line? The latest marketing analysis I have promised to have on her desk by the end of the day? To make me redundant? No, that's one thing I know she won't do; she needs me for this launch, and I have been working on it since the beginning.

'Of course, we shall be sorry to lose you,' June from HR says as Jessica nods in agreement. I stare at her in amazement, but her look of concern remains like her foundation: expertly applied and not shifting for anything.

So how wrong can you be? It is 4.05 p.m., and I am out of a job. I still cannot quite believe it. Near to tears, I switch off my computer and pick up my bag, trying to avoid the pitying looks from my fellow workers. The pharmaceutical business is a paranoid one and fears that I may pass confidential launch strategies and study results to competitors means I don't even get to work a notice; I am not even allowed to tidy up my emails or files. I remove the rotting banana from my top drawer and then put it back again in a vain attempt at revenge. Donna attempts to console me and I reassure her I'm okay, although she and everyone else can see I'm clearly not as I stumble out towards my soon-to-be-taken-away car. I don't remember the drive home and suddenly find myself standing in the middle of my living room feeling lost. What the hell happened? I try to erase the sight of Jessica's attempts to look sad and concerned for the benefit of June. Unavoidable, a valuable member of the team, essential streamlining, an impossible choice, a good reference, redundancy; the words are jumbled and I try to make sense of them as they float in and out of view.

'I'm sure you understand, Maddy,' Jessica had said, closing a file on her desk with a snap. 'Oh, and before you go, can you just email me those Cliquo files.'

I nodded, because the power of speech had been removed along with my security pass. This is not how it was meant to be, I wasn't ready to leave. Okay, I haven't enjoyed it over the past year, but I wasn't ready, not yet. I feel cheated; my moment of sticking two fingers up at Jessica as I handed in my resignation for a better job or a fantasy life making millions from cakes has now been taken away.

I can't quite believe that I'm out of a job. I deal with it

by pouring myself a large glass of wine, and cleaning the bathroom, because I don't know what else to do. Having not eaten all day, the wine goes straight to my head and I end up crying my eyes out and phoning everyone in a drunken state. They are all sympathetic, saying things like, 'It could be the best thing that has happened to you', to which I want to respond, 'Yeah, right, tell that to my mortgage company.' Mum offers to travel down to be with me and it takes all of my strength to say no. Ben promises not to tell Dad (I don't know why this is important, but it is) and invites me round to tea which I decline. Instead, I polish off the bottle of wine, eat a giant bag of Doritos, a bag of Maltesers and some chocolate ice cream.

The next morning I wake up with the king of hangovers. I gingerly pick up the phone, knowing that any sudden movement may tip me over the edge. I consider phoning in sick, and then I remember. I have nowhere to go. With a thumping head and waves of sickness, I spend the day watching myriad dreadful chat shows, daytime soaps and children's TV. I am now one of the million or so unemployed and I still can't quite believe it. Surely I will wake up soon and realise it's all been a horrible nightmare. Moo phones me to check that I am okay.

'Maddy, I know you feel like shit at the moment but try and think of all this as something positive.'

'How can losing my job be perceived as something positive?' I ask, sniffling away.

'Because maybe it's a sign that now is the time to create a new future for yourself. Sometimes we all need a push to do that and your push has come now. Didn't you say that you're getting some redundancy money?'

'Yes,' I mumble, curling a strand of hair round and round my fingers.

'Well, what about the cake business? What about Sugar and Spice? You often hear of successful businesses coming into fruition following redundancy,' Moo says enthusiastically. 'You've been saying for long enough that you were at a crossroads. Well, now is your chance to take the road that goes the opposite way. Maybe now is the time for us to actually do it.'

'Are you being serious?'

'Yeah. I think I am. Let's go for it.'

'What, you and me starting our own business?' I ask, laughing for the first time all day.

'Why not? Obviously, with me still working, I won't be able to commit one hundred per cent, but between the two of us I'm sure we could do something. Come on, Maddy, you have always talked about doing something like this.'

'But I wouldn't know where to start.'

'Well, without sounding harsh, you have two months on full pay to get your arse in gear and find out! Bear, say hello to Auntie Maddy.'

I sing hello down the phone. A snuffling noise and heavy breathing followed by crying is my reward and the sound of Moo laughing.

'His nose was running and now it's all over the phone,' she tells me. 'I have to go. As you can hear, he's now crying for no apparent reason at all. Love you, and think about what I've said. Ring me if you need me. Byeee.'

The next few days I wander aimlessly around the house, watch rubbish TV and spend money I'm not earning any more. Knowing I have to do something, I look through job websites but the thought of returning to something similar just depresses me further. Do I really want to do the same thing until I am too old to do anything else, and if not, what? Bake cakes? The prospect seems ridiculous and I send my CV through to agencies with a heavy heart. As I search through the Internet for something to ignite a sense of passion I find myself checking to see if the name Sugar and Spice has been registered. It hasn't, and for some ludicrous reason I register it under my name. More and more, as Lorraine Kelly chortles on about something and nothing, I find my mind wandering towards cakes and wondering how an ex-product manager for pharmaceuticals would market a sponge cake.

On the fifth day of being unemployed I am lying awake in the early hours of the morning, as has become my habit. I lie there and think about what Moo said. Do I want to get another job and continue on the treadmill, or do I want to take hold of my dream with both hands and see what happens? Should I suck it and see? I have a little redundancy money to keep me going for a while, and perhaps everyone is right and this is the best thing that could have happened to me.

I pull the covers tightly round me, and snuggle down like a little animal. I feel a calmness drift over me and sleep is not far behind. I dream of icing-sugar clouds, sticky fingers, anticipation, warm, enveloping, comforting. Melt-in-the-mouth, golden, light, dark, fluffy, dense, bitter, heavenly, luscious, scrumptious, pure, unadulterated pleasure, and laughter, sweet and delicious.

The next morning I wake up and feel a fluttering in the pit of my stomach. It is different from the big, black butterflies that have been there for the past few months, feeding from my fear and disappointment. These are different, a gentle fluttering with the most delicate of light blue wings; like someone tickling the palm of your hand.

It feels nice. I stand in front of the mirror and immediately wish I hadn't. Someone grey and tired stares back at me but I choose to ignore her.

Stand up straight.

Okay.

I am me, and I am wonderful.

I have the power within me.

I can do this.

I will be successful.

People love my cakes.

I think.

Is that cellulite?

I phone Moo. 'You're right. Let's do it!'

'What?' Moo asks.

'Sugar and Spice!'

'Hurray. That's fabulous news. So where do we start?'

'Well, I've registered the name but apart from that, I have no idea!' I respond, laughing.

'Sugar and Spice dot com. It sounds good. So, when we have made our first million I can open the first of my performing arts schools for underprivileged children,' she says.

'Wow! I was thinking more of buying a Malibu beach-front home next door to Brad Pitt,' I respond. 'But I would donate to Children in Need,' I add, feeling guilty and thinking that I really should do that anyway. This year I will.

'But until then we carry on with our careers and build it up gradually.'

Deep down I don't think either of us really believes that it will actually come to anything. I mean, let's face it, we would be mad to start a business baking cakes. Wouldn't we?

*

I attempt to search the Internet for information on setting up your own business. I trawl through information, clicking on anything that is associated with starting up your own business, absorbing it all until my eyes are sore. I am amazed and more than a little scared by everything I need to consider before our business can begin in earnest: things like registering the company, setting up payment procedures, insurance, health and safety, food hygiene and company stationery. Baking the cakes, it would seem, is going to be the easy part.

First things first, though; I need to get my food hygiene certificate and I enrol on a course. It turns out to be as boring as I thought it might be and I spend the day trying to summon up some enthusiasm for spores, bacteria and anti-bacterial wipes. As with most courses it could have been condensed into a morning and by three o'clock I'm thinking about whether Gordon Ramsay would cook a better cake than me on *The F Word* instead of listening to Brenda talk about rotten eggs. There is a little exam at the end that asks questions like 'What would you do if you had a mouse?' Call it Mickey and tell him he will have to go and play somewhere else? I suddenly worry that I might not pass.

The weather is bleak and cold, the evenings are dark and there is nothing to look forward to except the promise of warmer days, when the sun streams through your bedroom window and it doesn't take heavy-lifting equipment to get you out of bed. I don't mind though, because I feel as if I'm in my own little secret world that's warm and full of golden sponge. I pore over recipes, research packaging companies and look into approaching a bank about a business loan or overdraft to get things going. Moo and I spend what seems like hours on the phone talking about predictions, markets, costs, percentages and prospective cake recipes. Every now and then, the old fears return and I wonder if I really am living in la la land. It's all well and good making the odd cake for family and friends but to actually think about baking in quantities of more than two at a time, and then selling them to people, is another thing altogether. My habit of asking if the cake is okay at least fifteen times will have to be curbed. I can't imagine it will instil too much confidence in customers if I phone them with a barrage of: 'No, but is it really okay?' 'Are you sure I didn't use too much butter?' 'You don't have to say you like it if you don't. I won't be offended.'

A week later, Donna and the rest of the team have arranged a leaving lunch at the local pub. They are all enthusiastic and positive about my tentative plans and I want to hug everyone, cry, and generally make an emotional nuisance of myself.

'And these are for you.' Donna hands me a bouquet of flowers.

'Oh, how lovely,' I gush, and stick my nose into the middle of the arrangement. 'And they smell gorgeous, and oh, yellow roses are my favourite. Thank you, thank you. You are all so special and I am going to miss you. No, really I am.'

Everyone looks blankly at me, slightly embarrassed by my over-the-top, Gwyneth Paltrow at the Oscars moment. I react as I always do – by blushing.

What is it about me and blushing? I'm thirty-one, for heaven's sake, not fifteen! Whenever it happens, I cover my face with my hands so that nobody can see, but it really only makes matters worse and people end up just standing around embarrassed whilst I talk behind my hands.

Donna gives me a warm hug.

'I'm really going to miss you,' she says. 'But I think you're better off out of it.'

I nod, and agree that it is going to be fabulous. Waving frantically I say goodbye to my career-driven colleagues with their ever-increasing emails, the unmanageable to-do lists, the obligatory late nights in the office and the Vampire Queen who is thankfully nowhere to be seen, before heading out into the wide, unstable world that awaits me.

Later at home, the higher plane I'm on shakes a little and then completely gives way.

I'm scared.

What if I don't even sell ONE cake?

Interview in *Red* magazine

'Maddy, you are famous for battling against the odds and a multimillion-pound slimming industry to persuade us all to eat cake and your second book has recently been published about your experiences. Were you always so confident that you would be successful?'

'Well, there were a few doubts at the beginning but I can honestly say that I always had a belief that I could do it.'

'But you gave up a successful career to follow a dream many said wouldn't work ... Most people would find that quite daunting.'

'Yes, but whenever I had doubts I knew the alternative was something I couldn't go back to. Look fear in the eyes and then tell her to bugger off.'

This would be edited out later.

I have to rush off quickly after the photo shot of me and Frog playing ball in my spring-flower-filled garden. The same flowers that produce the ingredient for my skin-care range. Did I not mention that? Anyway, Virgin is having a tough time and I promised I would help Richard out. Damn, I will have to ring and cancel lunch with Manolo. As his new muse, I am the inspiration for his new range of sexy shoes. He will be so upset.

VICTORIA SANDWICH

Simple to make and absolutely delicious. So, get your food processor out and forget those horrid little things in the supermarkets.

Ingredients

225g (9oz) unsalted butter   225g (9oz) caster sugar

1 teaspoon vanilla extract   4 large eggs

225g (9oz) self-raising flour   3–4 tablespoons milk

1 teaspoon baking powder

(if using the processor method)

Method

Grease and line 2 × 18cm (7 inch) tins and preheat oven to 180°C/350°F/gas mark 4. Put all ingredients in food processor except the milk and process until you get a smooth batter. Pour the milk in gradually through the funnel until the mixture has soft dropping consistency. Pour into tins and bake for approximately 25 minutes or until the cakes are coming away at the edges or springy to touch. Leave in tins on wire rack for 10 minutes before turning out to cool completely. Spread lashings of jam in the middle and a sprinkle of caster sugar on the top. Mmmmm, delicious.

Add two tablespoons of bad news

I sit and wait impatiently in an absurdly low chair, designed to make me feel small and inferior. Today I am seeing someone about a bank loan and wearing my best suit, the one with the pinstripes, and, carrying a folder, I look and feel as if I am going for a job interview. With The Bear not very well, Moo has had to stay at home and without her I feel really nervous. I take a deep breath and try to summon up the 'I am gorgeous' and 'today is my day' positive feelings I'm still working on and hum. Humming is something I do when I want to drown out negative thoughts. It's like turning the music up really loudly. I gaze at the posters on the wall that promise people like me the world, or at least a hassle-free loan from a customer-friendly bank.

'Miss Brown, sorry for the wait. Would you like to follow me?' a young girl without a smile says, and walks away. I struggle to get out of the chair and hurry after her. We sit in a sterile cubicle with a plastic plant and she hands me her business card. It tells me she has a degree in business studies and I presume the letters after her name are meant to reassure me that she knows what she is talking about, that she will have at her fingertips everything I need to know about cash-flow forecasts and percentages. I soon discover that if she does have the information, she is keeping it, and any enthusiasm she may feel, very close to her chest. As if she has seen it all before, she flicks through my business plan without reading a line. I want to shake her violently. Doesn't she know how many hours I have spent doing this, or perhaps more importantly, how dangerous I am without my morning carbohydrate fix?

She looks at me and my anger is quickly disguised with a hopeful smile, but Miss MBA clearly doesn't care about me, or my business plan. She looks at the clock on the wall; it is nearly time for lunch, and I can tell she is planning her trip to the sandwich department at M & S. Shuffling the pages of my business plan together, she pushes them across the table.

'What a quaint idea. Unfortunately, Miss Brown, nothing can be done at this point without proof of ID from Moo,' she says, and a smile is still not forthcoming. Why didn't she tell me this over the phone before I put on my best suit and came all this way? Clearly, the only decision that will be made today is whether to go for a tuna or a chicken sandwich.

As I get up to leave, the smile she eventually gives me is like weak tea. Miss MBA obviously doesn't realise how close she is to having a plastic Yam Yam tree rammed down her throat. I leave feeling disappointed and despondent and, with my bottom lip dragging on the floor, I make my way over to Lou's favourite place in the whole world.

Bicester Shopping Village is a designer discount

heaven and I have arranged to meet her for lunch at her other favourite place, Pret a Manger. Over a crayfish sandwich we discuss her so far unsuccessful search for the perfect pair of shoes for a friend's wedding, and the mystery of my suddenly very itchy skin. We conclude I've developed either an allergy or fleas. God, what if it's the latter? How do you tell a new man in your life that particular gem? We can't sleep together darling, because I have a teeny weenie flea problem. Maybe I've developed an allergy to flour.

I absent-mindedly scratch my back. It's the weather, it's your soap powder, it's stress; the suggestions are end-less, but whatever the reason, it's driving me to distraction.

'You need to get rid of the itching before the dinner party. It's not attractive,' Lou instructs and looks at me as if she has just scraped me off her boots. We hug and she totters off in a pair of fabulously high heels that the rest of us mere mortals would last two minutes in. Even when she was heavily pregnant with her little girl Chloe, she insisted on wearing heels. In fact, thinking about it, I don't think I have ever seen her in flat shoes. Not the most practical of women to be with but definitely the most fun. I watch her go and marvel along with all the other women she passes, a grudging admiration on their faces.

I pop into the local chemist's in search of the cream Lou suggested might help. I scour the shelves but with no luck and eventually ask the woman behind the desk for Canesten for babies. She gives me a blank look.

'Sorry, love, I'm new and I've never heard of it.'

'It's for itchy skin. My friend recommended it,' I explain, but her subsequent search through the skin-cream shelf draws a blank. By this time, a queue has formed behind me and I can hear tutting noises. The woman eventually calls for the pharmacist. He comes halfway down the stairs, clearly irritated at being disturbed from his more important task of counting pills. Leaning over from his vantage point on the stairs he asks what I want Canesten for. I repeat what I have just told his colleague: that I have an itch and I have been recommended Canesten for babies cream.

'Canesten is for feminine itches,' he informs me in what should have been a whisper but, alas, wasn't.

'No, no, it's not that kind of itch,' I stutter and begin to blush. I just know that everyone behind me is thinking, 'Oh yeah.'

'Well, what kind of itch is it?' he asks, 'because Canesten is usually used for thrush.'

He says THRUSH as if in capital letters, the TH and the SH emphasised for all to hear, echoing around the now strangely silent chemist's and drifting out on to the high street. I want to die of shame. With my face as red as a beetroot and a cold film of sweat running down my back, I make my excuses and practically run out, leaving at least six burly builders looking down at their shoes as I pass.

I call Lou. After she has finished laughing, she tells me it was Sudocrem for babies I should have asked for. I decide to put up with the itching for now.

A few days later, I return to the bank armed with a signature, proof of ID from Moo and a sulk on. It's Valentine's Day and the lack of a card so far has made me feel unloved and a little depressed. I was hoping some mystery admirer might proclaim his undying love or at least a little something from James, but nothing; zilch, a big fat zero has appeared. I hope that Miss MBA will be nice to me, because today, if I can't have love, I at least want nice. Unfortunately she has not had an enthusiasm transplant since our last meeting and flicks through my business plan in a non-committal 'why do I have to deal with these stupid morons who think they can just start a business when they clearly have no idea' way.

'You need to fill in your cash-flow forecast,' she says flatly.

'Yes, I was hoping we could talk about that. You see, I'm not very good with numbers and I wondered if you could help me. It all looks like gobbledygook to me,' I reply, laughing in a 'silly me' fashion that is supposed to make her feel empathy towards me. It doesn't even warrant a smile from her pursed, Chanel-covered lips. I consider going for the no Valentine sympathy vote but the bunch of red roses on her desk lead me to believe that this will only make her feel more superior. Can you hate someone you barely know?

'It's quite simple,' she informs me.

So is rocket science to a rocket scientist, I want to say, before punching her.

It's two o'clock in the morning, the numbers in front of me are blurring and my calculations are not making sense. I give up. The perfect end to a shitty day.

I decide to go and stay with Moo for the weekend because a) I'm bored of my own company, b) I'm depressed that I must be the only person in the world who didn't get a Valentine's card, c) we need to talk about the business and d) she has made the mistake of inviting me.

Moo lives two and a half hours away in Suffolk, but the drive is worth it, and if I leave early in the morning, it is positively pleasurable. The roads are empty and I look set to break Moo's land-speed record of two hours. I sing at the top of my voice as the morning sun rises, and briefly covers everything with a golden glow, creating an Indian Sari landscape, before disappearing again to leave us with a cold and grey February day. I push my lovely Audi, courtesy of Pharmagenica who still haven't taken it back, into warp speed. One hour and fifty minutes later I turn into the small village they have made their home. I spot Bob pushing The Bear in his pram and pull over to say hi. With his nose red from the cold, large blue gloved hands and rather alarmingly bright yellow beanie hat he looks a little like a clown.

'Did you wet the bed?' he asks, the cold air pouring like smoke from his mouth.

'Morning, Bob,' I reply, ignoring his obscure Stoke humour.

'You're a bit on the early side,' he says, looking at his watch. The wife won't be best pleased. We had a heavy night with The Bear and slept in late. I've left her hoovering in a panic,' he informs me as The Bear sucks on a biscuit. The conversation clearly over, Bob begins to walk away.

'What shall I do?' I ask after him.

'Drive round the block a few times,' he calls out without looking around.

So I do, but my desperation for a cup of tea overrides the fear of Moo in a bad mood and I only manage to stave off my arrival for a further twenty minutes.

Moo is indeed in a panic and looks near to tears. 'I haven't had a chance to do the housework all week. In fact, it's a miracle I got through this week at all. Yesterday I fell asleep whilst sitting on the loo at work,' she tells me, shaking her head in disbelief. She looks pale and tired.

I hug her and put the kettle on, then raid the bread bin to make some much needed toast. Bob arrives a little while later and makes a 'what took you so long' joke. I wasn't going to say anything but Moo prises it out of us and Bob is told off. She sends him off to clear the dog mess from the garden, which I feel is a little harsh in the circumstances; it has started to rain and we all know what happens to dog poo when it rains. I cuddle The Bear, shifting his huge weight from one hip to another.

'Is everything okay?' I ask, trying to reach for my slice of toast.

'No!' Moo exclaims, grabbing it before I do and ripping bites from it as if she is a prehistoric cave dweller devouring a chicken leg.

'What's wrong?' I ask, watching my toast disappear.

'I'll show you what's wrong,' she spits, storming out of the room. She comes back with a huge ceramic cow and places it heavily on the table.

'Nice,' I comment, my mind working overtime on ways to get to the toaster and make another slice of toast with one hand.

'My Valentine present!' she says angrily and, before I can answer, she launches into an angry and tearful rant: 'What does he think I am? A big fat cow? Is that what he thinks?'

I don't know what to say. It is, as she says, a big fat cow.

Bob walks in looking cold and wet. He takes off his Wellington boots and hat and blows his nose noisily.

'I see she's shown you the cow.'

Take him at face value and Bob seems like a regular guy. Not bad looking, average height and build, mousy brown hair that has been shaved close to his head before it disappears altogether and unremarkable but kind brown eyes. Bob is a seed cake, a seemingly plain and unassuming variety that resembles a Madeira cake. The surprise comes when you look a little closer and bite into it. The addition of caraway seeds make it an altogether different flavour to the one you expected and Bob's droll humour and the ability to make people laugh transforms him from one you might forget to a 'there is something about him'. A bit like Eddie Izzard but without the skirt and lipstick. No wonder Moo married him. He is a man of few words, but what he lacks in quantity he makes up for in quality. His chosen words are weighted in inflections, accent, sarcasm, nuances – you name it, it's in there. So when he says, 'I see she's shown you the cow', he means 'It didn't take her long, all of ten minutes but, frankly, I thought it would be a lot quicker . . . So you see the hoovering was only part of the problem, the main one being me because I've been a complete arse on the good husband front, when I thought I was doing well just remembering it was Valentine's Day, and she likes those ceramic models, she said so, but what I didn't know was that Valentine presents are a different thing altogether and hold much more significance than other presents so, as you can see, I'm in the dog house.'

We all stand looking at the cow, its weight threatening to buckle the legs of the kitchen table, and I almost wish that it did tricks, like a moo sound when you pull an udder or something.

'It's different,' I comment, as my stomach growls noisily from the loss of toast, but from the look on Moo's face, this is clearly inadequate. I decide to try a different tack.

'Actually, it's quite nice and, let's face it, it could have been worse. You could have been me and received nothing or, worse still, a bunch of artificially coloured flowers from the garage,' I suggest, but Moo is not convinced and scowls at Bob who takes the cow away, his shoulders slumped in dejection. To punish him further she writes a list and sends him to Tesco. I put my free arm around my sister, the one that wants desperately to make some more toast. The Bear is getting heavier and I am getting weaker by the minute.

'I don't think he meant that you were a big fat cow. Yes, it's an unusual choice of present but you always said you were attracted to his slightly unconventional ways,' I venture, laughing.

'Yes, but not on bloody Valentine's Day.' She begins to laugh, and wipes a couple of escaped tears away. 'And now we've got to that point when I want him to put his arms around me so that I can forgive him but he won't because I've told him to bugger off each time he's tried to in the last twenty-four hours.'

Bob and Moo met when she held a drama workshop at the school Bob works at as a maths teacher. With a history of unsuitable men that included temperamental actors, musicians and flamboyant directors, quiet and unassuming Bob was not an obvious choice for Moo. The fact that he was the first man to resist her charms sealed his fate and by the end of the week-long workshop, Moo had decided he was the man she was to marry.

'Let's make him a cake,' I suggest, 'but first, let's have some toast.' I pass the huge dead weight that is The Bear back to his mum and make a dash for the toaster.

Moo and I talk nonsense, which is something we excel at, in between talking 'business', which is something we don't. During the business bits we alternate between her all-empowering confidence in our abilities as business-women, to my worried 'what if', 'how are we going to', and 'not sure if we can' mentality. Following my trauma, we agree to give Miss MBA the heave ho and pen a letter to tell her how disappointed we were, that we intend to take our non-existent business elsewhere. Hah! Moo has also found a colleague at work who can design our website for a couple of hundred pounds rather than the thousands we had envisaged.

Bob returns with the shopping and a mysterious little red bag. Inside is a small box containing some beautiful gold earrings and Moo begins to cry. While she is hugging her husband, I busy myself with a banana and pecan cake. An hour later, the smell of baking and feelings of contentment fill the kitchen as we sit down to a slice of cake. Moo smiles like a contented cat, her new earrings glowing in the fading winter afternoon light. Aah, the miracle of cake and something small and expensive.

Whilst we play with The Bear, Bob gets his calculator out and does the cash-flow forecast for us. I like Bob, he is always so generous about the frequent weekends I spend here, although I suspect it has a lot to do with having an excuse to buy *OK!* magazine and someone else to practise his magic tricks on.

'He's good with numbers,' Moo informs me, smiling at her husband scribbling away.

'Is that why you married him?'

'He's also very good in bed,' she adds, making Bob blush and punch the numbers into his calculator with extra vigour.

Later, Moo has invited a fellow psychic over to give me a reading and she busily prepares the dining room for her arrival. The Bear has eaten his own body weight in food and has been tucked up in bed. Bob is upstairs working and I delve into the *OK!* he bought earlier, amusing myself with the latest gossip and pictures of celebrities flaunting their cellulite on sun-drenched beaches. Our psychic arrives half an hour late blaming the traffic and I resist the temptation to ask why she hadn't seen it coming. The scene is set, with scented candles, glass crystals casting their colours across the walls, and soothing ambient music playing in the background. As Alice gets herself ready, breathing heavily and fluttering her eyes, Moo and I sit quietly, watching and waiting.

Despite the fact that I know psychics are normal people like you and me, I find Alice is a bit of a disappointment. I always think it adds to the experience if they display a little flamboyance or a touch of eccentricity in the way of a richly embroidered floor-length coat, hair the colour of raven wings or a pair of purple alligator-skin shoes; in fact, anything that makes them stand out from us mere mortals. Alice has none of these; she is dressed in a pale green jumper with navy trousers that are too short and very sensible navy court shoes that are not high enough to be high heels but not low enough to be pumps. They are the harmless librarian of the shoe world, the sort that people in banks wear because they have to. Her only concession to a touch of madness is a mass of frizzy, shoulder-length, mousey brown hair that has never heard the word serum spoken in its presence.

As I wait for her to start I begin to feel a little nervous, but before I have the chance to make my escape she lifts her hands up, palms upwards, and suddenly begins to speak, her eyes fixed on a point over my left shoulder.

'There is a light . . .'

I look around, but I don't see anything.

'You have been in darkness but now there is light . . .'

Aah, that kind of light.

'You must believe in yourself and follow the light . . .'

I fidget, hoping that the whole evening won't be so ambiguous. I want facts. Hard facts!

'There is a man.'

My ears prick up. At last!

'I told you!' Moo nudges me proudly.

'What's he like?' I ask.

'He is swarthy or Scottish.'

'Swarthy or Scottish?' I repeat, a little too high pitched for comfort. Moo motions for me to lower the volume.

'I'm sorry, but that's all I can give you,' Alice says in a stern voice.

'But which one do you think? I'd rather have Scottish than swarthy,' I say in a panic.

'That's all they are telling me,' she says, before closing her eyes again.

'What about children?' I ask, because I can't help myself. I need to know. Moo reaches over and squeezes my hand and we both wait anxiously as Alice takes a deep breath. She looks past my shoulder again.

'I see you in a garden. It is surrounded by a white picket fence and your husband is doing some DIY and . . . I think there are two children playing in the garden.'

'You think?' I ask. 'Are they mine?' I don't like the hint of uncertainty in her voice.

'I don't know. They might not be, I can't be sure,' she says.

'Oh great! So whose are they? Are they the neighbour's kids or maybe they are the local glue sniffers having a surreal moment with my vegetables?'

Alice begins to shake and her eyes roll back in her

head. I look at Moo for reassurance and she just grasps my hand even more tightly.

'You are afraid,' Alice says in a deep, almost masculine voice, her eyes flickering beneath her lids.

I am now.

'I am with you.'

She flares her nostrils and licks her lips.

'You hear footsteps on your landing. It is me.'

Great. Not only am I scared of the dark, now I have to worry about some spirit lurking about when I go to the toilet in the middle of the night.

'Do not be afraid. I am your spirit guide. I have your grandmother and grandfather here. They also watch over you.'

God, how many people are there on my landing?

Alice is revived with a cup of tea, a slice of cake and sixty pounds before going home, and I am left with the prospect of ending up with someone swarthy, with somebody else's kids and having to put my dressing gown on to go to the toilet in the middle of the night.

The next day as Moo tries to negotiate a better price with a delivery company, I spend time playing with The Bear. What kind of cake will he become? A banana cake? What will he choose to do? None of us knows what The Bear will dream of or whether he will at all. I met a girl who said she didn't have any dreams and I thought it was the saddest thing I had ever heard, but perhaps she will be the happier person, contented with her lot.

'Bastards!' Moo exclaims, slamming the phone down. 'Because we haven't got a history of trading they wouldn't budge from the standard rate. I tried everything, from a free cake to sex!'

'Moo!' I exclaim. She still manages to shock me. Bob walks into the room and asks what we are laughing at.

'Nothing, darling, just offering my body in exchange for a twenty per cent discount,' she says, hugging him.

'Did you offer cake as well?' he asks, smiling. Moo nods.

'Then I guess you did your best,' he says, planting a kiss on her forehead before disappearing again.

'Let's hope we have more success with the boxes and the bank,' Moo says, removing The Bear from my lap. 'But this time you can offer the sex part.'

We head off to Boxing Clever, the box manufacturer we have located following hours of trawling the Internet. After getting lost and driving ten miles out of our way, we arrive at a small industrial unit in the middle of nowhere. We are met by a tiny old man who looks as if he has never seen daylight, let alone two females. He ushers us into a unit full of boxes in all kinds of shapes and sizes. He has one eye that permanently looks to the right of us, which is a little off-putting, but in a bizarre way more than a little fascinating. I try desperately not to stare but much to Moo's amusement I find myself constantly moving position in case he can't see me.

'The widths of the middle make all the difference. You see these wavy bits, well, they hold the strength of the box,' he says looking at me, or maybe it's Moo.

'Fascinating. Isn't that fascinating, Maddy?' Moo urges, but I have been drifting off. I have a low-attention threshold and I'm too excited by the prospect that they can do the boxes we want: strong white ones that will withstand pretty much anything.

We end up ordering fifty but then worry about where we are going to put them. Moo's shed and my dining room seem to be the only option, which isn't ideal, but even the prospect of my lovely little house becoming a box warehouse doesn't dampen the feelings of excitement I feel building inside me. This is a milestone; a step in the right direction and now it feels like less of a game and more of a . . . more of a business. Wow!

I can't stop smiling as we head off to our second meeting of the day with a woman called Anita at the HSBC. The Bear, bored with boxes, is sleeping soundly and Moo prays that he will stay that way for the next half-hour. It is dangerously past his feed time, but bless him, he sleeps until ten minutes before the end when he shouts (probably something like 'Where the bloody hell is my dinner!') and is sick on Anita's desk. By then we don't care because she has said yes to the business account and yes to the overdraft. In fact, she does it in such a matter-of-fact way that when she goes out of the room Moo kicks me and whispers, 'Is that it, have we got it?'

'Yes, I think so, but I'm not sure,' I reply.

'I'm not sure either,' Moo says, wiping the sick off with the hanky she keeps in her sleeve. 'Perhaps we should ask when she comes back.'

Anita comes back, we ask, and she says yes once again. Yes, we have a business account in the name of Sugar and Spice, and yes, we have a £3000 overdraft.

Hurray!

The three of us celebrate with a cappuccino, a bottle of milk and a toasted teacake each, although we decide that The Bear is still too young for sultanas and I eat his too. Shame, but it's really in his best interests! Before I head home, we work on the text and instructions for the website so that Moo's friend can begin work on it.

'I can't believe that we are actually going to do this.

That Sugar and Spice is a real business,' I laugh. This is it. We are starting a business and if the HSBC believe in us, then I guess we should too. Bloody hell!

'It's kind of scary, isn't it?' Moo comments. 'But good scary,' she adds quickly as my eyes widen with panic. I push the bad, scary feelings away and pretend to be someone else who is brave.

'A toast to Sugar and Spice, our successful new company.'

'To us,' Moo says and our coffee cups meet a little too enthusiastically and mine develops a crack down the side. Hurray!

My journey home is made longer than usual by a snowfall and by the time I get back my bladder is the size of a football. There is a message from Ben on the answering machine and I listen to it as I pee for England. It goes on for ever and ever and I wonder how I held it all in.

'I've got the coal, you bring the carrot,' Ben's voice calls out.

The five year old in me returns as I pop my hat and scarf on and make my way round with a cucumber because I don't have any carrots. As we live just round the corner from each other in the pretty market town of Stoney Mills it's easy for me to pop round for a chat, a brotherly hug or to get my lawn mower fixed. Situated between the counties of Buckinghamshire and Northamptonshire, Stoney Mills is not far from the area we grew up in, and after spending most of our adolescent years planning our escape it seems ironic that we have both returned.

An hour later we admire our handiwork and, flushed with success, we do a high five; the cucumber isn't the ideal nose but a ringed doughnut as a belly button was a flash of brilliance.

We head back into the warmth, our noses red from the cold. Ben gives me an impromptu hug.

'All right, mate?' he asks, releasing me.

I look at him and smile. He has developed a little grey at the sides. I think it suits him.

'I'm fine.'

Unconvinced, he looks at me as if I'm hiding something.

'Honestly, I'm fine,' I, say, trying to reassure him that I'm not about to dissolve in a flood of tears.

'I worry about you,' he says, hugging me close to him again.

'I know. So do I,' I admit.

It amuses me that lately he, my baby brother, has felt the need to be my protector. In fact, he worries far too much about me nowadays and my ability to survive in this big bad world. I think he has forgotten the fact that I seem to have survived okay thus far. It's nice that we are close, that he cares so much and I know his heart is in the right place. The memory of him phoning to tell me he had a baby daughter still makes me go all gooey inside. I cried tears of happiness for him as I had for Moo three weeks earlier, whilst my body and mind still adjusted to the fact that this miracle of life would now not be happening to me.

The doctor said that it happened to thousands of women, that there was nothing I could have done, but the guilt remained. The counsellor I eventually went to see told me I had to accept the grief, but I fought it all the way, pushing it all to the back of my mind with a forced smile and increased workload. However, that is in the past, and as the doctor said, it happens to lots of women. Now, as I look at Ben, I get the urge to put my hand up and quietly, but forcefully, say, 'Yes, a few things have happened over the past couple of years that have caused me to cry an awful lot and yes, I'm grateful for all of your help because otherwise, without you, Mum and Moo I couldn't have got through it all, but . . . but I'm okay now thanks. I'M OKAY NOW and I think I can take it from here.' Because I'm pretty sure I can. Oh bugger it, I'm not sure at all and that's why I decide to keep quiet. I want to ruffle his hair but I can't reach. At over six foot, I wouldn't reach it even on my tiptoes.

Meeting my brother for the first time, you would be forgiven for thinking he was a perfectly balanced normal individual. But Ben is a Battenberg cake and, as cakes go, these are pretty complicated. There is the square shape, for a start, the marzipan surround and the different flavoured pink and yellow sponge pieces all held together by apricot jam. Despite his attempts at being a sensible grown-up responsible for the protection of every female on the planet except, of course, Moo, who doesn't need protecting from anything, deep down he is still my mad baby brother whose apricot jam isn't always there.

Freya arrives home with The Princess from a day out with her baby group. She should have been back earlier but, because of the snow, it has taken her a couple of hours to get home. Ben lights the fire and puts the kettle on while I have a little cuddle with The Princess, who has yet to discover the sheer magic of snow, shoes and shopping. As the fire crackles and pops into life, we sit down to a cup of tea and yet another mince pie.

Feeling all warm and snuggly with the world and with

our okay from the bank, I decide now is a good time to come clean about the business. I say it all too quickly, hardly pausing for breath while Ben and Freya listen intently without saying a word. They seem to be thinking of a suitable response; one that doesn't include 'Are you mad?!' which means I continue to rabbit on and on and on to fill the silence and delay the inevitable.

'Life is too short and sometimes you just have to take risks, don't you . . . Perhaps I have lost the plot a little but . . . cakes. Like flowers . . . I know . . . it sounds like a stupid idea . . . So . . . Do you think we're mad?'

When I finally finish there is an awful silence. Freya removes the clip from her hair and lets it fall like the women on the L'Oréal adverts. Thankfully, she doesn't swish from side to side otherwise I would have to kill her. Ben is frowning and his thick bushy eyebrows look as if they have moulded into one.

'Are you mad?' he asks, but I'm not sure if he is repeating my original question or whether he is asking me because he thinks I am. I wonder if Richard Branson had to go through this.

'Well, are we?' I ask.

'Yes,' he says, removing the top off a mince pie and eating it.

'Yes?' I repeat.

'Yes!' Ben reiterates, stuffing the remainder of the mince pie into his mouth.

'That's it?' I ask, a little disappointed.

'What do you want me to say? You're bonkers, a raving lunatic, you've lost the plot. You're insane. You're a few sandwiches short of a picnic. You're living in la la land. I could go on but you've heard it all before.'

He is smiling and I don't take it personally. He has

been saying the same thing to me since we were kids but Freya is clearly mortified.

'Don't talk to your sister like that,' she reprimands and then turns back to me with an apologetic smile.

'Don't take any notice, Maddy. I think it's a wonderful idea. We both do. Don't we?' She looks at Ben, urging him to say the right thing. He complies and nods sheepishly. Clearly satisfied with her husband's response she reclips her hair in that annoyingly easy way I can never get the hang of, before clearing the cups away and heading towards the kitchen. When she has gone Ben shakes his head, points his finger in my direction and mouths the word 'Cuckoo' at me.

I throw a cushion at him but the seed has been sown and I begin to wonder if he is right. The Princess picks up the knitted belt from my trendy Top Shop cardigan and wipes her nose on it. Unfortunately, or fortunately, depending on the way you look at it, my cardigan is green, which means I cannot see where the offending contents from her nose are.

'Do you want to stay for dinner?' Freya calls out.

This puts me into a little bit of a dilemma. Freya is a wonderful cook but a dedicated carnivore and I'm not sure if vegetarians are that common in Sweden. Her previous comments of: 'But vegetarians eat chicken?' and 'Oh, it's only a little piece of meat' make me nervous. I can't very well ask her what's on offer before I accept, so I just do what I always do, say yes and proceed with caution.

While Ben bathes The Princess, I sit at the kitchen table with a large glass of wine as Freya prepares our mystery dinner.

'Will you do decorated birthday and wedding cakes?'

she asks, expertly chopping an onion. She has long slender hands and tiny wrists; like a Sindy Doll.

'No, just traditional teatime cakes,' I reply, looking at my own hands. I really must do something with my cuticles. Biting them off is clearly not working.

'But you'll have one with a happy birthday message on it?' Freya asks.

'No,' I confirm.

'Oh.'

I can hear the disappointment in her voice.

'Well, as I said, I'm sure it will be a huge success,' she confirms but I can tell she is now wondering if Ben had a point. With her long model legs, cheekbones to die for, and disgustingly healthy-looking, shoulder-length blond hair, it is no wonder my brother fell in love with her at first sight.

Ben was working in the City, his life a succession of bars, pubs and girlfriends, the only constant in his life the crowd of practical-joke-loving, rugby-playing friends he staggered around with. Within a year of meeting Freya, he had left London, started working with Dad in the family business and thrown himself into a life of domestic bliss. Freya is calm, unruffled and always in control, which is sometimes quite scary to the permanently ruffled, out of control amongst us. I sometimes wonder if her glacial coolness is a cultural thing and if all Swedes have the ability to remain unfazed when confronted by ten friends coming round for dinner, Christmas shopping, packing for a holiday and putting long hair into one of those coiled, chignon things she so effortlessly wears. I would probably hate her if I didn't love her so much. Freya is an orange sponge cake, which is based on the recipe for a Victoria sandwich. With the addition of orange and a light, pale buttercream filling, it is transformed into a delightful-looking and particularly fragrant cake much loved by everyone who tries it. Just like Freya herself.

After what turns out to be a harmless but very spicy vegetable curry Ben opens another bottle of wine and we continue talking about my plans for the future.

'Seriously, Maddy. Have you really thought about all this?' Ben asks with a concerned look on his face. It's very similar to the look he has when The Princess won't drink her milk.

'As much as I can without scaring myself half to death,' I respond, trying to keep the conversation light.

'Okay, let me put it another way. Do you think you should be embarking on something like this right now? It will mean a lot of work, it's financially risky and it will give you a lot of stress.'

'No, I don't know if it's a good idea but I'm willing to take the risk. I can't be afraid for ever,' I tell him, thinking that in reality I probably could. It would be a lot easier.

When I get home, I phone Moo.

'Do you think we're mad starting the business?' I ask, wiping an imaginary smear from the coffee table with my sleeve.

'Yes, of course we are,' Moo replies. 'But we would be mad if we didn't,' she adds hopefully.

'Yes. That's what I thought,' I say.

'Bye.'

'Bye.'

I wonder what Ben and Freya really think, and if they will ever really tell me. Part of me wishes I hadn't said anything but I know that as much as Ben might think that his sisters have finally lost the plot, he will be our biggest supporter. When Dad left, he saw it as his responsibility to be the man of the house and grew up overnight; a little boy acting like a big man looking after two females who seemed to cry an awful lot (Moo never cried). If I think about it, nothing has changed, he is still the ten year old trying to be a grown-up and I am still crying at every opportunity, although, to be fair, it is getting less. As if on cue, he phones and pretends to be somebody Scottish called Mr Beeg Heed who wants a cake shaped like a haggis.

The phone rings again almost immediately.

'Oh, by the way, I forgot to tell you . . . my medium friend Alice phoned back to say *he* is not far away; in fact, *he* is just around the corner . . .' Moo says.

'Who?'

'Scottish, swarthy bloke . . . your chocolate cake.'

'Oh, him. Gosh, do I need to put lipstick on, shave my legs and wear my sexiest knickers?' I ask excitedly.

'Sorry, no specifics, but it could all happen very soon,' she says.

'How soon are we talking?'

'Soon, that's all I know, so yes to shaving your legs but I think putting your sexiest knickers on is being a little presumptuous and, if you ask me, just a little bit slutty. At least wait until the second date.'

I put 'Smother myself with fake tan' on my to-do list.

Note to self: Do not apply fake tan in future when looking after the Frog because a) dog hair sticks to fake tan and b) he likes the taste of it and has licked it off my feet and ankles. James has gone to Prague for the weekend and the Frog is staying with me. He is already testing the limits of my patience as he wanders around aimlessly, ruining my attempts at gorgeousness and whining intermittently. I should be working on the design for a flyer but decide to take him out for a walk instead with the hope that it will tire him out.

We make slow progress as he ambles along, swaying as he goes. His vision is not what it used to be, which means kerbs are mountains to be climbed or jumped off, depending on which way we are going, and catch the stick is not what it used to be now that I have to run after it and bring it back myself. Despite the cold, it's good to be outside, feeling the wind on my face and breathing in the clean air. Didn't Davina McCall meet her husband whilst out walking her dog? I bet she looked good in her woolly hat, though, like the models in the Accessorize adverts who always look so cool, laughing and kicking leaves in their little beanie hats whereas I always seem to look like a mad, socially challenged person.

I try out different design techniques for our first flyer on the computer. We don't have the money to hire a professional design company so the job is left to me and I'm getting nowhere fast. Moo and I have decided that the company image should involve dark chocolate brown, cream and pale pink; the colours of cake or, as Ben points out, the Neapolitan ice cream we had as kids. The colour options provided by the computer are either too harsh or too bright, the designs uninspiring. Feeling frustrated with my lack of progress I decide a *Blue Peter* moment is called for and I rush out to the shops to buy a selection of wrapping papers, material and a pot of glue. After lots of experimenting with material and paper stuck around pieces of text, I ponder my options from the twenty-six that are on the floor in front of me. Frog wanders over, licks my arm (great, another white mark) and makes an alternative bed out of four of them. I decide on the vintage pink-rose fabric that looks like an old-fashioned tablecloth. Hurray, we now have our first flyer and I rush down to the copier shop.

'Cool ... do you do a Snickers bar cake?' the young boy from behind the counter asks.

'No,' I reply, mystified as to whether there is such a thing.

'Oh,' he replies and begins to shuffle away, the tiny flicker of interest extinguished almost as quickly as it had appeared. He begins to take copies of my flyer, leaving me to ponder on the possibilities of a Snickers bar cake. Ten minutes later, he hands me my precious cargo and I say a cheery goodbye.

I have been worried about Frog's state of health for some time now, and I book him in for an appointment at the vet's. Frog knows he is somewhere he doesn't really want to be and begins to make a hasty retreat as soon as we walk through the door. The vet appears, and gives him a couple of treats and some tummy tickles. It's not long before Frog is putty in his hands and allowing him to make a thorough examination. The Frog and I are very similar in lots of ways! He tells me that yes, he is an old bastard (his words, not mine – he's Australian!) but I wouldn't put my granny down if she was doddery and a bit uncomfortable with rheumatism, would I? I think it's best that I don't answer this obvious trick question, and instead shake my head in a vague, non-committal way.

There is something attractive about a man who is good with animals, and I am impressed by the way he gently handles Frog. Unfortunately he has a beard and a bit of a beer belly, reminding me of Rolf Harris, and, good with animals or not, I wouldn't take him home either. He tells me Frog also has a bit of doggy Alzheimer's and that would explain the confusion. Combine that with his lack of vision and he tells me it's not really surprising Frog gets upset sometimes and whines for no apparent reason. I leave the vet's feeling guilty for shouting at him at half past five in the morning when he suddenly begins to howl his wake-up call, giving me a heart attack and waking the whole neighbourhood. Bless him.

My guilt over the Frog lasts until a quarter past five this morning when he wakes me again with a blood-curdling howl. I get up and walk blindly into his water bowl and flood the kitchen floor. The words I mutter to myself do not include 'Bless him'. But now that I'm up early and there's no one to drag me back to bed, I get to work baking the cakes we have agreed to include in our range. James, who is a photographer for an obscure nature magazine, has agreed to take the photographs for the website.

James arrives looking a little jaded and murmurs something about too many beers on an empty stomach and a blonde called Tammy. Who the hell calls their daughter Tammy? I used to have a dancing Pippa doll called Tammy. I mutter away to myself while grating a lemon a little too vigorously for the last cake on my list. There is more zest on the work surface than in the bowl and, as always, I wonder how I seem to manage to make so much mess. I could never be a TV cook.

'And has Tammy left school yet?' I ask and laugh at my own brilliant quick-witted humour, but the remark goes unnoticed as James has fallen asleep with the Frog lying on top of him. They look kind of cute, both snoring loudly, their limbs intertwined, and I get a warm feeling in the pit of my stomach. It has always amazed me that for someone who doesn't want kids James absolutely adores Frog. He is his little dark shadow, swaying close behind as they wander to the pub to share a packet of chicken crisps. I think James would have made a good dad, and I experience a little pang over lost opportunities. It's funny how things change, but I can't imagine us making a go of it now. Our friendship is better. I walk back into the kitchen and remove the last cake from the oven. The smell wafts through, causing Frog to sniff the air and investigate, waking James up in the process.

With five cakes ready and waiting on the dining-room table, we set up with a few props, which include vases of flowers, paper doilies and old-fashioned decorative plates. The next few hours are spent photographing them in different positions: with a fork, with the flowers behind them, without the flowers, on a plate, on a cake stand, with a cup of tea, with a slice of lemon, with a teapot. I lose the feeling in my right arm from holding the living-room lamp and a piece of kitchen foil at various angles. By the end of it, I am glad I am neither a photographer's assistant nor a supermodel, not that the latter was an option. James downloads the images on to my computer and I am truly amazed by how fabulous the cakes look.

'Wow, they look fantastic,' I enthuse, clicking through the photos, the website forming in my mind as I do so. I hug him excitedly.

'Thanks for doing this for me. Let me cook you dinner as a small token of my appreciation,' I suggest.

'No need to cook. Sleeping with me will be just fine,' he says with a smirk and I want to slap him. The lovely gooey feelings of earlier disappear as I wonder how he can be so heartless.

'Don't ask. Don't get. And legally I am still entitled to my conjugal rights,' he teases, tucking into a slice of Earl Grey Tea cake, but my sense of humour has left me and I wander back into the kitchen unable to look at him.

'This is really good. Can I have another slice?' He wanders into the kitchen.

'No, you'll ruin your dinner,' I say, wanting to punish him in some pathetic small way. Okay, I am a little pre-menstrual, which means nothing seems particularly funny at the moment, but even so, it was a little insensitive. I sometimes wonder if he really is as heartless as he appears, or if he has chosen to forget what happened the last time we slept together. I am not ready to forget. Not yet, anyway. It's something we never touch on, dancing around the issue like an unexplained death in the family, although to all intents and purposes I guess that's exactly what it was.

James looks at me, confused by my sudden change in temperament. Do I say something? He smiles at me sheepishly and I decide to let it go. It will only upset me and, anyway, the photos look fabulous.

Now that the photos are ready I log on to the website Moo's friend has been working on. As the page downloads, I begin to feel excited by the prospect of seeing a vision in cream with the words 'Sugar and Spice' in dark brown text, and tempting words like 'delicious' and 'mouth-watering'; a website that is irresistible to all who log on, ensuring lots of orders. Instead, I am confronted by something a child would do. The home page is a bright, shocking shade of purple, none of the text I spent so long writing has been used and, worst of all, and I can barely contain my anger, in big, bold fuchsia-pink are the words 'Crappy Cakes'! If this is a joke, I'm not laughing. Without the website we cannot distribute the flyers, without the flyers we cannot launch the business. I pick up the phone and dial, my fingers nearly punching the numbers out of their sockets.

'It's purple . . .' I say, and begin to pace up and down the length of the house.

'What's purple?' Moo asks.

'THE WEBSITE!'

'Oh,' Moo says in response. Is that all she can say?

'And if that's not bad enough, it says "Crappy Cakes"! I mean, is that supposed to be funny?' I fume. Moo is unusually silent on the other end of the phone.

'It's bright bloody purple! And shocking pink!' I say, wanting to drive the point home even more. 'It was supposed to be finished this week!' I remind her, feeling a little close to tears. I begin to pull the petals off the winter chrysanthemums that I bought earlier to cheer myself up.

'I'll speak to him,' Moo says calmly.

'Will you?' I ask forlornly, the disappointment weighing down on me so that I slump down, my head nearly touching the table.

'Yes.'

'You'll get it sorted?' I ask, needing more reassurance.

'Yes,' Moo confirms, and I nod to myself, knowing that she will. This is just a glitch, because Moo always gets things sorted.

A week later and with the packaging delivered and courier company ready to go I figure we are nearly ready to launch Sugar and Spice. Our very own business! We have done it and I still can't quite believe it. It's all happened unbeliev-ably quickly and I have been so busy buying equipment, cake tins and ingredients that I haven't had a chance to really contemplate what is about to happen to us. With the heading '*Sugar and Spice and all things nice. That's what mums are made of*', our flyers are ready to go and we are on target for our planned launch before Mother's Day. All we need to do now is go live with the website. I phone Moo, barely able to contain my excitement.

'Hello, business partner,' I sing down the phone but Moo's response does not match mine. Her voice is tired and almost inaudible.

'Maddy, the website hasn't been done,' she says matter-of-factly and my heart hits the floor.

'But . . .' I don't know what to say. 'I thought it was being sorted out. How can we launch the company without the website?' I ask, my bright little bubble bursting. 'You said you were going to talk to him,' I add.

'I know, but I just haven't had the chance,' Moo says flatly.

'But why didn't you tell me? I'm all ready to distribute the flyers.'

'I'm sorry, but The Bear caught a tummy bug,' she tells me and I immediately feel guilty. Unfortunately, it's not enough to soften my frustration and anger.

'If you'd told me, I could have phoned the guy myself. I hadn't heard from you so I just assumed everything was on track.'

'I know, but to be perfectly honest, Sugar and Spice was not at the top of my list of things to do,' she retorts angrily.

'That's fair enough but a phone call would have been nice. We're supposed to be business partners!' I snap back.

'Look! The company may be the most important thing

to you right now but it isn't to me. I am a mother, first and foremost, and The Bear takes priority,' Moo says, her voice hard and unforgiving.

I don't say anything because right now I can't think of an answer. She's right; the business is everything to me. I haven't felt so passionate about something in a long time, and right now, it's the only thing I have. It's my light at the end of the tunnel. A feeling of tiredness suddenly overwhelms me and I am tempted to just put the phone down, climb into bed and pull the covers over my head.

'Oh, what the hell, you wouldn't understand,' Moo snaps and I feel as if she has just slapped me around the face.

No, I wouldn't understand. How could I?

'Let's just forget it, shall we? It was a bad idea from the start,' I snap and put the phone down before letting my hot, angry tears fall.

I wake feeling groggy with a stiff neck from falling asleep on the sofa. The rain that lashes at the window doesn't make me feel any more positive about the day ahead. I move around in a daze, not really concentrating. All I can think about is the business and Moo. The frustration and anger from yesterday has disappeared, leaving a nagging worry that we are letting the business affect our relationship. The last thing I want is to fall out over this. I pick up the phone.

'Moo, I'm sorry for overreacting.'

'Me too,' Moo says. 'I hate it when we argue and I'm sorry for being such a crap business partner. When I'm not working The Bear takes up all of my time and sometimes it's really, really hard,' she continues, her voice wobbly with emotion.

'I need to take you down the pub,' I suggest.

'Sounds great,' Moo says, laughing.

'And in the meantime I will find someone else to do the website,' I tell her sounding more confident than I feel. I start to fiddle with my more-frizz-than-glossy shoulder-length hair, something I tend to do when lost in thought or nervous. My fingers are caught in a tangle at the back of my neck and I tug in an attempt to loosen it. The tangle comes out along with an alarmingly large amount of hair. Have I a bald patch at the back now? I seem to remember there was some research done a little while ago that said if you had a good hair day then you would have a more successful day at work. Maybe I should have included a personal hairdresser in my business plan.

'Thanks, Maddy. I've gotta go, it's Bear's teatime. Love you,' Moo says and is gone, leaving me to wonder how I will find someone to design our website for peanuts and get it done before Mother's Day. All those flyers. What a waste! I'm probably losing my hair with worry! Oh God!

I search the Internet for someone who will design our website and eventually find a company who promise to deliver the goods for a reasonable price, not the many thousands I had originally anticipated. After what seems like tons of emails back and forth discussing my requirements with a very helpful New Zealand chap, they promise to have it up and running in no time for £300. Unwilling to take it out of the bank account and use money we need for running costs, I agree with Moo to fund it from cashing in an ISA I have been paying into for the last five years. The total sum of £3000 will be deposited into our business account, which is not the usual £25,000–100,000 that it ordinarily takes to get a business off the ground, but it's a start and when we are a success the business can pay me back. Did you hear that? I said when, not if! All thoughts of a holiday, a pair of beautiful brown soft leather boots and a new rug are pushed to the back of my mind as I remind myself it will be an investment for the future.

James arrives to move my kitchen sink so that I can install a bigger cooker and helps himself to a large piece of cake; another chocolate cake, this time with a shot of espresso added for strength and intensity. My man has to be strong in the face of adversity and I am banking on him to help me out when he arrives. James dismisses my complaints about it not being anything special. Should I tell him I am attempting to make the perfect cake for the perfect man? Probably not a good idea. Every man thinks that they are the perfect one. He has reassured me that the kitchen will be a simple job, but I still find it traumatic and try to ignore the dust and debris that threatens to upset me even more than the failure of baking the chocolate cake to beat all chocolate cakes. When James eventually finishes, I regard the extra space he has created with wonder; all I have to do now is buy a bigger cooker and my problems will be solved.

'Thanks. You're a star and the best nearly ex-husband a woman could have,' I tell him.

'Hey, it's worth it for the cake. Bloody marvellous,' he declares, helping himself to another slice.

'I'm glad we're friends,' I say, looking up at him and smiling.

He pulls me over and squeezes me into the side of him so that my head is nearly under his armpit.

'Me too.'

I wrap the whole cake up for him, much to his delight,

before he rushes off to help another female in need of his services. He has a date with a blonde. I don't, so I agree to look after the Frog and decide to catch up on my phone calls before clearing up.

As I put the phone down to Lou, the doorbell rings and I step over the debris that litters the floor to answer it. A tiny ginger-haired man who looks like a shrew stares back at me and introduces himself as Mr Mallard, the Environmental Health Inspector. I stand there open mouthed.

'We had an appointment at six p.m.,' he says, holding out his ID card.

'We did?' I ask. We did. Oh, shit!

'Could you just hang on one moment?' I shut the door before he has a chance to argue.

The Frog is in the middle of the debris, collapsed and snoring on the kitchen floor. I try to persuade him that it would be to his advantage to move upstairs, but for once he is quite happy where he is. Mr Mallard shouts my name through the letterbox and I shout back that I will be two minutes. With some difficulty I pick up the Frog and carry him up to my bedroom where I plonk him on my bed. He cannot quite believe his luck.

'Don't get used to it, buddy,' I say, and close the door.

Mr Mallard's red and pinched little face tells me that he is not a happy man.

'Sorry, I had left an elderly neighbour in the garden and she panics if I leave her on her own,' I bluster breathlessly. 'Please, come in.'

My heart hits the floor as he takes out a clipboard and coughs with authority. He walks into the kitchen and we both stand there, looking at the devastation in silence.

'I'm having work done to improve my facilities,' I explain.

He doesn't say anything but just nods before writing something on his clipboard.

'Obviously it won't be like this when I start cooking,' I stammer, trying to steer him towards my carefully labelled ingredients that have thankfully missed the dust cloud.

'Would you like a cup of tea, or perhaps a slice of chocolate cake?' I offer, and then remember I have given it all to James. 'A biscuit?' A little hospitality may sway things in my favour. Perhaps I should just let him feel my tits and be done with it!

'No, thank you, Miss Brown. Now, I assume you have done a risk-assessment sheet?' I nod that yes, I have, and reluctantly leave him to search for it in the upstairs office. The Frog is whining and I open my bedroom door to give him a quick fuss before returning to my pending tray. After what seems like ages, I eventually find it and return triumphant.

'Sorry about that. It was filed under very important, which is the red file and not the green one.'

'I thought I could hear a whining sound?' Mr Mallard says, looking suspicious.

'Whining?' I squeak.

'Yes, whining. Like an animal.' Mr Mallard narrows his eyes, and I swear his nose twitches.

'Oh, I think next door have a dog. Would you like to see my equipment?' I ask hopefully, but it sounds as if I'm suggesting something that has nothing to do with my sparkling new mixer and utensils.

'That won't be necessary,' he says, looking at me as if I'm a butterfly he's about to stick a pin into. I answer all of his questions, trying to remember everything I learned on the food hygiene course: spores, bacteria, mice – these are all my enemies, and I recite the ways I will avoid them, although I'm not entirely sure I could really kill a mouse when it came down to it. Mr Mallard tells me that my risk-assessment sheet is flawed. I've failed to include a section about oven temperatures. I want to shout at him that he should be looking at my fingernails instead and the fact that I have bought myself a hairnet and that I use anti-bacterial soap and . . . oh, what the hell, he's not interested. As long as I have it written down then it appears I am okay. So the local takeaway could be using utensils they lick or scratch their bums with but if they said they didn't on their risk-assessment sheet then it would all be okay? How scary is that? I will never eat out again.

'Well, Miss Brown, I feel unable to issue your certificate at the present time. I will return again, and hopefully this' – he points to the mess – 'will be sorted out and your risk-assessment sheet will be rectified. I'll see myself out.'

I want to flick the end of his little shrew nose. Bastard mouse of a man! I needed that certificate.

Now I don't know what happens, but one minute he's walking and then the next minute he's doing what looks like an impressive break dance. By some miracle he manages to stay upright, but not before his file and papers have fallen to the floor and he seems to have suffered what looks like a rather painful groin injury.

'Oh God, are you okay?' I ask, trying to gather his stuff together.

He pushes away my attempts to help him. 'I slipped on . . .'

I follow his eyes to a brown substance. The Frog!

'Oh shit!'

'Precisely, Miss Brown.'

'Oh, Mr Mallard. I'm so sorry. It's that elderly neighbour I was telling you about. It's such a shame, but sometimes she just can't control herself. I'll make sure she's kept away from the premises in future.'

'This is highly irregular. I will return,' he says, smoothing the little hair he has left. 'And I hope that when I do, we will not see a repeat of this ... this farce,' he snaps, and limps out.

Is there anything else anyone wants to throw my way? Go on, get it over with because I know they come in threes and I don't want to wait. Bring it on!!!

I pick up my post from the floor and my attention is drawn to a rather official-looking envelope. Intrigued, I open it and my jaw drops. It's my decree absolute, which means I'm now divorced. I knew it was going through but it has still taken me by surprise. It feels like a very final act, like a door left ajar finally closing. My God, can this week get any worse? Feeling sad and dejected I slump in front of the TV; any energy I had for the business to-do list has been sucked away. The phone rings and surprises me out of my self pity.

'Does this mean I don't get to call you wifey any more?' James asks.

'I guess so, although I rather liked it,' I say, fiddling with my hair.

'I suppose I can't demand my conjugal rights either now, can I?' he laughs.

'Do you fancy coming round?' I ask suddenly, not wishing to be alone, to be reassured that things will not change between us.

'Sorry, out with the blonde.'

'Oh, okay,' I say, disappointed, my hair twiddled beyond repair.

'You sound sad,' James says after a short silence.

'Mmmmm . . . just feels a little weird, that's all,' I say, unsure of how I should be feeling about all of this. Sad? Happy? Relieved?

'I know what you mean,' he says, and I get the impression he wants to say more but doesn't.

With a heavy heart and near to tears I am in bed by ten. What a shitty week! I can't stop thinking how sad it is that we are finally divorced. We have been through so much together. James took me on my first holiday abroad when I was twenty-one, and later we spent six months travelling around Australia, New Zealand and Thailand. We dreamt of returning to Noosa or Byron Bay to live; of driving a camper van full of golden, freckled children; Frog with a bandana around his neck, surf boards on the top and a smile on our faces. Should we have stuck it out a little longer and tried a bit harder to make it work? If I hadn't lost the baby, would we have tried again? Probably not; a baby doesn't make a relationship work and it's probably for the best. One door closes so that another one can open.

With this in mind I decide to try another chocolate cake recipe. Tonight is Lou's dinner party and maybe, just maybe, this Dave will turn out to be gorgeous and full of the right ingredients. He will also love the fact that I can bake a good cake and can make my elbows do funny things. So what kind? The coffee didn't work so well . . . I sensed too much sarcasm there instead of strength . . . what about a chocolate fudge topping . . . no, too sickly sweet and eager to please; not my kind of man at all. Banana and chocolate? Bananas are a manly fruit, good for you . . . It's worth a try.

I arrive feeling nervous, but chide myself for being such a wimp. As I wait for the door to be answered I check I haven't got any dirt on my heels and recite in my mind the mantra for the evening: They are not going to bite me. I won't be expected to do a PowerPoint presentation on my life's aspirations. What's the worst that could happen? He hates my cake and has a moustache?

It WILL be a pleasant evening.

But the moustache would have to go!

Lou hugs me and I hand her the cake. I sneeze from the heavy perfume she is wearing as I follow her into the house she shares with her partner Carl. It is like walking into the pages of a glossy interiors magazine with its plush cream carpeting, and mood lighting at the touch of a switch. It has the feel of a luxurious boutique hotel and I have to stop myself from lounging on the extraordinarily long leather sofas and ordering a Manhattan cocktail, although I'm always a little scared to use the white towels in the bathroom. I follow Lou into the dining room and scan the faces already assembled. I immediately feel better at the sight of Mac grinning at me like an idiot.

I have known Mac longer than I have known Lou and every so often we meet up to tell each other we get better with age. A freelance writer, he is a cross between Louis Theroux and George Clooney, an irresistible mix of intelligence and good looks that mean the women love him. Or so he keeps telling us. Thick, dark wavy hair, chocolate Labrador eyes and tanned skin mean he is often mistaken for being Italian, but his rather wonderful Romanesque nose is the clue that his roots are, in fact, Jewish. Mac is a coffee and walnut cake and if he wasn't my friend and I hadn't seen him in a pair of knicker-bockers during his New Romantic stage, I would probably be a little in love with him. He is, by his own admission, a bit of a tart, although this is not how he wants it to be; it is a consequence of his quest to find the perfect woman. As he goes from one gorgeous brunette to another, all he dreams of is a little house in the country with his beautiful wife (approved by his mother of course) and equally beautiful children who are aesthetically perfect; direct from a Calvin Klein advert. The woman next to him looks as if she is that woman; sexy and gorgeous and, by the look on her face, she clearly adores him.

'And this is Maddy.' Lou introduces me as if I am the evening's entertainment. The rest of the table, a seemingly cliquey group of friends and neighbours who have known each other for years, look up from their conversations and wave. They are the posh cakes you find in the window of a patisserie in Hampstead Heath: rectangle sponge and cream concoctions, embellished with elaborate chocolate and fruit decorations. They are the sort that look impressive, but once eaten you feel disappointed and just a little nauseous. There is Felicity, who is an interior designer, and her husband Richard who runs his own architectural practice. Felicity likes to be called Fliss and Richard likes to be called Richard, but everyone calls him Rick except Fliss, who calls him Wichey. Pass the sick bag. Fliss and Rick are joined at the hip and finish sentences for each other; she strokes his arm as if he is her pet cat and puts her head on his shoulder, nuzzling into him between courses. They haven't got any kids yet but they are trying 'and having lots of fun, aren't we, Tiger?' Ruth and Mike both work in the city, and have just had their first child. This means they have just swapped their matching midnight blue BMW 5 series with leather interior and personalised plates for an SUV that has all the safety features of a jumbo jet. 'Does it come with in-flight entertainment?' I ask flippantly and am treated to a look from Ruth that would wilt sunflowers. Apparently it does; there are TV screens in the front-seat headrests for when Phoebe wants to watch *Tweenies*, and yes, it does have refreshments via a plug-in facility in the back for a bottle cool box. Ruth and Mike form their own little groupette at the end of the table with Tony and Karen who have just had twins through IVF. Over a Provençal-inspired cassoulet we are treated to graphic accounts of IVF and the birthing process but, determined not to be put off my food, I close my ears to it and try not to look at Mac who keeps pulling faces at me.

Dave, the other single person, turns out to be nothing like 'my type'. He doesn't have a moustache but does have a rather annoying habit of being an expert on everything. I make my excuses and leave the table to find Lou in the kitchen. As always, she is being the hostess with the mostest without breaking into the sweat that would accompany any attempt from me to do the same. Thank heavens my house isn't big enough to invite people round for dinner.

'So what do you think of him?' she asks me.

'Not my type,' I reply, trying to think of something nice to say. 'I mean, he's pleasant enough but . . . oh God, Lou, what were you thinking?'

'Sorry, Maddy. He's someone Carl works with and he

promised me he would be perfect for you.' She hands me the coffee to take back through.

'I've got my new knickers on tonight; I even exfoliated,' I say, sounding like a disappointed child.

'I'll cross him off the list, although I have to admit he wasn't on the top. Phil couldn't make it. You would really have liked Phil!'

'You have a list?' I ask, mortified, but Lou's answer is lost in the chatter of the table.

As I return to my seat, I am disappointed to find that the conversation has turned to the dehumanisation of race and culture through history. With nothing clever to add, I zone out. It's not that I don't like a little bit of intellectual conversation over dinner, but there is a limit and at some point it would be nice to just talk bollocks! My mind wanders to more important things and I think of my lovely knickers going to waste. At what age do you stop wearing g-strings and those lovely little lacy shorts? Is there an age limit or do you just know that now is the time to go big? I must ask Mum, although someone who wears tights under her jeans is probably not a reliable source.

'What are you thinking about?' a voice asks, and I turn to find Dave looking at me with a quizzical look on his face.

'Knickers,' I say before thinking and the whole table stops talking. Knickers, it would appear, are a lot more interesting to everyone than baby formula and world politics. I glance over at Mac who has his head in his hands. Luckily I am saved from further explanation by the appearance of Lou.

'Maddy has made a cake and in the absence of dessert I thought we could all have a slice with our coffees,' Lou declares, setting it down on the table. The posh cakes look panic-stricken.

'Oh, I can't eat wheat.'

'Has it got sugar in it?'

'No fruit, I'm afraid. Did you know it's a carbohydrate?'

'Not for me, I have no more points left.'

Lou looks to Tony, who has the rotund features of someone who can be counted on to say yes to dessert.

'No, thanks. Chocolate gives me migraine,' he says.

'Oh,' Lou says quietly, her immaculate hostessing reputation now in question. Carl and Mac rescue the situation by asking for extra large slices and I make a mental note to be for ever in their debt.

'Make that three,' I say in defiance. Bastards, the lot of them! I proceed to tuck in enthusiastically in a futile bid to let them know what they are missing.

'Aren't you having any?' I ask Dave accusingly.

'No. I don't like sweet things.'

See, I knew he wasn't my type.

Dave is a Madeira cake. That all-important chemistry is clearly missing and I count the minutes until I can politely go home, change into my pyjamas and catch Jonathan Ross. Don't get me wrong, Madeira cake is okay and for some it is enough, but I want something that is deliciously irresistible, a real cut-it-and-come-again cake. Back to the mixing bowl.

Jonathan Ross Interview

'So, Maddy, are you still single or is there a man in your life?'

'No, Jonathan, there isn't a special someone in

my life at the moment.'

'I can't imagine a beautiful lady like you will be on her own for long.'

'Oh, you're too kind, but yes, I do believe the man of my dreams is out there somewhere.'

'And you'll be ready with one of your delicious cakes.'

'Yes. Chocolate cake, I think. After all, chocolate is the food of love.' I smile.

'Well, I ask you, what man could resist the combination of you and chocolate cake?'

I blush in what I hope is a rather attractive and endearing way.

'Except, of course, Mr Pitt here, who, like me, is a big fan of your Victoria sandwich cakes. In fact, he was complaining earlier that he can't get hold of any in the States. Do you have plans to expand?'

'I shall let you and Brad into a little secret. We plan to open our first stores in New York and Beverly Hills next month.'

'That's fantastic news, but hopefully we won't be losing you to the US?'

'Heavens, no!' I laugh, not too loudly (I've had a laugh coach). 'I'm really a home bird at heart.'

'Good. Well, until next time, thank you for joining me tonight. I think Brad and Jack will agree with me when I say you look ravishing and it's been a real treat talking to you.'

'The pleasure was all mine, Jonathan, and I promise I'll personally make you and Brad a Victoria sandwich,' I say and wander back to the green room.

'I would like to thank my guests, Maddy Brown,

Brad Pitt and Jack Nicholson, and hope you'll join me next week.'

Brad leans over and says something that makes me smile shyly as Angelina looks on jealously.

BANANA AND PECAN LOAF

I don't know why, but I don't think I have found a man who doesn't love this cake. You can use walnuts instead of pecans, if you prefer. To make it really special replace 50g (2oz) flour with good quality cocoa powder and some chocolate chunks on top. Irresistible.

Ingredients

175g (7oz) plain flour

2 teaspoons baking powder

½ teaspoon bicarbonate of soda

½ teaspoon salt

125g (5oz) unsalted melted butter

150g (6oz) soft, dark brown sugar

2 large eggs

4 small, ripe bananas

75g (3oz) pecans

100g (4oz) sultanas

1 teaspoon vanilla extract

demerara sugar for the topping

Method

Preheat oven to 170°C/325°F/gas mark 3. Line a 23 × 13 × 7cm (9½ × 5 × 3 inch) loaf tin. Put flour, baking powder, bicarbonate of soda and salt in a bowl and combine well. In a separate bowl beat melted butter and sugar together, then beat eggs in one at a time. Add mashed bananas. With a wooden spoon, stir in pecans, sultanas and vanilla extract. Add flour mixture a third at a time, stirring well each time. Sprinkle a generous helping of demerara sugar on top for a crunchy topping. Put into tin and bake in oven for 1–1hr 15 minutes. Leave in the tin on a rack to cool.

One big decision

The winter weather seems to be disappearing at long last and we are being treated to bursts of early spring sunshine. It makes everyone smile just a little bit more than they were a couple of weeks ago, including me. But typically, just as I get my spring/summer wardrobe out, it rains, the temperature plunges and I end up freezing to death, which is exactly what I am doing now as I tread the streets of Stoney Mills delivering flyers through people's doors. My legs are aching, my hands are sore from letterboxes that bite back and my nose is running from the cold. Nothing, though, can dampen my spirits. This is it! The long-awaited launch of Sugar and Spice to the waiting world.

Yesterday morning, the New Zealander had phoned with the news that the website was up and running. As I nervously clicked on the different links, the text and James's amazing photos came to life in gorgeous hues of cream, chocolate brown and the palest of pinks, the words 'Sugar and Spice, deliciously different' were there for all to see and I wanted to scream with excitement and relief.

I phoned him back to tell him that I wanted to marry him but he assured me that would not be necessary, a cheque would suffice.

I print off a list of local businesses for a mail-out I plan to do, email the organiser of the local May Day Fair about the possibility of having a stand, design an advert and phone the local newspaper about placing it in next week's edition. Then it's out with a car full of free cakes to hand out to local businesses with some flyers.

I arrive back home to a message from the organiser of the May Day Fair. I phone him back and I'm a little disappointed when he tells me he already has a stall with fruitcakes and flapjacks.

'But what about fairy cakes? Kids love them,' I suggest, thinking on my feet. I need to have a platform to launch the company locally and this would be ideal.

'That's a lot of fairy cakes,' he says warily, which is exactly what Moo says when I phone her later.

'But that's potentially three hundred fairy cakes,' Moo laughs loudly down the phone.

'Mmm, it does sound rather a lot,' I reply, trying to calculate how long it would take to bake that many, but giving up. I wish I could understand numbers. I wish I could sing. I wish I had long legs.

'That's a lot of fairy cakes!' Moo is still laughing.

'I know. I didn't quite expect the event to be that big,' I say, feeling a little like a fool. I pace around the living room as I talk, wiping dust from the surfaces with my finger and then regretting it as I realise how little housework I have done lately.

'I mean, I think it's a great idea, but have you really thought about this?' Moo asks.

'No,' I admit, but I am thinking about it now, and there's a hot flush creeping up my back, underneath my arms and settling on to my cheeks.

'Have you worked out how long it will take to bake that many?'

'No,' I reply.

'That's a lot of fairy cakes,' Moo says again.

'So you keep saying.'

'Good job you have that bigger cooker coming,' she points out.

'Mmmm . . .' I reply, getting a duster out.

Mr Mallard, the health inspector, returns as promised. This time I manage to lure him into a smile with a fairy cake from the batch I am testing and impress him with my amendments to my risk-assessment sheet. The Frog is safely with James and I'm prepared for every emergency including weevils in my flour and what colour plaster to use if I cut my hand. Apparently it has to be blue. His little nose twitches in approval and I press a flyer into his sweaty little palm before he leaves. Hurray! Everything is finally falling into place, and not before time. My salary from Pharmagenica officially stops at the end of this month and then it's sink or swim. Probably not a good analogy, as I can't swim.

I check the website and answering machine. There are no enquiries or orders and I try not to feel too disappointed, but it's hard not to. I feel like a spurned lover waiting for that all-important call. I consult my to-do list and set to work baking fairy cakes like a mad woman. Soon the kitchen is full of bowls of butter coming up to room temperature, eggs waiting patiently for their turn in the proceedings, and flour sieved within an inch of its life.

My disappointment at the lack of orders is forgotten as I lose myself in the sheer joy of baking.

An unexpected burst of sunshine pours through the window as Ricky from the Kaiser Chiefs sings to me alone. I spoon the mixture into the pretty, flowery cases my fairies will be wearing for their big day out. Whilst the little lovelies bake in the oven, Ricky and I have a smooch around the living room. The aroma of vanilla and sweet golden sponge fill the house and I suddenly feel ravenous. Within five minutes of the first batch being removed, I test one, and then another, just to make sure.

I have eaten three, or is that six, fairy cakes? I force myself out for a run; well, a power walk and then a run; and then, oh, look at Mrs Duck with her six fluffy little chicks! I spend twenty minutes marvelling at Mrs Duck's parenting skills and then struggle to start running again. My calf muscles are hurting, my lungs are crying out for mercy, and my face is red, but I feel good, sure that I've been out for at least two hours. The clock on the kitchen wall tells me it has only been forty-five minutes. Minus the ducks, that's . . . oh, what the hell, I look as if I've been out there for two hours.

There's a thin layer of fog covering everything as I drive through Cambridgeshire. The muted greens, blues and browns blend into one and I feel as if I'm driving through a watercolour painting. I'm looking forward to seeing Moo and discussing things face to face. I haven't seen her since the website fiasco and sometimes phones, like emails, are the worst form of communication, especially when it involves emotional and business issues. Perhaps that's why I like it so much, the ability to hide behind a mask of indifference; the 'I may be upset but nobody can see me' mentality. As Moo says, and I have to agree, it's so much easier to make a judgement call when you can see the whites of people's eyes.

I arrive to find Bob and Moo looking pale and exhausted, with huge, dark circles under their eyes. The Bear is doing Bear things, unaware of the effect he is having on his parents, and devours a bowl full of Weetabix the size of America. Bob sits at the table still in his milk-stained dressing gown, while Moo almost slumps over The Bear's high chair in a baggy, crumpled sweatshirt that looks as if it will house ten men. I feel positively over-dressed for a change. I know things are bad when The Bear smears a spoonful of Weetabix in Moo's hair, but she doesn't notice, or if she does, she doesn't care. I set to work quickly providing tea and toast first aid before suggesting I take The Bear out so that Moo and Bob can grab forty winks. They nod gratefully and I can hear Moo snoring even before The Bear and I are out of the front door.

'Everything okay?' Moo asks on our return an hour later. She takes The Bear off me and plants a gentle kiss on his soft blond head.

'Yes, everything's fine. No trouble at all,' I respond before collapsing into a chair. Moo laughs but it's not the huge, infectious belly laugh I am used to; it has the resonance of someone who is struggling to find anything to laugh about. Everything about her is tired and weary; from the hunched shoulders, the oversized dark clothes, and grey pallor of her face. Even her usually glossy hair is limp and greasy.

When The Bear has gone to bed, I insist on dragging Moo out to the pub, despite her initial protests that she has nothing to wear and her hair needs washing. We eventually wander down to the Pig and Pocket, a rather dark and dingy-looking pub with a grubby patterned carpet and stained tables. Despite this, it seems very popular with the locals and we find it hard to find a free table. After a couple of glasses of wine and discussions on everything from The Bear's eating habits, hairdressers, to how Davina McCall lost all that weight after having her baby, Moo suddenly looks serious and takes a deep breath. She looks as if she's trying to summon up the energy from somewhere and I can see from the expression on her face that whatever she's about to say, it's not good.

'You're pregnant again?' I ask.

'No.'

'Bob's having an affair?'

'No, nothing like that.' Moo shakes her head and smiles briefly, but it doesn't reach her eyes. 'Look, Maddy, I don't quite know how to tell you this, but since the website fiasco I've been thinking about the business a lot and I've come to a decision.' She takes another deep breath. 'I don't want to be part of the business any more.'

'What do you mean?' I ask, confused. Here I was thinking we were going to talk about ways of making it work for both of us, and now? Now I don't know what's going on.

'I mean right now, I'm trying to hold down a job and be mum to The Bear. It's just impossible to give Sugar and Spice the time it deserves.' Moo empties her wine glass before continuing. Her hand is shaking a little and she seems to be shrinking before my very eyes.

'I want to be one of those superwomen who have it all, I really do, but I just can't. For the first time in my life I feel out of control and have no idea who I am any more and what I'm doing. All I can think about is teething, sleep and not going out with puréed food on my top.'

I look at the turmoil evident in her face and don't know what to say. Moo has always been one of those superwomen without really giving it any thought. She has never been fazed by anything in her life, always tackling everything life throws at her with a loud laugh of derision and a can-do attitude. Funny, but I always assumed she would deal with motherhood in the same confident, no-nonsense, what's-all-the-fuss-about way.

'The truth is, I never expected us to get to this point so fast,' Moo says, breaking into one of her beautiful smiles that cause the opposite sex to stop and smile back.

'Moo?' I want someone to press the rewind button.

'You're going to have to do it without me, Maddy. I'm sorry, really I am,' she tells me, her face serious again. She places her hand on top of mine. I feel disoriented, as if the rug has been pulled from beneath my feet.

'But I can't do it without you,' I say with certainty.

'I'm sorry,' she says again. 'It was always your dream, anyway. It was never mine, and you'll be fine, Maddy. You don't need me really.' Moo attempts to reassure me as she always has done, but I am having none of it. I shake my head in denial as my brave, kick-ass new world dissolves in front of me. She doesn't seem to realise that she is wrong; completely wrong. Of course I need her. This was never something I would do on my own. It was always meant to be a family thing; something Moo and I could do to make a difference to both our lives. I don't want to do it on my own. I'm not even sure that I can.

'I'm sorry, Maddy,' Moo says as if she hasn't said it enough.

Not half as sorry as I am.

'It's okay,' I reply, and get up to order another couple of glasses of wine and a packet of cheese and onion crisps. As I stand waiting for the barman, I turn and smile at Moo. She smiles back, reassuringly, but I cannot help feeling very much alone. Sisters Baking it for Themselves has turned into deluded lone girl with no one to bake for.

'You'd better make those large glasses,' I call over to the barman.

I drive home the next morning feeling shocked and severely disappointed at Moo's decision. Everything I have been working towards over the last couple of months has been for the two of us, and my vision for the future had Moo by my side, telling me it would work. Moo has always been the confident go-getter; not me. What am I going to do? WHAT AM I GOING TO DO?

As March draws to a close the landscape has begun to shed its drab grey winter coat, replacing it with splashes of bright yellow forsythia, butter-coloured daffodils and tiny buds of luscious lime green. The air has changed from a damp, smoky grey to something lighter and brighter; the delicate scent of spring flowers creating a freshness that fabric conditioners always promise, but never quite deliver. This does little to lift my spirits as I wonder what I'm going to do. The simnel cake I'm making for an Easter get-together at Dad and Susan's is sensing my unhappiness. Cakes, like me, are sensitive little creatures. The spoon flips out of my hand and falls behind the cooker. I don't know how it happened, but it has. This is on top of the egg that jumped out my hand, the contents sliding down between the worktop and the fridge, and the sieve (obviously twin sister to the spoon and egg) flicking half its contents on to the floor and my top. I take a deep breath and try to focus. I want the cake to be perfect; not just because I want the approval of the one person who never gives it, but also for proof that it's all going to be okay. I blowtorch the marzipan on top and burn it. For heaven's sake, it's Dad, not the bloody Prime Minister! Oh, but if only life was that simple.

I was fifteen years old, a girl turning into a woman, and he was the first man to leave me, the first to break my heart. His distance and apparent disinterest over the subsequent years left me wondering what was wrong with me, and even now I find myself trying to make him feel I am worthy of his love. Moo tells me it's all about self worth and she is, as always, right. It's a cycle I'm determined to break, but not right now, because now I want this bloody fucking bastard of a cake to be perfect for him. Breathe . . .

Dressed, I look at myself in the mirror and try to think good, positive thoughts.

I CAN do this.

The cake will be fabulous.

And so will I.

Hair up or down?

My thighs look really big in these trousers.

Don't look round . . . it's best not to know.

Oh God.

I'll wear a skirt!

Now I look as if I'm going to work.

Jeans. Best to be comfortable.

On my arrival, Dad hugs me and gives me a quick kiss on the cheek, the bristles from his beard lightly scratching my face. Dad is a big man, over six foot tall with the build of a rugby player, and his hug threatens to break my ribs.

He looks younger than his fifty-nine years and is proud that he hardly has any grey in his cinnamon-coloured hair, which I guess is important to somebody with a wife who is almost twenty years his junior.

'Sorry I'm late,' I say.

'Not a problem,' he says, but I know from the look on his face that it is. He hates bad timekeeping. I take a deep breath and follow him into the dining room, which is already full of chatter and laughter. There are at least four different conversations going on at once and it always amazes me how much noise seven people can make. The babies are passed around for their continuous supply of hugs and kisses as we all marvel at how much they have grown. Dad holds court over the gathering like The Godfather, his voice and laugh louder than all of ours put together. He is a double-choc-chip muffin, the large American kind that you can't possibly eat all in one go, and, like Moo, adds value to any gathering with his larger-than-life personality.

'You're not going to do anything silly, are you? Promise me you won't give up on Sugar and Spice,' Moo says when we have a moment to ourselves.

'I don't know, Moo. I really don't,' I respond, because I don't.

After dinner, I produce the cake with a little tah dah accompanied by Moo clapping. Dad proceeds to subject me to a barrage of questions about the business and I trip over my words. As I become tongue-tied and my confidence seeps further down the scale, I realise that where he is concerned my need for approval is still based on a young girl's need for her father's unconditional love. I get the impression he thinks I'm just playing a childhood game of baking cakes. Well, what did I expect? A 'my beautiful girl, I'm so proud of you?' In your wildest dreams, Maddy Brown.

Ben winks at me, produces a bottle of champagne and proposes a toast to the new company. Everyone clinks their glasses and I glance at Moo to check that she is okay. I was worried that our relationship would change, but she seems perfectly happy and is smiling along with everyone else. I feel like a fraud. Here they all are toasting the future success of Sugar and Spice and I'm not even sure that I will carry on.

'So, have you got yourself a man, yet?' Dad turns to me.

'No,' I respond wearily.

'You need to get out more,' Dad says as if it's the most obvious solution to my perceived predicament. Over thirty with no boyfriend! Stop the world, there's a spinster in the room. Without a partner to talk football with or a grandchild to add to the proceedings, Dad, for one, doesn't quite know what to do with me. After the miscarriage, people fell into three categories: they either sympathised and talked freely about it, or they couldn't quite understand why it had hit me so hard (although I suspect this is similar to finding out your husband is having an affair; until it happens to you . . .), or, just like Dad, they acted as if it had never happened. To be fair, this was made more difficult by my own mood changes that swayed between the three categories independently of those around me, rarely meeting in the middle. Dad kept his distance, both emotionally and physically, which is hardly surprising. It was the only thing he and James ever had in common.

I stuff a huge piece of cake into my mouth.

'You should try Internet dating,' Susan suggests and I

grimace. Susan is a carrot cake. The one with the frosted topping. She has a tan, curly blond hair and her cleavage is permanently on display. She must be at least a thirty-six-inch triple F and, at barely five feet tall, she looks as if she will topple over at any minute. Initially, of course, I hated her, but now I don't, although I might actually like her more if she didn't keep talking about her hugely successful PR-type daughter. The one who commutes between London and New York and is dating the most handsome man on the planet.

'Baker seeks dough? Sponge looking for her cream filling?' Bob suggests and receives a nudge from Moo.

'Not long,' Moo says to me as if she has read my mind.

'Well tell *him* to bloody hurry up,' I tell her. 'I'm getting old and bitter.'

Talking of being bitter, there is a message from Mum on my return. I phone her back but immediately wish I hadn't as she goes into guilt overdrive about being on her own over Easter whilst we were at Dad's.

'So, what have you been up to?' I ask.

'Nothing much; I was going to visit, but I knew you'd be busy,' she says. I don't respond because I know that she was fully aware we were all going over to Dad's and, sure enough, she says, 'And Freya told me you were all going to your father's.' Ooh, that's another reprimand. It was Freya, and not me, who told her.

'We arranged it a long time ago and, to be fair, we haven't been round there for ages,' I say, trying to justify this apparent betrayal.

'I suppose SHE cooked a nice meal for you all?' Mum spits, the contempt for 'that woman with the breasts' clearly audible in her voice.

'It wasn't that nice, really. Your cooking is better.' I attempt to reassure her. We have all become wise to the fact that anything to do with Dad must be carefully edited. With the guilt mounting, I find myself cracking under the pressure and, despite knowing that in the fledgling weeks of the company I shouldn't really be going anywhere, I offer to visit. What is wrong with me? Moo and Ben would have just ignored it. Me? I'm just a sucker for guilt.

I put the phone down and open the post. There is a letter from the car lease firm and they are taking my beautiful company car away ... oh no. An empty answering machine and quiet website make the news hard to take. My beautiful flyers and free cakes have had little effect. No orders equals no money. Perhaps now is the time to call it a day ... with Moo gone I'm not sure I can do this any more. As I stare at the beautiful photos on the website, I wonder if I'm the only one to have done so. What a waste. The phone rings and I consider not answering it, but then think that perhaps something awful has happened. Not that I am feeling negative and doom laden right now or anything!

'Fancy going out with the most desirable man in the area? I have a window and it's Maddy shaped,' Mac says and makes me smile. Nobody has died.

'No, thanks, I'm tired and I think I'm going to have an early night.'

'Oh, come on. You're going to look like a cake soon, with unattractive sponge legs, chocolate fingers' – Mac laughs at his own brilliance and it makes me laugh even though it feels as if my mouth has forgotten how to – 'and we haven't celebrated your mad new business yet.'

'Bugger the business!' I say bitterly.

'Okay, I'm coming round to collect you and I expect

you to look gorgeous. I have a reputation to maintain. No egg-white stains, or people will think I've been getting excited over your fairy cakes.'

Thank God for Mac. He gets me very, VERY drunk on chocolate martinis in honour of my now obsessive search for the perfect cake recipe. Of course he thinks it's ridiculous and proof, if proof were needed, that I've lost the plot and need someone to have sex with, fast. He offered to do the dirty deed himself to put me out of my misery but I could see his heart wasn't in it and I declined. We laughed, talked rubbish and, at some point in the evening, I forget exactly what it was that I was worrying about.

The next morning I wake up with a hangover and can hardly get out of bed. It's just as well I have no orders. Oh well, tomorrow I shall look for another job. Right now, though, I might have to go back for a little lie down. I'm meant to be meeting Lou for some shopping, but first I need to stay very still. I shuffle back to bed but before I can snuggle down I am stopped by a knock on the door. I try to ignore it, but the person on the other side is persistent. I put on my misshapen faded hooded sweatshirt that is something of a security blanket and wearily make my way through the hall and open the door. Standing there, with the sunshine streaming in all around him, is an angel sent from heaven. Temporarily blinded, I have to shield my eyes against the brightness. The vision before me moves position so that his body blocks the sun. He is not an angel but, just as welcome, a gorgeous Dundee cake, all golden and full of fruit. Is it *him*? He doesn't look swarthy or particularly Scottish, but he's delicious-looking in a blue shirt, faded Levi's, tanned arms and hair the colour of sand. He stands there with a quizzical look on his face, and smiles at me as if amused by something. I smile back and then remember I have my Tigger pyjama bottoms on. A force-eight blush immediately appears and I rub my face, conscious that I probably still have sleep in my eyes and a pillow crease across my cheek.

'Ronnie Johnson?' he asks.

'No,' I reply, puzzled, wishing I were.

'Oh. I thought she lived here,' he says, looking a little disappointed.

Won't I do?

'No, sorry, but I think you may have got the wrong house,' I say. Is it too late to say that I have had a temporary memory loss, and that yes, I *am* Ronnie Johnson?

'Is this number eleven?' he asks.

'No, this is number ten,' I reply, beginning to hate my neighbour for knowing someone as gorgeous as this when I don't.

'Oh, I'm so sorry. There was no number on the door,' he says, looking embarrassed.

'My numbers fell off yesterday,' I tell him, smiling my brightest, most seductive smile.

'Sorry to have bothered you,' he says, moving away, and unless I'm very much mistaken, there's a slight touch of relief in his voice. I reluctantly close the door and wander back into the house. Well, if that was *him*, it wasn't love at first sight – well, not for him anyway! I catch sight of my reflection in the mirror above the fireplace and it stops me in my tracks. Staring back at me is a mad-looking woman with dark circles of smudged mascara and hair sticking up in all directions from all the hairspray I used last night. How will I tell Moo that I have blown it? The first gorgeous man who comes within striking distance and I ruin it by looking like a mad person on Prozac. What if it really was him?

Lou thinks this is hilarious. She has no time for predictions and assures me that it wasn't him.

'It's not like the man of your dreams is just going to knock on your door,' she says, waving a blood-red talon at me and nearly taking my eye out in the process. I nod in agreement. After three hours of trailing around behind Lou as she tries on at least fifteen different outfits and twenty-three pairs of shoes, I'm feeling decidedly weak. My responses have changed from 'Oh, that really suits you' or 'No, the brown looks better' to 'Mmmm' or 'What did you say?' to eventually 'I'm just going to wait outside.'

I need sugar, fast. Luckily, Lou has an emergency can of Coke in her bag and as she disappears into yet another changing room, I sit on a bench outside, soaking in the sugar. The fizziness fills my mouth, making my tongue tingle, and my eyes water. It reminds me of the paper bags of multicoloured sherbet we had as kids; sucking the sherbet off our fingers until they became stained yellow. The shoe shop is the sweet shop of my adulthood and, with my sugar levels renewed, I find myself rushing into what Lou has promised is the last shop of the day. In my experience, this could be an empty promise as her capacity to shop knows no boundaries. The season's 'must haves' must be hers, with no exception, and there's still a pair of shoes-worth left on her credit card.

My senses immediately come alive with bright candy colours, shiny reds, sequins and fine Italian leather in chocolate brown. The sweet jars of my childhood have been replaced with Perspex shelves full of beautiful creations that will surely make us more beautiful, and our lives infinitely better. We wander around touching, admiring, lusting, calculating how much pocket money we have left to spend. My attention is immediately drawn to a pair of exquisite silver sandals with the most impractical of heels. They are the tinsel that decorated the Christmas trees of my childhood, the tiny silver balls on a fairy cake. Excitedly, I take off my boots and slip them on to my feet, admiring the effect in the mirror. I'm sexy and gorgeous, a Kylie-like disco diva, although the black socks don't really do them justice. How will *he* be able to resist me wearing these babies?

Lou appears clutching a pair of equally unsuitable red-sequinned shoes. They look like something Dorothy from *The Wizard of Oz* would wear on her slutty days.

'I have to have these,' I say with conviction.

'They're gorgeous, but I hate to ask, when would you wear them?' Lou asks.

'Every girl should have a pair of silver dancing shoes,' I tell her, doing a little twirl to test their effectiveness. Perfect.

'When was the last time you went dancing?' Lou asks, and my bright, sexy, gorgeous world disappears as fast as the sugar hit and I come crashing back down to a world without silver glitter balls.

'But I might, if I have these,' I murmur, sounding like a little girl who is about to have her lolly stolen from her.

'I don't mean to bring you down, sweetie, but you're not exactly flush at the moment and without a salary coming in . . .'

'Since when have you been so sensible?' I say sulkily.

'Isn't that what friends are for?' she says, walking up and down in her Dorothy shoes.

As much as I don't want to hear it, she is saying the same things as the little voice in my head, the one that tells me I should be spending the little money I have left on a pair of sensible boots and getting a plumber out to fix the annoying dripping tap in the bathroom. This no-salary business is no fun, no fun at all.

'If it makes you feel any better, I won't buy these,' Lou says, reluctantly placing the red shoes back on the display case. As we walk away, she gazes back at them as if they are made of precious rubies and will be snatched away by the Wicked Witch of the West. We leave the shop despondent, justifying our decision and congratulating ourselves on being so sensible. We only manage to get two hundred yards before Lou stops me in my tracks.

'Hoovering!' she says, and I look at her as if she has gone mad.

'Forget the dancing. Every girl should have a pair of sparkly silver hoovering shoes,' she declares, taking my hand and dragging me back to the shop.

Hoovering shoes. How fabulous!

With shopping bags all around us Lou and I make a toast to a successful shopping day.

'So why did you change your mind about my silver shoes?' I ask her while we pore over the menu of Pizza Express. Highly calorific and full of carbohydrates, it is perfect post-shopping food.

'Because life is too short to take the sensible option every time and with shoes there is very rarely a sensible option to consider,' Lou replies. She looks fabulous today, in a tight-fitting black leather jacket that complements her curves and narrow jeans tucked into absurdly high, black leather boots.

'And if you are going to bag a man you have to have some shoes to do it with,' she says and I groan at the prospect of meeting another one on her list.

'Cheers. To hoovering shoes and ruby reds.' I raise my glass to her. 'When will you wear yours?' I ask, trying to think of an occasion that would warrant such a pair of shoes.

'My pole-dancing lessons. I start on Monday.'

'Aahh.' Of course, now why didn't I think of that?

'Carl can't wait.' Lou raises her eyes to the heavens.

'What will you use as a pole at home?'

'Oh, I don't know. A broomstick, and I can always use the kitchen table as a stage, but I'll need to do a weight-bearing test first,' she says matter-of-factly.

'What are you going to have?' I ask as we scan the menu. With a hangover still hovering I am starving. My body is screaming out for something unhealthy.

'I don't know. Salad, I think. I'm trying to be good.'

'Me too. I'll have salad as well,' I agree, trying to hide the disappointment in my voice.

'Mmm, that pizza smells lovely, though.' Lou looks up as a waiter wafts one past us.

'We could always share one?' I suggest hopefully.

'Yes, let's share one,' Lou says as we both continue to look at the menu. 'Although I am pretty hungry . . .'

'And they are smaller than they used to be . . .' I add helpfully.

'Sod it! Let's have a pizza each.'

As our stomachs groan and our shoes glow softly in their boxes at our feet, I bring up the subject of the business.

'But I don't think I can do it on my own without Moo,' I say, shaking my head in despair.

'Why not?' Lou questions me as if I have said

something really very stupid. She may have a point because, when I think about it, I can't come up with a convincing answer.

'Just think, if it's a success, the silver shoes will be Jimmy Choos and it won't be a case of shall I buy them, it will be a case of shall I buy one or two pairs!' Lou says, holding up her glass for another toast.

'A nice thought, but I don't think there is a fortune to be made in cakes,' I say, clinking her glass. I feel surprisingly merry on one glass of wine. The excitement of a pair of silver shoes has made me a little light-headed, although there is the argument that I am just topping up last night's quantity.

'Look at Nigella Lawson. And the men love her,' Lou says.

'Yes, but I'm not offering sex with my cupcakes.'

'Perhaps you should be. Let's face it, your sex life is pretty dismal at the moment,' Lou points out, and laughs at her cruel observation.

'I'm not quite that desperate just yet and Environmental Health might have something to say about it. All those fluids.'

'It might add something to the texture of your icing.'

'Urgh, you are disgusting!' I say, laughing so much that I begin to choke on my wine.

'But it might not be a bad marketing ploy. A slice of something you fancy! A fumble and a fruit cake!'

Our coffee arrives and we pay the bill. Lou takes out her compact to check that there are no stray bits of spinach in her teeth. Happy there is nothing to offend she snaps it shut and turns to look at me with a look I imagine stalls the most eager of sales reps in the drinks industry.

'The thing is, Maddy, you mustn't see Moo's departure as a negative thing. See it as an opportunity, an opportunity to shine like the star you are, to dance the light fantastic in your silver shoes. Remember you're the woman who increased sales of that drug . . . ?'

'Genolipten,' I prompt.

'That's it, Genolipten. You ran that campaign and sales increased by thirty per cent, if I remember rightly. You did that, Maddy, nobody else.'

'That was a long time ago,' I respond, thinking back to the launch that had me throwing up minutes before presenting to three hundred of the top consultants in their field. But the applause afterwards . . . I remember feeling like Madonna on a world tour.

'The person who did that is still there, you just need to find her again.' Lou looks at me and smiles. 'Wasn't that the YMCA conference?'

I nod, remembering celebrating with a little too much champagne and doing the YMCA dance in front of the same consultants that night. Oh, the shame of it.

'Anyway, I want to be your first order. I need an Earl Grey Tea cake for Carl's birthday.'

'Are you sure?' I ask.

'Of course,' she confirms, getting up and gathering her bags. 'By the way, you have a rather attractive cappuccinoesque moustache.'

Grazia Interview

Me on the front cover wearing my silver shoes with the headline 'Forget Sienna Miller: We Talk to Maddy Brown, Head of Sugar and Spice'.

'How have your friends and family reacted to

your success with Sugar and Spice?'

'They've all been so supportive and many of them are involved directly with the company. My sister, Moo, as you know, is co-founder and executive director. She is currently working on our children's baking range. The company marketing director is my oldest friend, Lou, and she is liasing with Stella McCartney to design some funky aprons and my father is in charge of sales. Mum runs one of our tearooms in Cornwall and my brother and his wife are the people responsible for business development. In fact, my brother is at the moment discussing the possibility of a TV series.'

'Is that what keeps you grounded through the whirlwind success Sugar and Spice has become?'

'I'm sure it helps. One minute I'm on the phone to Nicole Kidman and asking her if she wants pink or yellow flowers on her fairy cakes, the next I'm doing the washing up at my sister's. She never lets me get away with being a prima donna.'

'And how do you feel when magazines call you a style icon; when what you wear becomes the must-have purchase for women everywhere?'

'I find it flattering. I just wear what makes me feel comfortable and if people like that, then that's great.'

'And Chloé have named a handbag after you?'

'Yes, it has lots of inside pockets and room for a small Tupperware of fairy cakes.'

'Your jeans are great, can we ask where you got them from?'

'Oh, these? I designed them myself.'

The sultanas and raisins look as if they have had botox. They went in all wrinkled like old women and have now emerged plump, gorgeous and smooth, their little skins nearly bursting with goodness. I wonder if Earl Grey Tea, butter and sugar would have the same effect on my skin. God, I need it. The sleepless nights worrying about what to do now Moo is out of the picture have meant I look like one of the 'before' raisins. I wonder for the umpteenth time what I am going to do. Safety in numbers, isn't that what they say, and I did feel safe with Moo by my side, convinced that with her there it could only be a success. I may be the eldest but it was Moo who had the first boyfriend, was the first to leave home, the first to get a job and the first to get pregnant. Everything I have done I have looked to her for direction, like a lighthouse lighting the way. Now some bastard has turned the bulb off and I feel shipwrecked. Even with Lou's words of encouragement I am scared of the what ifs. Could I make a success out of Sugar and Spice on my own?

I pop the Earl Grey Tea cake I have made for Carl into the oven and consider giving it all up now, before it gets out of hand. Nothing lost, nothing gained. I could just go back to my life before this crazy idea and put it down to experience. But what life? Since losing the baby I have felt lost and, if I'm honest, have wallowed in self-pity. The business has been a life saver, giving me focus and making me feel as if I am once again taking control of my destiny. I phone Mum and ask her what she thinks I should do.

'*Faites vigoureux, chérie,*' she tells me and I respond with a thank you but am none the wiser. I pace up and down, a bad-cop-versus-good-cop routine playing out in my head. It was just a silly idea and it's best to finish it all now before it goes any further . . . but, I have worked so hard to get this far, and didn't I sort out the website on my own? Well, surely I could do it again? Couldn't I?

I remove the cake from the oven and the warmth of sweet cooked fruit fills the kitchen; it looks and smells absolutely delicious. I stand back and survey my creation. Give up? How could I deny the world my Earl Grey Tea cake?

With my momentous decision made and the fact that my car is being taken away tomorrow, I have asked Ben to help me choose something else; something cheap and practical, something good for transporting cakes. God, I never thought I would hear myself say that. As I open the door I notice a piece of paper on the floor: *'Got hold of Ronnie so thanks for your help. If you fancy going out for a drink, ring me on 07977863444. My name is Greg, by the way.'*

Oh my God!

What do I do now? Do I ring him? I pick up the phone and try not to hyperventilate.

'Hello?'

'Somebody has just given me their number to ring. A man . . . and he is gorgeous. What do I do?' I scream down the phone.

'Ring him now, you stupid mare. It could be *him*,' Moo says excitedly.

I pace up and down before dialling the number. Each ring is like a slow torture.

'Greg speaking.'

'Hi, Greg. It's . . . urm . . . the girl [who am I trying to kid?] from number ten. You left me your number?' I stumble over my words, feeling like a schoolgirl.

'Hi, girl from number ten. Do you have a name?'

'Maddy.' I giggle stupidly.

'Well, Maddy, I'm glad you rang. Do you fancy going out for a drink tomorrow night?'

'Ummm . . . well . . . yes, I'd love to,' I stammer. Since when do I have a speech impediment?

'I'll be there at eight. See ya,' he says brightly and is gone.

Is that it? I guess it is. Wow! I have date! I have a date tomorrow night with a gorgeous man! Oh my God, what am I going to wear? Fake tan, I need fake tan. I also need to paint my fingernails and toenails, rub those horrid hard bits from my heels and find my favourite black knickers with the baby pink bows on them.

No, stop! It's a first night out. He will not be sucking on my heels or seeing my knickers! However, it's always good to be prepared.

I peer into car windows and try to concentrate on what Ben is telling me instead of thinking of my hot date. I almost tell him but then stop myself. I cannot face the twenty questions I know I will get, but it's so hard. I am practically bursting with it all. He tells me to leave everything to him as he strides across the salesroom floor to bargain with a rather spotty-looking child with a suit on. I haven't the energy to argue as I try not to look at all the shiny new cars. A nice new Golf in metallic-blue with air-conditioning, CD player and alloy wheels? The reality of my financial situation means that I can only just stretch to a ten-year-old Astra van without any of the above. Soon I will not only be without my beautiful company car but the fuel card, AA membership and paid tax and insurance that went with it. Now I will have to pay for it all myself and the thought depresses me, but not half as much as driving a van. Yes, it's practical, and yes, I have to be sensible with my money, and yes, it makes sense for delivering cakes but no matter how much you try and put a positive spin on it, the truth is there is nothing exciting or sexy about being a white-van woman. Ben gives me the thumbs up and I try to look enthusiastic and grateful as the baby-faced salesman hands me the keys. Driving it home, I am pleasantly surprised. It's actually not that bad, although it would be a whole lot better if I had some cakes to deliver.

The van is now parked outside the house and is soon forgotten as a knock at the door confirms his arrival. I quickly spray on some more perfume, although I suspect I have overdone it a little, and check my appearance. Not bad. I am wearing the black wraparound dress over jeans (wasn't going to wear stockings on a first date – the key is to look gorgeous but not as if you have tried too hard, though this is coming from someone who can't remember her last date!) and my silver hoovering shoes. Okay, take a deep breath, shoulders back. You look gorgeous.

'Hi. Ready?' he asks, and I nod. I have to take a deep breath again to calm my nerves. He is very good-looking.

'You scrub up well,' he says with an easy laugh and I respond with a sheepish grin, remembering our first meeting.

'What made you ask me out when I looked like such a freak?' I laugh as we wander down the high street.

'Because I have a thing about women in pyjamas,' he says, and smiles. He has a cheeky smile and exudes confidence, or is it arrogance? I like a man with a sense of humour.

The evening is spent talking and laughing easily. By the time he has walked me home, I am a little tipsy and my jaw is aching from smiling so much. He lightly kisses me on the lips and then, before I know it, we are in full snog mode. He tastes of beer and fruit pastilles.

'Are you going to invite me in for coffee?' he asks when we eventually pull away. My legs feel like jelly. Yes? No? Yes? No? Yes? Oh God! I shake my head no. Right now there is a very loud voice telling me to just pull him in, but part of me also wants the whole romantic thing of leading up to it. If Greg is *him*, then I want it to be right.

'I have to get up early,' I say as an excuse.

'I'll ring you,' he says, smiling, and saunters off without looking back. From the doorway I watch him go and I have to use all of my willpower to stop myself from calling out 'Forget I said no. Come back and kiss me until my lips are sore, throw me on the kitchen floor and rip my knickers off with your teeth. Please!!!' Well, it has been a long time, and it could be the last time before I revert back to virginity.

As I get ready for bed, I realise I have had my knickers on inside out all evening. Thank goodness I didn't invite him in for coffee. Not that I would have slept with him on the first date, of course!

EARL GREY TEA CAKE

This cake becomes even more lovely and moist over time, so if you can resist it, leave it for a day or two before tucking in.

Ingredients

150g (5oz) butter

175 (6oz) light muscovado sugar

250ml (8fl.oz) fairly strong Earl Grey Tea

250g (9oz) dried fruit (sultanas, raisins, chopped apricots/ prunes)

200g (9oz) self-raising flour

Finely grated zest and juice of 1 unwaxed lemon

1 large egg

50–75g (2–3oz) walnuts

5 demerara sugar lumps, coarsely crushed

Method

Grease and line base of an 18cm (7 inch) tin and preheat oven to 180°C/350°F/gas mark 4. Place the butter, sugar, tea and fruit in a saucepan and bring slowly to the boil – stir then simmer for 5 minutes. Cool thoroughly. Sift flour into fruit–tea mixture and beat in. Mix in lemon zest and juice, beaten egg and walnuts. Pour into tin and scatter crushed sugar lumps over the top and bake for 1–1 hour 15 minutes. Leave to cool in the tin before removing.

300 fairy cakes

Everybody loves a fairy cake: they are the Doris Day of the cake world; fluffy blondes with pretty, pastel-coloured dresses and sugary sweetness. Moo, Mum and I are surrounded by them as we ice the three hundred I am hoping to sell tomorrow at the May Day Fair. Mum has wandered back into the kitchen to make another batch.

I managed to persuade her to come here instead of me driving over to hers. She is looking decidedly frumpy in an oversized cardigan, checked trousers and boots that look very similar to the ones my neighbour, Mrs Miggins, who is eighty-five years old, wears; I get the impression she has come to the conclusion that she is now an old woman and should act and dress accordingly. The break-up of a ten-year relationship a couple of years ago hasn't helped and she took it hard. It must be difficult to be on your own again at her age. At least now she is painting again and has a nice little part-time job in a gallery near to home, but the attractive, vibrant woman I know is in there has been replaced by someone who has given up. I resolve to do something about it. A trendy hair cut, some new clothes and, who knows, she could find herself an older version of Greg. Maybe we could have a double wedding.

'What do you think? Fifty pence each and three for a pound?' I ask.

'Sounds about right,' Moo confirms. Oh, the precision of it all!

'Thanks for helping this weekend,' I say and put a sticky hand on hers.

'I needed the break,' she replies, and for a moment, I think she is going to cry. She brushes a stray hair from her face and looks down as if struggling with her thoughts.

'Are you okay?' I ask, concerned. I am not used to this side of Moo. I've always been the cry baby whereas she has always just laughed or shouted at whatever or whoever was upsetting her.

'Yes. I'm okay, really I am,' she says, looking up and giving me a weak smile. 'If I'm honest, I needed some time out from everything: work, baby, Bob. I try so hard to give them all one hundred per cent but fail dismally. I feel as if I'm being drained of every little piece of me. I'm irritable all the time and most days I'm too tired to hold a proper conversation.'

She violently shakes some hundreds and thousands on to a cake so that it ends up smothered. Without the lipstick and eyeliner on, which once upon a time she wouldn't leave the house without, she looks unnaturally pale, like one of those desperate drug addicts on *Casualty*. Is this what motherhood does to you? If Lou was here she would immediately prescribe an emergency dose of fake tan.

'And I'm FAT! I can't seem to shift that last stone and none of my old clothes fit me!' Moo throws a fairy cake across the room and I try not to laugh. That's more like it:

Moo the drama queen. As a child she would throw herself face down on the bed and refuse to eat or speak to anyone at even the slightest whiff of a 'no'. She roughly wipes her eyes with her sleeve, desperately trying not to let the tears fall but failing dismally. They come thick and fast: big fat droplets that run down her cheeks and fall on to the table. Colour bleeds from the sprinkles caught in the downpour, causing a tiny rainbow sea. I get up and put my arm around her as the tears continue to fall and her shoulders heave with the effort.

'You are not fat. Stop putting pressure on yourself to be the perfect woman all of the time. Lots of women struggle with their weight immediately afterwards.'

'Posh, Madonna, Sarah Jessica Parker?' Moo points out.

'Er, yes. But three words spring to mind: starvation, personal trainer and a nanny. Get real, Moo.'

Mum walks in at the sound of one of her brood crying.

'Oh, Michelle, darling . . .' she says and kisses her on the head. 'In the absence of some decent coffee here, how about I make us all a nice cup of tea?'

Moo nods and sniffles, looking like a child at nursery. The table is now covered in hundreds and thousands from her violent shaking and it looks pretty, like a speckled painting in bright hues of pink, blue and yellow.

'It is like an affair; the worst kind . . . you love until your heart will break . . . all for a smile or the sound of your name uttered from their lips,' Mum shouts from the kitchen.

I look at Moo who shakes her head.

'When did you have an affair?' I ask, not sure that I want to know the answer.

'I did have a life before your father robbed me of it . . .

his name was Jean-Luc . . . but that's by the by,' Mum says, bringing in two mugs of tea. 'What you have to remember darling, is that the first year is always hard and you should think yourself lucky . . . at least Bob helps out; your father was never around.'

We ignore this remark.

'Freya doesn't seem to find it hard,' Moo challenges, and Mum doesn't have an answer because she is right; Freya seems to have taken to it all like a duck to water and emerged half a stone lighter. Life can be so unfair sometimes. I get the impression, though, that even if Freya was struggling, she would never let on.

'She did give up work straight away,' I offer in way of explanation, 'and she is Swedish.' Although what relevance this last factor has on all of this is not really clear to either of us. As if on cue, Freya arrives, looking as fresh as a daisy, to lend a helping hand. She looks at Moo's bloodshot eyes and asks if she is okay. Moo confirms that, yes, she is fine, just a little tired, and I sense that she wants to change the subject. I ask Freya what miracle skin-care products she uses to make her skin glow and immediately wish I hadn't. Her answer makes me feel just as cheated as Moo.

'Oh, nothing, just soap and water.'

Life really is unfair.

Lou arrives with a pair of latex gloves on to protect her nails. She has offered to help but refuses to wear a hair net so sits there and talks beauty regimes with Freya instead. She is horrified at the suggestion of soap and water and proceeds to give us the low-down on the latest must-have beauty products. I use this opportunity to join Mum in the kitchen and try a little Trinny and Susannah psychology on her.

'You know, I really liked your hair when it was short,' I suggest.

'What's wrong with my hair like this?' Mum immediately stops whisking. Oh God!

'Nothing is wrong with it. It's just . . .' What do I say? It's just that a blue rinse and a Zimmer frame would finish off the way you look right now?

'I just like you with short hair better, it really suits you.' Phew!

Mum looks at me with suspicion before breaking the eggs into the mixture.

'We could go shopping later, if you want. Marks and Spencer have a fantastic new range of classic but funky separates in right now,' I suggest, sounding like their advert on TV.

'I suppose you want me to dress like a twenty year old, like that woman with the breasts? Well, some of us have more dignity,' Mum shouts over the sound of the hand mixer.

'No, I just thought it might be fun to go shopping and try some things on,' I suggest lamely.

'We haven't got time,' she says with a look that says this particular conversation is over and I nod, knowing that for now, like the eggs, I am beaten. I wander back to the icing.

'I've bought you some Clarins Beauty Flash Balm because you're looking a bit haggard,' Lou tells me, 'and you need to look good for your next date – it's like a mini facelift.'

'Thanks . . . I think.'

'So, have you heard from him?' Moo asks.

'No,' I answer despondently. I don't admit to checking my phone on the hour, every hour.

'He'll ring, it's just the four-day rule,' Lou informs us all with authority.

I hope she is right.

The first fifty cakes we iced with careful precision, each sprinkle shaken to ensure consistent coverage, but the last fifty are not so lucky. We slap on the icing with wild abandon and sprinkle without even looking. There is icing all over our hands and aprons, with hundreds and thousands rolling along the wooden floor waiting for a tragic accident to happen. When we have finished, I produce a bottle of champagne from my fridge that has been waiting for just such an occasion and we toast to the first public outing for Sugar and Spice. Before long, we are giggling about nothing in particular and have eaten too many of the fairy cakes. Lou leaves first but not before she suggests taking Mum for a makeover next time she visits. To my surprise, Mum thinks it's a wonderful idea. I give up! She is staying at Freya's and not long after Lou they leave together. Moo and I check everything is in place for the morning, although how effectively is anyone's guess. We make our way to bed, tired from our little icing production line and more than a little tipsy. Moo sleeps in my bed and I get the blow-up mattress out to put in the spare bedroom. Blowing up a mattress when half pissed is not a good idea and by the morning I am flat on the floor, having forgotten to put the stoppers in.

The May Day Fair is a yearly event in my hometown. The main street is closed to traffic, and stalls fill every available space. They are always the same: a church tombola, a second-hand book stall run by the local Rotary club, a WI stall with jams and preserves and about six charity raffle stalls. Surrounded by a backdrop of town houses, pretty Victorian cottages and brightly coloured bunting, the local green becomes a mini music festival. Folk musicians emerge from wherever it is they remain for the rest of the year, their beards an inch longer and their breeches an inch shorter, to play in front of an appreciative audience. This is the public launch for Sugar and Spice and, too excited to sleep, I am awake with the dawn chorus. I pull open the curtains and my heart lifts as the early morning sunshine pours in, promising a beautiful and successful day. Hurray! Hurray! I practically jump out of bed and begin to gather my little fairy friends around me whilst Moo grumbles about me ruining the first lie-in she has had for months.

We arrive at the green to a flurry of activity as an eclectic range of stalls are erected all around us. There is a woman selling pottery who will be next to us, a plant stall, one full of brightly coloured tie-dyed clothes and wooden jewellery, a couple of girls selling essential oils and relaxation tapes, and a rather odd-looking man selling collectors' comic books. By ten, we are ready to go, and although our tarpaulin, held on by miles of gaffer tape, threatens to collapse at any moment, our stall is resplendent with an impressive banner, pretty floral tablecloths, delicate china and coloured glass cake stands. The table is positively groaning under the weight of fairy cakes with sprinkles, jelly tots and sugar flowers in all kinds of mouth-watering pastel colours. There are chocolate ones, lemon ones, some with Smarties and, under pressure from James, football-inspired George Cross ones. It looks fabulous!

Fabulous!

The music starts and soon the green is full of people in

T-shirts, shorts and summery dresses. Children giggle as they excitedly run around, losing summer hats and ice creams in the process, while their parents enjoy the music. Some get up and dance while others lie on blankets, soaking up the unexpected sun or reading the Sunday papers with a picnic.

Children love our fairy cakes, and parents apologise as little fingers are poked in their middles while they decide which ones to choose. Strangely, the little boys love the pink ones with the sprinkles on, while the girls always go for the chocolate ones, although Moo has a point when she comments that this is quite normal and is the beginning of lifelong fascinations for men and women. The pink ones with sprinkles turn into blondes with big tits, and the chocolate? George Clooney, Mr Darcy and Johnny Depp, of course.

I feel like I did when I was a child playing pretend post offices with Moo, and I throw myself into it with gusto as if I'd been born to run a stall. Inspired, I make a mental note to investigate doing a farmers' market on a regular basis. A steady flow of friends and family visit the stand including Mum, Ben, Freya and The Princess, who sucks the icing off the top of a cake before handing the remaining soggy sponge back to me with a sour look on her face. Mac and a stick-thin brunette called Rebecca say a brief hello and buy a couple of cakes, although by the look on her face she is not a great fan of cake, or, I suspect, any type of food. Egged on by Mac, she begins to take tiny mouthfuls like a bird but it's almost painful, like watching someone eat a raw brussel sprout. The things we do for a new man in our life. I must ask him about her later tonight.

James and Frog settle themselves down on the grass behind the stand, James sipping a bottle of beer, watching the blondes go by with Frog never far away, snuffling for stray cakes dropped by little hands. I'm glad things don't seem to have changed much between us since the divorce became final. We haven't talked about it, but then that's the way we are; like the miscarriage, it is another thing that has been brushed under the carpet. I look at him and think how strange life is; it's as if we were never married and I wonder if there will be a time when he will not be part of my life at all. He looks up and smiles at me before waving to Lou who arrives with Carl and Chloe. As the rest of us wilt in the heat she looks like an exotic tropical plant with a brightly patterned halter-neck dress in vibrant blues and greens, matching mules and designer sunglasses. She should be in Cannes, not the local green, and people double take as if they are not sure if she is a film star or not. As Carl and James talk football results, Lou attempts to supervise Chloe, who is determined to poke her finger in each and every cake.

'Look at the pretty pink ones.' Lou points them out to her daughter. 'They are the same colour as your shoes.'

Chloe has other ideas and greedily takes two chocolate ones. Within minutes her pretty pale pink dress is covered and she is grinning at me with a chocolate-smeared grin. Lou shakes her head in despair and pulls out a pair of tiny jeans and a T-shirt from her bag for Chloe to change into. Despite her attempts at dressing her three-year-old daughter in delicate little princess dresses, Chloe refuses to be drawn into the feminine world her mother inhabits and is a tomboy through and through. Secretly I suspect that this is how it should be. There is only room for one princess per family.

As Lou glides off, her perfectly tanned shoulders

glistening in the sun, Moo and I can only watch and wonder how she makes it look so easy.

'Don't you feel a little dowdy and plain next to her?' Moo asks.

'Thanks, but yes, I do,' I reply, licking the ice cream Moo has brought back.

By 6.00 p.m. our stand is practically empty except for a few stray fairy cakes that Moo packs away to take back for The Bear. The green begins to empty as sunburnt faces and shoulders make their way home. It has been a hectic, uplifting and exhausting day and I feel on a high as we pack up and count the takings. The grand total is £130.00. It will thankfully cover my costs, but if I looked too closely at the man-hours I have spent baking it doesn't really add up to a profit. It has been productive in other ways, though; more people now know about Sugar and Spice, and some even came back to tell me how lovely the cakes were and that they would definitely be placing an order. I resisted the urge to demand a written confirmation. After much hugging and kissing, Moo and Mum make their way home and I wander back with a sense of achievement.

Tired, but feeling on a high after my busy day, I take a quick shower before meeting Lou and Mac for a drink. With only half an hour to get ready, I stand in front of my wardrobe and wait for some inspiration. Nothing seems right and I angrily throw things on the bed before deciding on a pair of jeans, and my trusty white shirt. I do a quick check in the mirror and persuade myself I look stunning.

I should have known better. Lou looks stunning in a slashed-to-the-cleavage top I seem to remember seeing

Liz Hurley wearing in *OK!* magazine the other day and Mac, the epitome of man tart, is looking sexy in brown and black stripes. I feel positively dowdy next to them and for once, my shirt has failed me.

As always, Lou and I are fascinated by Mac's love life, relentlessly probing for little titbits of information on each girl that passes through his life; always wondering if, in Mac's world, the perfect woman actually exists and whether his mother would accept her.

'So tell us about Rebecca,' I say.

'Oh.' Mac screws his nose up. 'Mad as a box of frogs, totally obsessed with the gym and her diet. And . . . she has really pokey-out hipbones. No, Rebecca has got to go.'

'What happened to Ingrid?' Lou asks.

'She had the most stunning blue eyes, if I remember rightly,' I confirm.

'Big feet,' Mac states, as if this explains everything.

'What do you mean, big feet?' we ask in unison.

'She had big feet. They were horrible, so I ended it.' Mac closes his eyes and shakes his head as if he is trying to erase the memory.

'But all tall girls with legs up to their armpits have big feet,' I observe, wishing that it was something I had to worry about.

'Mac, you're crazy! Ingrid was bright, funny and gorgeous,' Lou says, looking to the heavens in disbelief.

'I know, but I couldn't stop thinking about her feet and in my mind they just kept growing.' He wears a pained expression, as if speaking about them causes him acute distress.

'What happened to Carrie, the South African solicitor?' I ask him.

'Oh, bushy eyebrows, and then there was the accent, of course.'

'Of course,' I say incredulously.

Mac has a desire to be with a certain type of woman. A woman who for the last fifteen years has inhabited the same dream, the one where Mac is the man in tights and she hangs on to him for safety. Fluttering those huge, dark, cow-like lashes, she turns to him with a breathless voice, 'Oh, Superman.'

'Does the perfect woman or man exist?' I ask, wondering if I should be considering the Madeira cakes of this world, and whether my chocolate cake man is an improbable fantasy. Bloody Greg is turning out to be one . . . improbable, not cake like.

'No,' Lou states with authority. 'But if someone is right for you then they become as near perfect as it ever gets.'

'Mmmmm . . . But in Mac's case?' I ask as if he isn't there.

'Mac, of course, is a different matter. He has totally unrealistic expectations and unless she has the physical attributes of Teri Hatcher, every girl he meets doesn't stand a chance,' Lou says, slurring a little.

'Hey, are you saying that I am that shallow?' Mac says, looking a little put out. His hurt puppy-dog expression is probably causing every woman in the room to consider rushing over and hugging him to their bosom.

Lou and I look at each other for a split second before nodding yes.

'Ooooh, I nearly forgot. Carl and I are having a little barbecue on Monday. You should both come.' Lou slurs a little and Mac and I exchange a look that questions the use of the word 'little'. Lou's barbecues have the same reputation and a similar guest list to Elton John's parties.

'And talking of perfection, I think I may have found just the man for you.' Lou waves a finger at me, her eyes not quite focusing. 'Gorgeous-looking, successful solicitor, split up with his girlfriend six months ago, and he has a lovely old cottage on the outskirts of Oxford,' she says excitedly as if she has found the perfect rug for her living room.

'Good sense of humour, likes outside pursuits and his favourite song is "Hello" by Lionel Richie?' I groan but Lou just smiles at me indulgently before getting up and heading towards the bar for another round of drinks. She smiles indulgently at the men who gaze at her with tongues hanging out at the thought of nestling their heads between her magnificent breasts.

I can hear ringing but my fuggy, hungover brain thinks I'm still dreaming and I decide to ignore it. Suddenly, the realisation that it is the phone kicks in and I bolt out of bed as if I have been scorched. By the time I get to the phone the answer machine has clicked off. Now I am in a dilemma. Do I wait and hope that they will phone back, or do I dial 1471? I cannot wait; I am too excited and nervous about my potential first order. I dial 1471 and call back the number I've jotted down.

'Hello,' I say with my best business-type voice. 'This is Sugar and Spice. You called a minute ago?'

Some snotty-nosed kid answers with a nonchalant, 'Oh, I dialled the wrong number,' and hangs up.

Bastard!

God, my head hurts.

I check my phone again but there is nothing from Greg. I don't understand it and despite going over the evening a thousand times in my mind I can't think of anything that could have potentially put him off. Maybe I laughed a little too loudly, or wasn't that interesting; I was a bit quiet, but that was nerves and I don't remember doing anything embarrassing. Whatever I did or didn't do, it was enough to make him not want to see me again. Perhaps he wasn't my chocolate cake after all. I turn my thoughts to the eligible man Lou has promised me and decide to try another recipe. Mmmmm . . . perhaps I need something to spice it up a little. I am thinking exotic, dark velvety seduction. A touch of Cointreau or brandy?

Instead of smelling of cake mixture, I arrive at Lou's with the aroma of Chanel. My what-to-wear dilemma was answered by Freya who has lent me a pretty fifties-inspired floral tea dress in pastel blues and greens that she wore when she was five months' pregnant and which fits me perfectly. I have teamed it with a small blue cardigan and flip-flops and, ignoring the fact that I am wearing what amounts to maternity wear, I feel pretty good. As I place the chocolate and Cointreau cake with a dusting of cocoa powder in the kitchen, Lou drags me to one side.

'Dooby whatsit is here,' she whispers.

'Dooby whatsit?' I ask, puzzled.

'You know, the guy I was telling you about, the solicitor,' she says and drags me out into the garden before I have the chance to protest, or check my hair.

'Look who's arrived,' Lou announces, and to my horror, everyone turns around to look at me. This is not something I cope with very well, and I soon begin to feel the beginnings of a full force-ten blush. This increases to a force-fifteen when Dooby whatsit turns out to be utterly gorgeous and looks straight at me as if he is waiting to see if I do tricks. If only Bob was here to produce a rabbit from under my skirt. I make an emergency dash to the toilet to check my hair, and wait for the blush to disappear. Nine minutes later, I emerge with a more manageable force-three that could be mistaken for a radiant glow. I manage to keep my composure, but as I feel Dooby's eyes follow me, a force-eight is not far away. I manage to bypass the Hampstead sponge cakes and head for Mac, who is nursing a burger and beer with a rather sullen-looking Rebecca by his side. I look at him with a silent question and he shrugs his shoulder in despair. She is thin, very thin; in fact, as Lou pointed out earlier, she is too thin (not that we are jealous or anything), although her feet are not particularly big and she seems to be pretty perfect in any other way. Well, she would be if she smiled a bit more and didn't keep checking on her reflection in the patio doors.

Just knowing that a good-looking man is somewhere very near gives the proceedings an unexpected frisson, heightening my appetite and enjoyment factor considerably. I nibble on all the things the GMTV diet expert told me to avoid earlier in the week and try to ignore the daggers Rebecca shoots at me as I attempt to make small talk. She is not a happy bunny, and nor, by the look of things, is Mac. I search for an escape but Lou is being a social butterfly, flitting from guest to guest, dressed in what the magazines are calling mouth-watering brights. This summer, if you're anyone worth your fashion-slave salt, you must ignore the fact that there is a danger of looking like a packet of Starburst and should dress yourself in corals, limes, oranges and yellows. For the pale-skinned amongst us it's a recipe for disaster. I smile a gracious smile, make my excuses and sit down on the grass with little Chloe who is already covered in mud from playing hide and seek in the bushes with Carl. As I try to work out how her electronic keyboard works she attempts to stick a ketchup-covered sausage into my ear, which is a little distracting, but I persevere, turning the keyboard this way and that. It's more complicated than my DVD machine and I look around for something else to take her attention away, before becoming aware of an expensive pair of shoes next to me. I look up to find a vision of dark hair and even darker eyes.

'The switch is on the side,' he says, smiling to reveal a set of beautiful white teeth.

'Thanks,' I reply as I attempt to remove myself from Chloe, who is now waving her sausage around like Darth Vader. I stand up and rub off the ketchup I can feel on my left cheek and smile what I hope is a winning smile.

'Donald Geddes. Lou has told me all about you,' he says and inwardly I groan at the thought of what she has said and why someone so gorgeous should have such a naff name. He doesn't look like a Donald, more like a Ralph pronounced Raif. The thought occurs to me though that Donald is a vaguely Scottish-sounding name.

'You make a great cake,' he says, pointing to his plate. I simper with delight and imagine him taking me away from all this for a romantic dinner for two. Chloe and her keyboard are quickly forgotten as we begin the start of something potentially beautiful. And it is beautiful, for the first thirty-five minutes, but then something happens and I find myself transfixed by my quickly disappearing chocolate cake that I still haven't sampled yet. Donald is beautiful, but he makes the mistake of relying on it to see him through the fact that he has no real personality. He doesn't get my humour and I don't get his, and I quickly become bored as he talks at me about himself. He is a

Devil's Food cake, all gorgeous, sugary frosting; the sort that makes you feel a little sick after a while and the little cocoa-powder moustache he has acquired does nothing for me. My mind has wandered to a slice of a different kind and I make my excuses, narrowly beating Lou's nan to the last piece of cake. Mmmmm, not bad, but like Donald, it's not the one.

After having consumed my own body weight in food I say goodbye to Mac who looks as if he is struggling as much as Rebecca is with the slice of cake that remains untouched on her plate.

'Not Lois Lane?' I whisper and he shakes his head mournfully. I leave him to it, and do air kissing and hugs with Lou and Carl before making my way home.

The next morning the Sugar and Spice phone rings and I'm not sure what to do. Is it going to be some other little shit with a wrong number? I pick it up nervously, and a woman asks if she could possibly order forty-eight fairy cakes for a nursery birthday party tomorrow afternoon.

'I know it's short notice, but you would really be helping me out if you could fit it in,' she says apologetically.

'Let me see what we can do,' I say, pretending to look through my non-existent, full order book.

'Yes, I think we can do that for you,' I say, as if I'm doing her a huge favour. Oh dear, I will never go to heaven. Wow! I have just received my first order from a complete stranger! I phone Moo and we both scream with excitement.

'That's forty-eight times fifty pence . . . ?'

'Twenty-four pounds!' Moo exclaims excitedly and we both scream again as if I've just won the lottery. It's not much, but it's a start and at a cost of approximately ten pence per cake that's not a bad profit margin.

'What are you going to do about Mum, though?'

Shit and bugger! In my excitement, I had completely forgotten we had planned to be there for her birthday, which also happens to be tomorrow. What kind of bad daughter am I?

'She is not going to be happy!' Moo echoes my train of thought. 'Not happy at all . . .'

'Mmmmm,' I murmur, already dreading the phone call I'm going to have to make to Mum. Surely she will understand?

'Ooooh, I'm so pleased. Look, I've got to go, The Bear is determined to kill one of the rabbits, but keep me informed.'

I put the phone down and spend the next twenty minutes hovering over it, trying to summon up the courage to phone Mum.

'Mum . . .'

'Hello, darling. I was just thinking about you. I've been making some Madeleine cakes for tomorrow. I can remember being addicted to them when I was pregnant with you,' she tells me and I feel so very, very bad. Deep breath and . . .

'Mum, I can't make it tomorrow.' There, I said it. A silence follows, which is bad, but infinitely better than her putting the phone down on me, which is what I fully expected. I attempt to fill the silence with my excuse.

'I've just had my first order. Can you believe it? I'm so excited. They want the cakes for tomorrow and, of course, I couldn't say no. Not to my first order, Mum. You understand, don't you?' I ramble on, barely pausing for breath.

'You have to do what you feel is right, Maddy,' she says slowly. This is where I should be falling on my sword.

'You know I want to be with you, Mum, but I have to do this. It's too important for the business.'

'If that's what's important to you. I'll take the Madeleines around to Mrs Darwin,' she says, sounding like a sulky child.

'Moo and Ben will be with you,' I remind her, wiping the already clean kitchen surfaces over with a cloth. It stops me from fiddling my hair away into complete baldness.

'It would have been nice to have my whole family around me. But if you're too busy . . .'

'It's not that I'm too busy, I just feel that I have to make this sacrifice for the business,' I say lamely.

'As I said. If that's what's important to you, Maddy,' she remarks before putting the phone down. Well, that went well! When did I become responsible for her happiness? I'm surprised she didn't make the comment that I always seem to make it for Dad's birthday, but I guess that will come later. This guilt trip will be a long one. I will send her a cake and hopefully she will forgive me in the fullness of time.

I attempt to banish the guilt cloud that has settled over my kitchen and soon have forty-eight golden beauties cooling on a rack. It takes me longer than is absolutely necessary to ice them but it is the turning point I have been waiting for, and I want them to be perfect. As I carefully place the dolly mixtures and chocolate buttons on top of each one I check my mobile every now and then in case Greg has texted me – nothing! He kissed me. Surely that means he likes me. So why hasn't he rung? Perhaps he has changed his mind? Oh, shut up, Maddy! I turn my attention back to my cakes, chiding myself for acting like a schoolgirl and eat the remaining dolly mixtures – except the green jelly one. Like the green fruit pastille and wine gum, there is no place for them and far too many in a packet.

With something to deliver, my van transforms into something I resent driving into the most wonderful thing on four wheels and I resolve to get some sign writing for the sides: 'Sugar and Spice and all things nice delivered to your door' or something like that. I deliver the cakes as if I'm giving away a box of newborn puppies. A pleasant young girl hands me a cheque, smiles and closes the door. Unable to tear myself away I hover there for a moment, feeling like a new parent, wanting to hold their little fairy hands and check they exceed all expectations on their first day at school. I resist the urge to knock on the door to ask if I can watch them being eaten, and drive off with my first cheque shining brightly on the passenger seat. When I get home, there are a couple of messages on the phone; one is another order for more fairy cakes and the other is from a reporter from the local newspaper who, after seeing me at the May Day Fair, wants to do an interview with me. I feel ecstatic. Is this the start of things? Today the *Buckinghamshire Post*, tomorrow the front cover of *Vogue* in a couture gown, surrounded by cupcakes in mouth-watering pastel colours.

I phone the reporter back and we talk about the business and the recent fair. She comments that fairy cakes are really 'in' at the moment, that apparently Sarah Jessica Parker loves them. I'm tempted to say, 'Yes, we fly them over to her New York pad in pink designer Tupperware with her initials engraved on the top', but I'm sure Ms Parker has lawyers who protect her against people like me, in the way of a lawsuit. I respond with a 'Mmmmm . . . how fascinating', because if anyone believes SJP eats fairy cakes with her size-six figure they are severely delusional. I bet she doesn't even lick the icing off.

Graham Norton Interview

'So, sweetie, tell me all about the Vanilla Fairy Cake diet. There seems to be a whole number of celebrities extolling its virtues,' Graham says and I wonder how long it will be before he makes a double entendre.

'Yes, it's quite remarkable. It all happened by accident, really, but it has really taken off.'

'So, what does the diet consist of? Lots of fairies?' Graham laughs.

'It's really quite simple. You have a fairy cake at eleven a.m., then another one at three p.m. and finally a couple in the evening.'

'Sounds fabulous, but what about taking exercise?'

'Oh, there's no need for exercise. It really is the perfect way to lose weight. Eat lots of fairy cakes and watch the pounds fall off,' I tell him, producing a plate from under my chair and offering him one.

'Darling, can I just say you certainly look good on this fabulous diet.'

'You are too kind,' I reply, smiling. The slim-fitting dress Sarah Jessica Parker lent me for the occasion certainly does fit like a dream.

In my excitement I don't hear the door go and practically fall into the arms of Greg on my way out to tell Ben and Freya the good news.

'Oh, hello,' is all I can manage, fighting the blush that threatens.

'Sorry I haven't been in contact, it's been a bit hectic . . . Here, these are for you,' Greg says, handing me a bunch of daffodils. Butter-yellow, they are perfect. He is perfect.

'They're lovely, thank you . . . do you want to come in?' I ask, giving up to the blush.

'No thanks, I have to go. That's what I came round to tell you. I'm away for a little while with work, but I'd like to take you out again when I come back.'

'That would be lovely,' I respond, gazing into the daffodils. 'I'll bake you a cake.'

He kisses me on the cheek.

'Sounds great. Speak soon.'

And he is gone, leaving me on a little cushion of air; as light as a perfect sponge. It may have been short and sweet, but I don't care. He was here, bought me flowers, and he kissed me on the cheek. That's practically a date!

FAIRY CAKES

Aah, everybody loves a fairy cake. There are countless ways you can decorate them: dolly mixtures, candy flowers, chocolate sprinkles, the list is endless. I'm particularly fond of the way the Americans do it: butter and icing sugar whisked to within an inch of their life and topped with sprinkles. The Magnolia Bakery in New York is the place to sample the very best.

Ingredients

125g (5oz) unsalted butter, softened

2 large eggs

½ teaspoon vanilla extract

125g (5oz) caster sugar

125g (5oz) self-raising flour

2–3 tablespoons milk

For the icing:

185g (6oz) icing sugar

3–4 tablespoons lemon juice

Method

Preheat oven to 200°C/400°F/gas mark 6. Put all ingredients except the milk into the food processor and blitz until smooth. Add the milk down the funnel until a soft dropping consistency is achieved. Spoon mixture into cake cases until about three quarters filled. Bake in the centre of oven for 15–20 minutes or until the cakes are golden on top. Leave to cool on wire rack – cut off mounded tops so that you have a flat base for icing.

One smile and a couple of blushes

This morning my toaster flashes and is then gone to the big toaster dump in the sky. A day without my morning breakfast ritual and the repercussions could be huge. I have come to realise that there are some things that are so ingrained in my life that it might appear a little obsessive. How will Greg take to these little foibles of mine? Perhaps I should make him a 'need to know' danger list:

1. Breakfast is essential to my good humour for the day.
2. Public toilets are something I try to avoid and, on the same subject, a clean bathroom is a must. It may appear clean to you, but without shiny taps and spotless surfaces my spiritual well-being is severely disrupted.
3. 3.00 p.m. is slice of cake time. This is non-negotiable. Any earlier and it is too near lunch, any later and it is too close to dinner.
4. Do not question the fact that the vast number of shoes and handbags stay in my wardrobe because

they are too lovely and special to wear.
5. Once a month I become an emotional, angry monster. Do not take this personally.
6. Horror films give me nightmares and no matter how much I love you I will not watch them with you.
7. I will also not go camping. See number 2.
8. I am a control freak.
9. I am very sensitive and will take things personally. See number 5.
10. I get miserable and irritable when I am cold or hungry.
11. Oh, and I have a verruca called Veronica who follows me everywhere.

Maybe I'll wait. He will find it all out soon enough anyway. I look at my daffodils and swoon a little. Lust on an empty stomach is not something to be recommended. Starving and toastless I find some muesli at the back of the cupboard, which is better than nothing, I suppose. All the magazines say that oats, grains and fruit are good for you; but then so, apparently, is colonic irrigation and I can't imagine enjoying that either. As I attempt to plough through my healthy breakfast, I do something else that will potentially churn my stomach just as much: I look at my bank statement. It is not good: forty-eight fairy cakes are not going to pay the mortgage and my redundancy pay will not last for ever. Twelve thousand pounds seemed a lot of money at the time but the fact that I had a hefty credit card bill to pay off, a bigger cooker, cooking equipment and a van to buy has not helped matters. The house insurance is up for renewal, the business insurance needs paying and I seem to get through over £1500 a month on living expenses. Perhaps I should be cutting down on my Green & Black's chocolate and buy normal toilet rolls instead of that lovely quilted stuff.

This, of course, is not how it is meant to be, and my fluffy, sponge-like cloud I've been floating on for the past few days deflates a little. Despite more leaflet drops, an advert in the local newspaper, a mail-out to all the businesses and nurseries in the area, and my stand at the May Day Fair, I have not been deluged with orders. In my bid for publicity I even sent a whisky cake to Terry Wogan at Radio 2 on his birthday, although that was a bit of a disaster and I don't really want to dwell on it; suffice to say I choked on my tea, spewing its contents everywhere when he said on air that it was a bit on the dry side. Although everyone said that success would be a long and slow process resulting from word of mouth and consistent exposure, part of me, the part that still believes in Father Christmas, expected Sugar and Spice to be an immediate success. Well, there is only one thing for it. I need to get another job to keep myself and the business going before I get myself into debt. I'm not going to let a little thing like money stop me now.

As I fill out the applications for a number of part-time jobs that require little of me in terms of commitment or time, I remind myself that I'm living my dream, that I have to do whatever it takes, that pride goes before a fall. In fact, anything that will inspire me to become a tearoom assistant or a stockroom girl.

I return from posting my job applications to a message on the answer machine from the Vampire Queen asking me to call her. Her voice sounds light and friendly and I immediately feel suspicious. God, what if they have made a mistake and they now want my redundancy money back? Do I phone her? I decide I won't and instead get on with the information pack I plan to send to all the national glossies. I also need to practise my best smile for the newspaper photographer who is due in five minutes. They want a picture to go with the interview.

A couple of days later I put on a suit that has been languishing in my wardrobe for the last couple of months and head towards a stately pile, opened to the public, called Carriage House. A woman with an abrupt manner telephoned to ask if I wanted to come for an interview. They need a part-time tearoom assistant . . . urgently . . . so urgently, in fact, that it doesn't seem to matter that I have no experience. An unexpected heatwave has hit with the temperatures hitting the nineties and by 10.00 a.m., it is already hot, and I can feel myself begin to perspire from the heavy material of my suit. As I drive slowly along the driveway, trying to miss the potholes and peacocks that seem to have no road sense at all, I feel as if I'm entering a world where men wear breeches and women float, their feet hidden by swathes of silk and lace. Perhaps I should be arriving in a carriage with my small basket of goodies and a letter of recommendation from my mother. I attempt to smooth out the wrinkles when I get out, but to no avail; I look, and feel, a little crumpled.

The building before me appears just as crumpled, with shadows of something that was once imposing and grand. Despite the peeling paint and crumbling brickwork there is still something quite beautiful about it. I walk through an archway past huge terracotta pots that look as if they have been in situ for hundreds of years bursting with flowers, bright and vibrant, some spilling over the sides in cascades of colour. A cobbled courtyard surrounded by old brick buildings leads to what I assume is the tearoom. It is crammed full of pine tables, each with a small glass vase containing a plastic rose.

A large woman, as wide as she is tall, is cleaning one of the tables. I make my way over and introduce myself. Her features are crammed into the lower part of her face, offset by a rather large expanse of forehead. Her short, grey permed hair makes her look old and matronly and I take a guess that she is in the region of sixty to sixty-five but I could be wrong. The stained green apron she is wearing stretches over a large tummy and bosom and there is a flush to her veined cheeks from the effort of clearing the tables. I smile at her but she doesn't smile back; instead, she looks me up and down, taking in my suit with clear disdain. I quickly realise, a little too late, that it was the wrong thing to wear for the post of tearoom assistant, but old habits die hard, and it didn't even cross my mind that I might be overdressed for an interview.

'This way,' she indicates, and I follow her through a door marked 'staff only'. There is no air circulation and the heat is unbearable from the two industrial-sized ovens that seem to take up most of one wall. All around there are fruit cakes, flapjacks and shortbread cooling on racks. Dot opens the door to a small office and indicates for me to sit down on a chair covered with paperwork. I pick it up and put it on a desk piled high with invoices, recipes and printed emails. I wait whilst Dot searches through a pile before finding my CV.

'So you bake cakes?' she asks accusingly as if I were selling drugs to children.

'Yes. I run my own company,' I reply, trying not to sound too proud and pompous.

'So it says here. Tell me, if you have your own company, why do you want another job?' Dot asks and I wish I knew the answer.

'It's a new company and I need something part time to pay the bills while it gets off the ground,' I say as pleasantly as I can. Dot looks at me and I'm sure I can see dislike behind those piggy eyes.

'Have your got your food hygiene certificate?' she asks abruptly.

'Yes,' I reply.

'When would you be able to start?' Dot asks, not looking at me as she gets up and turns towards the door.

'Pretty much straight away,' I respond as she opens the door to the office. The smell of baking wafts in and it makes me feel hungry. What I would do for a piece of flapjack now.

'Pretty much?' Dot turns round to face me with a frown on her face.

'Straight away,' I confirm.

She nods, the frown never leaving her face. Dot is a bloody great huge blob of a rock cake, all knobbly, and dry with tiny currants for eyes that peer suspiciously at me. I wonder if she has ever cracked a smile in her life or whether she was born to be miserable. Aren't fat people meant to be jolly? I heard that laughing can apparently help you lose weight by using the muscles in your stomach. Maybe I should suggest this to her? I look at the wrinkles around her mouth that only a lifetime of scowling can nurture. Mmmmm, perhaps not.

'Be here next Monday. Eight thirty a.m., no later, and no jewellery, no sandals, no nail varnish, and make sure your hair is tied back,' she demands before waddling off, her big fat arse straining against the fabric of her trousers.

I'm left standing there feeling slightly bemused. Was that it? Does this mean I have the job? The girl making the sandwiches must have read my thoughts and she laughs.

'Welcome to the team,' she says, and laughs again. It is a tiny, almost childlike laugh, like small silver bells ringing. It reminds me of Tinkerbell the fairy.

When I get home, I ring Moo to tell her my news, but of course, she already knows. Are there no surprises in the spirit world? There is another message from Jessica and reluctantly I dial her number. Best to get it over and done with.

'Aaah, Maddy, how nice to hear from you,' she simpers and I feel goose bumps rise on my arm. We make small talk; she tells me I am missed (I suspect through gritted teeth) and I exaggerate the success of Sugar and Spice before she eventually loses interest and cuts straight to the chase.

'The thing is, Maddy, we have been let down by a company supplying us with hand-made biscuits. We're giving a hamper to each doctor attending the launch symposium,' she tells me and I want to shout, 'WHAT! YOU MEAN MY LAUNCH? THE ONE I WORKED ON FOR EIGHTEEN MONTHS? *THAT* BLOODY LAUNCH???' but I don't because I am all mouth and no trousers.

'I know it's short notice, but we need thirty cakes. Brian from Medical suggested you might be able to do it?'

'The launch is in a week's time,' I say aloud and my mind goes into overdrive. A big part of me wants to say no, I want your launch symposium to be a disaster without me, but then I think of my bank statement and the business. I am also enjoying the vision of her squirming in her steel-toe-capped stilettos.

'Okay, what cake do you need?' I ask.

'A selection. I don't know, I'll leave it to you to decide,' Jessica says and I wonder if this is the first time she has ever said that to someone.

'Wouldn't it be better to have one type, say lemon drizzle? You know what hospital consultants are like: if one gets a chocolate one, then you'll have a riot on your hands as the others will think it's better than theirs,' I suggest, and there is silence as she digests this. She knows I'm right, but the point is whether she can bring herself to agree that I might be or whether she goes true to type and dismisses it.

'Yes, of course, you're absolutely right,' she says. Wow, another first, she must be desperate. 'I'll get the details emailed over to you.' I bet the old bag is spitting blood! Aahh revenge . . . Small, but oh, so sweet.

As the temperatures rise outside, a similar occurrence happens almost simultaneously in my kitchen. I open the door to take out another batch of the thirty lemon drizzle cakes I have begun baking and brace myself. The rush of heat threatens to burn my eyebrows off and melt my eyelashes into one big clump of mascara. It wasn't that long ago I was wearing power suits in air-conditioned environments, now I'm sweating in combats, an apron and a delightful hair net that causes my hair to develop strange kinks when I take it off.

I still cannot believe this is happening. I have gone from not having anything to bake, except cakes for photographs and test recipes, to now running around like a headless chicken wondering if I can make this many cakes. Things are not helped by the fact that at long last some of my efforts are paying off and I have had a couple of orders come through: one from a company that received a flyer and one from a woman who came to the stand at the fair. This is fantastic, but I could have done with them last week when I had nothing much on. It is all good experience, Moo tells me, and I believe her. Truly I do, despite being absolutely exhausted from waking up at 5.00 a.m. and not collapsing into bed until the small hours.

As I stop to take a breath and sit on my garden bench with a cup of tea, there is the feeling that even with the constant panic and tiredness, it feels good. Really good! Sitting here with the smell of baking wafting out into the garden, I feel strangely happy. For the first time in my life I feel in control – well, kind of; the chaos that surrounds me in the kitchen probably doesn't look very much like I am in control to the casual observer. Thankfully, there is no one here to witness the pile of washing up, cakes cooling on racks and traces of cake mixture on every surface.

I idly flick through the *Buckinghamshire Post*, enjoying my brief moment of peace and . . . Oh no! Why, oh why, is life so dreadfully cruel sometimes? Just when everything had a rosy glow to it! 'Local Company Has the Ingredients for Success' is the headline with a photo of me looking like Dracula's daughter! The article is good – a few misquotes, but I expected that – so, fingers crossed, it will generate some business. But why, oh why, did they use that photo? Couldn't they have done some air-brushing? Distraught, I put it face down so that I can't see it and go back to my lemon drizzles. I'm in the middle of making another batch when Freya phones to congratulate me on the article.

'I don't know what you're worried about. It's not like you're selling make-up. At least the cakes look nice,' she says. If this is meant to make me feel better, it doesn't. Yes, the cakes are the ones that should be looking gorgeous (which, thankfully, they do) but it would be quite nice if I did too. My only hope is that nobody will recognise me. As I put the phone down a text comes through from James.

'Nice photo, hun!'

'Bugger off!' I text back. He rings me immediately on my landline so that I can hear him laughing. When he has finished enjoying my discomfort, he reassures me that it doesn't look like me. This is little consolation.

'I was thinking about you the other morning. Terry Wogan was eating a whisky cake, and remarked that it was a bit on the dry side.'

'I know,' I reply, debating whether to make my confession.

'You should send him one of yours,' he suggests.

'It was mine!' I admit.

'What do you mean?' he asks, confused.

'I mean the bastards were talking about a cake I sent them. I was hoping for some good publicity. Thank God they didn't actually say our company name.'

I'm having trouble grating a lemon while balancing the phone under my chin.

'Oh,' James replies and I can tell he's trying not to laugh again. 'Not so good, then.'

'No! That's the last cake Terry gets from me and suffice to say I am no longer a Tig, Tog, or whatever I was,' I say, losing control of my lemon and dropping it into the cake mixture. 'Gotta go, having a lemon problem,' I say, putting the phone down. I fish the lemon out with a spoon and it makes a gloopy sound as it comes out. The sensible thing would be to wash the mixture off, but waste not, want not and I lick it off. The phone goes again and it's Mac.

'Is that you in the paper?'

'Yes,' I grudgingly admit.

'God, Maddy, you look like a member of the walking dead.'

'I know.' Oh God, this is so awful.

'The cakes look good, though,' he comments thoughtfully before bursting out laughing, I start laughing too because otherwise I would cry.

'Oh, by the way, Terry Wogan was eating a whisky cake the other day, but wasn't that impressed. You should send him one of yours,' Mac suggests and my laugh almost turns into a hysterical wail.

'Look, I've got to go, my mobile is ringing now. Somebody else to tell me my cake is prettier than I am!' I pick up my mobile.

'Yes! I know I look like Dracula's daughter!' I almost shout as I attempt to put the cakes in the oven with my free hand.

'Not the last time I saw you, you didn't.' Greg's voice causes me to jump and I burn my arm on the side of the cooker.

'Shit,' I shout in shock.

'Shall I call back?' he suggests.

No! Nooooo!

'No, it's all fine now, I just burnt my arm, that's all.'

'Well, I promise to kiss it better when I see you next.'

Oh yes please . . . and my inner thigh, I'm pretty sure that needs a kiss.

'I'm sure that will help the healing process enormously,' I respond, smiling.

'I have healing hands too,' he says and I can imagine

that cheeky grin of his. 'By the way, I was listening to Terry Wogan and . . .'

I listen as if for the first time.

Chris Moyles, Radio 1 *Breakfast Show* Interview

'My mate Maddy Brown is here!' Chris shouts into the microphone and everyone in the studio claps.

'So old Mr Wogan didn't think much of your cakes when you first started out?'

'No, he didn't,' I confirm.

'So, Maddy, I hear the most talked-about act at Glastonbury this year was the Sugar and Spice tea tent.'

'Oh yes. That was great fun. We also did the V Festival and we're due at Reading at the end of the month. I love it!'

'I know you do, babe . . .'

'Chris.' I admonish him for teasing me.

'So, what of the rumour that you've tamed the hard man of rock, Liam Gallagher, with your cakes?'

'Liam and Noel couldn't get enough of my lemon drizzle cake, which surprised me. I thought they would go for a more macho cake.'

'Hey, cake is the new rock and roll,' Chris declares. 'So, are we going to the pub later?'

'Definitely,' I say, hugging him.

It is my first day at the Carriage House Tearoom and for some unknown reason I feel really nervous. Dot has not miraculously transformed into a smiling, warm old woman full of the joys of life. Instead, she briskly instructs me on all of the things I am not allowed to do, including wearing the earrings I have forgotten to take off.

The most cakes I have baked in one go is four, not twelve and Amy, who it transpires is Dot's second in command is oblivious to my distress, assuming that I know what I am doing. I struggle with the large mixer, lose count of the number of eggs I have put in, and instead of softening the butter in the microwave I turn it into liquid. Amy watches me from the corner of her eye and I can see her thinking, 'Ha, so you've got your own business baking cakes, have you, little miss hot shot, but you can't cut it in the real world, can you?' Things get worse when Dot hands me a piece of paper and tells me to get on with it. It is an order for lunch needed for a meeting at the house later. The handwriting is barely legible and I have no idea what it says; it may as well be a secret code, for all I know. Amy points to a number on the top of the list.

'You need to speak to Matthew Tennant. He's in charge of the house restoration project,' she says before disappearing. I dial the number; a man answers the phone and confirms he is the person in question. He sounds young, not the stuffy elderly gentleman I was expecting.

'Your order for lunch today? Can you just go through it with me?' I ask.

'It's just the usual,' he replies.

'What's the usual?' I ask.

'Oh, you know, some sandwiches, crisps and fruit. The usual,' he says as if I should know. If only I did, but the last thing I want to do is ask Dot.

'Sorry, but I'm new and I don't know what the usual is,' I say helplessly.

'Oh, um . . . nor do I. I'll tell you what . . . sorry, I didn't catch your name?'

'Maddy.'

'Maddy, ask Tilly. She's really nice and will help you. I'm not to be relied on,' he says and laughs. He sounds friendly and after Dot and the sullen Amy, I am grateful for a friendly voice.

'Thanks,' I reply.

'But don't forget the Jaffa Cakes,' he calls out just as I am about to put the phone down.

'Jaffa Cakes?' I say, writing it down on my pad.

'Orange and chocolate biscuits.'

'I know what Jaffa Cakes are, thank you very much!'

'Sorry,' he replies and I feel bad for snapping at him.

I glimpse Dot watching me and say a hasty goodbye before setting off to find Tilly. She is serving behind the till but tells me all I need to know and, despite taking ages to find all the ingredients, I manage to get Matthew Tennant's lunch order off on time, although I'm not sure all is as it should be. God, even a simple thing like making sandwiches has become a mind-boggling experience. By the time I get home I am shattered and haven't the energy to do anything, let alone cook myself some dinner. After a large glass of wine and some toast I am in bed by 9.30 p.m. At 10.20 p.m., I am woken by my mobile at the side of my bed. I had forgotten to turn it off. It's a text message from Greg.

'Hi. Do you fancy going out for that drink?'

Yes! Yes! Yes! Of course, I don't say this. No! I will play hard to get and reply tomorrow. I last all of ten minutes before I pick up my mobile and type in the word 'yes'.

My second day begins a little less stressfully and I'm sent to clear the tables, which is a relief. At least nothing can go wrong out here, there are no cakes to ruin or procedures to muck up; even I can clear a table, and more importantly, I'm away from the constant disapproval of Dot. This is relatively easy, until a coach load of American tourists arrive en masse and consume every cake on the premises and three hundred cans of Diet Coke. One lady complains that there is not enough frosting in the Victoria sandwich and asks if it was named after Queen Victoria. Kailey, one of the young girls behind the till, pipes up that no, actually it was named after Victoria Beckham. I decide to ignore this exchange and proceed to rush around trying to clear the tables before a group of women from the Women's Institute arrives. No one helps me and I feel hot and sticky with the oppressive heat. Oh how I long for my flip-flops as my feet continue to swell uncomfortably in my shoes. Not for the first time today, I wonder how I got here. In the space of two months I have gone from the marketing department of an international pharmaceutical company with a budget of half a million pounds to being a tearoom assistant. I have to remind myself that this is a means to an end, that soon the business will be a huge success, and this will all be a distant memory.

As I carry the last tray to the loading trolley, the floor suddenly becomes an ice rink and I slip and lunge forward. For some unknown reason, despite the possibility that I will fall flat on my face, it suddenly becomes imperative that I keep hold of the tray. Unfortunately, a plate falls to the floor, smashing into pieces and a slice of half-eaten chocolate cake goes flying through the air. Bits of it land on a table occupied by a man and woman although, miraculously, they miss her and instead cover him, landing in his cappuccino and covering his top. Who wins the competition for most shocked look on their face? That would be me!

I rush over to the table and say sorry at least thirty times whilst attempting to wipe the man down with my cloth. The fact that I'm probably making it worse, rubbing it into the stone-coloured combat trousers and white T-shirt he is wearing, does not deter me. Why, oh why, did it have to be chocolate cake? Why couldn't it have been a Madeira or a lemon cake, then at least it wouldn't have looked so bad. I am absolutely mortified, and despite his reassurances that he is fine, I continue to apologise and wipe. I don't even have to look in the mirror to check if I am blushing or not, the heat searing through my skin confirms it. He is very gracious and even manages to laugh. He has an interesting, almost handsome face that lights up when he laughs, but this factor only makes me blush more. Why couldn't he have been an old man with a beard?

'You are going to have to stop wiping my trousers, otherwise there's a chance I'll start to enjoy it, and then people will start to talk about us,' he jokes, looking at me with blue eyes. They mirror the bright, summer sky outside and twinkle with amusement. For God's sake, Maddy, concentrate on his trousers! No, no, not his trousers. Oh, please God, get me out of here and I promise to do good things for as long as I live.

God comes in the shape of Dot who barks at me to get back into the kitchen. As I hurry through the door, head hung low, I hear the man tell her that it really is okay and not to be too hard on me. I fear it's too late. Without a word, but with a look that says a thousand things, including you're very close to not lasting the week, she puts me on to washing-up duty for the rest of the day. So much for an easy part-time job. This is like purgatory.

'How is it going?' Lou asks when I phone her later.

'This living the dream? It's not all it's cracked up to be,' I say wearily and tell her all about my cake incident. She laughs almost as much as Moo did earlier.

'You're meant to entice the men with cake, not throw it at them.'

'I know, and he was rather nice which made it worse. But you will be glad to hear all is not lost. I'm going out again with Greg.'

'Ooh, how exciting. I thought he had disappeared. What are you going to wear?'

'I have no idea.'

'I'll bring some things over.'

'Don't worry. I'll find something.'

'No, I insist. You can't be trusted,' Lou tells me and it seems churlish to argue.

The next morning Dot marches over to me as I enter my second hour of washing up.

'Tilly needs some help with the scones. Do you think you can do that without creating any major disasters?' she asks without waiting for an answer.

Tilly and I work well together as she talks and I listen. Blonde and petite with the frame of a ballet dancer, and a pretty face with a little snub nose, Tilly is a lemon fairy cake with gold dust sprinkled on top of white icing. Light and fluffy with a penchant for ballet shoes, she twirls around as she speaks. Within an hour, she has given me the low-down on everyone who works here, and the story of her last four failed romances. Our chatter is cut short when Tilly is called to help serve customers during the three o'clock teatime rush, leaving me to the rest of the scones. As I cut, I think of new ways to market Sugar and Spice. Maybe send a cake to the foodie magazines? As I'm lost in thought, somebody coughs behind me and I jump out of my skin, expecting it to be Dot. The perpetrator is leaning against the wall, watching me intently with a languid smile on his face.

'Hi. Matthew Tennant. We've spoken on the phone,' he says. I look at him open mouthed and he mistakes my lack of response for a lack of understanding.

'I wanted to say thank you for our lunch order. It was perfect. Lots of egg, but that's okay, because I like egg.'

I am barely listening, my ears are ringing, and I can feel a full force-twenty blush cover my whole face.

'But if I had known, I could have said that yesterday,' he says and his smile widens. Please no! No! No! No! Matthew Tennant, and the man from the chocolate incident yesterday, are one and the same. He is tall, six feet, maybe, and much better-looking than I remember.

My blush increases to an unprecedented force-thirty and I cover my face with floury hands, mumbling an apology behind them. When I finally remove my hands he is still smiling at me and I want the ground to open up and swallow me whole. I am saved from having to respond by Dot who appears with a stern look on her face, waving her hands at him to get out. She shoos him out of the kitchen clucking like a mother hen at her wayward chick, leaving me to wonder if I have flour on my face.

I get home shattered and downhearted but any promise of a restorative bath and glass of wine float away as I check the answer machine. There is an order for a lemon drizzle cake and I groan. I have had enough of bloody lemon drizzle cakes, but orders are good for business and I put my apron on and begin to get my ingredients together. The smell of lemon fills the evening air and I close my eyes, transported back to holidays in Italy, and evenings spent over glasses of sweet syrupy Limoncella. As always, baking a cake makes the world feel good and I sing as I whisk, forgetting about Matthew Tennant, well almost, and the traumatic events of the day. I decide to make an extra cake, one to entice Greg. I want to take things slowly and lemon is good to begin with. The chocolate can come later.

Greg turns up and whisks me away to the local Indian restaurant with no mention of why there has been so little contact since our last evening together. Perhaps he wants to take it slowly and is just as nervous about all this as I am, although, listening to him, nervous is not a word that immediately springs to mind. He recounts funny stories involving friends and Indian restaurants, and then asks me lots of questions about Sugar and Spice. He seems genuinely interested.

'What a great idea. I'm very impressed.'

'Thanks,' I answer bashfully. I like it that he is impressed. 'So what do you do?'

'I guess you could say I'm a bit of a troubleshooter in the world of the nerd.'

I haven't got a clue what he means.

'I'm an IT consultant.'

'Aah,' I answer. He doesn't look like your average IT bod: he can look me in the eye, for a start.

'I like it, though. I am my own boss and can pick and choose who I want to work with. I've worked with some big names,' he says, reeling off some big names I've never heard of.

'Me too,' I say. 'My mum, Auntie Vera . . .'

We both laugh, and the rest of the evening is spent

flirting over Tandoori King Prawns. His easy, confident manner is very sexy, and I find myself wondering what chocolate cake he is.

As we wander back, I'm already anticipating the kisses I'm pretty sure are going to come my way and feel a little frisson of excitement.

'I made you a lemon drizzle cake,' I tell him and hand him a slice with his coffee. He smiles and kisses me lightly on the lips before taking a bite.

'Mmmmm, this is good,' he says taking another bite and I smile triumphantly, thinking his kiss wasn't half bad either. As he tucks in I congratulate myself; I may not have a chest that makes all who see it weak at the knees, or legs up to my armpits, but I can sure as hell make up for it with a slice of something good and wholesome. His mobile rings but he switches it off and I'm glad that he doesn't want anything to disturb our evening together. After a few more lemony kisses I reluctantly drag myself away. I have an early start again tomorrow and I'm in no hurry to move to the next stage. He is very sexy, though . . . God, I had forgotten how much I enjoyed this kissing thing. He leaves, and as I close the door I feel gorgeous for the first time in too long.

LEMON DRIZZLE CAKE

This is a beautiful cake and especially good served in the garden on a sunny lazy Sunday afternoon. I don't think I have found one person who doesn't like this one.

Ingredients

225g (8oz) unsalted butter   zest of 2 unwaxed lemons
225g (8oz) caster sugar   275g (10oz) self-raising flour
4 large eggs   6–8 tablespoons milk

For the syrup:
Juice of 1 lemon
100g (4oz) icing sugar

Method

Grease and double-line tin – preheat oven to 180°C/350°F/ gas mark 4. Cream butter and sugar together. Add eggs and lemon zest, beating them in well. Add flour, folding in gently but thoroughly, and then the milk. Spoon into tin. Bake for approximately 1 hour or until golden and skewer comes out clean. Whilst cake is cooking, make the syrup. Put lemon juice and icing sugar into saucepan and heat gently until sugar dissolves. Take cake out of oven and puncture top of cake with skewer – pour syrup over it, ensuring middle and sides of cake absorb liquid. Ensure cake is completely cold before taking out of tin.

A handful of memories

The alarm goes off at 4.30 a.m. and I am sure it has made a dreadful mistake. Bleary eyed, I leave the house at 5.10, which for me is a miracle. I usually need at least an hour to have breakfast, try to do something with my hair and change my mind a minimum of three times about what to wear. With my foot to the floor, I race towards Norfolk in a bid to beat the weekend traffic of holidaygoers. The world hasn't woken up yet, the light is golden and soft, the air is clean, and it feels good to be alive.

By the time I arrive at 6.45 a.m., Snow Patrol are blasting the morning into wake-up mode and I am desperate for tea and toast. In a bid to woo the city dwellers who make their way to the pretty seaside towns every weekend, I have secured a stand at the regional food fair. I meet Moo there. Like a fairy godmother, she has managed to acquire free coffee and egg rolls from a food van nearby. As we eat and set up, Ben phones me on my mobile to check everything is okay before proceeding to go through a checklist of things I needed to remember for the day. I try to reassure him that I have everything under control and that Moo is here to supervise me in case I crumble under the pressure. I say this sarcastically, but it is lost on him, bless him.

As the first few customers arrive I tell Moo all about my second date with Greg and, like me, she is feeling positive about the possibilities.

'Chocolate cake?'

'Too early to say ... but it's looking good,' I reply. 'Anyway, how are things with you?'

Moo smiles at me with that dreamy look of someone who has just fallen in love.

'Good. The Bear has a few more teeth and he's so funny now. Bob is bringing him over later so you can see for yourself.'

'Is it getting any easier?' I ask. She still looks pale, the Moo of old with her colourful clothes, great pieces of jewellery and ornate clips in her hair has taken to wearing lots of black with her hair scraped back in a constant ponytail. She looks good but in an understated, almost anonymous way, and I miss her flamboyance.

'I'm still tired and overweight, consumed with guilt that I'm not a good mother by going to work and, for the first time in my life, not sure what I'm doing. I won't pretend to anyone, except Freya, of course, that I find it easy, but as soon as I look at my little boy's face and he smiles at me, everything is okay; even the fact that I can't get into my size-twelve jeans any more.' She smiles again and I hug her.

'You look gorgeous, you always do,' I tell her.

'That's what Bob says, bless him. Aaah, talk of the devil and he is sure to appear.'

Moo waves and walks over to lots of hugs from the two adoring men in her life. Moo brings The Bear over and I squeeze him tight, snuggling into his soft little head. It feels like a mole's head, not that I have had much experience of cuddling moles, but this is how I imagine they would feel and I can't resist stroking it, much to his annoyance. He has the same quick temper as his mum and looks more like her every day with his big round eyes and long eyelashes. I leave the three of them and head out amongst the crowds with slices of cake and flyers for a couple of hours.

It's a long day but I feel positive about being here. Hopefully people will tell their friends and maybe take a look at the website.

'So, how did we do?' I ask when the last of the customers have wandered away.

'Mmmmm . . . not bad. You've made the grand total of one hundred and eighty-seven pounds – oh, and three punnets of strawberries,' Moo confirms.

'Strawberries?'

'I did a swap with the fruit and veg man.'

'Well, together with the Pharmagenica order, it's a start, and from little acorns . . . plus, it's all experience,' I confirm, trying to sound more positive than I feel. 'Hey, a few months ago I wasn't sure I could make seven pounds from cakes, let alone over a hundred pounds! Let's celebrate with a cup of tea and check out this tearoom!'

As usual, we spend far too long trying to choose something from the impressive array of home-baked cakes that are on offer. I settle on a slice of coffee cake, whilst Bob and Moo both have slices of a rather huge Victoria sandwich. As we sit there tucking in, Moo and I do our usual grading process, picking the place to pieces. Bob laughs at us and asks why we don't just open up a tearoom ourselves.

'Oh, and how would I fit that in with working and looking after you and your son?' Moo asks, her eyes flashing. Bob responds by kissing her and immediately her anger dissolves. She turns to me with a serious look on her face.

'But you could, Maddy.'

I have to admit it is something I have been thinking of lately. After working in the Carriage Tearoom, I know the sort of thing I wouldn't like. I have always loved the idea of a funky, fabulous tearoom where people could drop in to drink coffee and tea, eat cake, talk, relax and read. In my dreams, it resembles the coffee shop in *Friends* and I have an uncanny resemblance to Jennifer Aniston, have lots of beautiful, funny friends, and a boyfriend who makes me laugh like Chandler. I think of Greg. He isn't a Chandler . . . but he is very kissable . . . *very* kissable.

We start to talk about how my little tearoom would be different from the rest, with old, comfortable chairs in vintage fabrics, fresh flowers from the garden on each table, second-hand books and magazines to read and, of course, lots of home-made cakes served on mismatched china picked up from the markets. We both agree that high tea at 3.00 p.m. should be on the menu, a bit like at The Ritz, with a cake stand full of tiny fairy cakes, scones and fruit cake. I'm getting excited just thinking about it. Perhaps I should seriously consider doing it. Mmmmm . . . I need to win the lottery first, though.

Interview with Parky

'So, Maddy, since we last spoke I believe you have recently opened another couple of tearooms; one in London, the other in New York?'

'Yes, I am always amazed at how quickly things have progressed. I have to pinch myself that it's all happening.'

'Do you like fairy cakes, Gwyneth?' Michael asks Ms Paltrow, who is sitting serenely next to me. I look at her and wait for her response. Bless her, she gushes that she absolutely adores them.

'So, is there anything else left for Sugar and Spice to conquer?'

'Michael, you know I often wonder the same thing myself. I always think that I will take a break but then something else happens. We are currently working with Jo Malone to create a range of room fragrances that smell of freshly baked cakes and a skin cream based on our fairy-cake mixture. It's all very exciting.'

I flick my newly highlighted hair. I have already given the number of my colourist to Gwyneth.

When I get home there are two letters: one from the courier company demanding payment for its last invoice and the other from the wholesaler telling me that they will not set up an account because I am a new business; all orders will have to be paid up front for six months. How? If I haven't any money, how? Oh God, what a mess. I am backed into a corner with no visible way out and the butterflies flutter inside my stomach as the panic rises. There's a steady, if slow, trickle of orders now coming through, which I guess is better than nothing but the lack of payment from Pharmagenica for the lemon drizzle cakes has seriously affected my cash flow. Despite my reluctance to speak to the Vampire Queen, I have swallowed my pride and left a couple of messages but, surprise, surprise, she hasn't come back to me. The business account is looking decidedly sad after paying for the ingredients and courier charges and I try not to panic about the fact that I have used up my emergency, keeping-going fund. Thankfully, things at the tearoom are a little easier as I get used to what Dot expects of me, although I still can't get to grips with how someone can be so grumpy and downright rude to people.

Today, though, I am finding it hard as my mind wanders to other things. It's a year to the day when I lost the baby and for all my attempts to treat it as another normal day, my emotions are getting the better of me and I feel a dark cloud descend. The unbearable heat in the kitchen doesn't help, sapping my already low energy levels, and I struggle to keep going. Even Tilly's brightness washes over me. When Dot eventually decides I have earned a lunch break at 2.30 p.m., I decide to escape into the garden for a little solitary thinking. I wander around inhaling the scent of fragrant honey from buddleia bushes covered in butterflies, and my skin tingles as the sun caresses it. As I close my eyes and stand there in the silence, I contemplate lying on the grass and falling asleep. Today I want to sleep. Today I want to forget and lose myself in the beauty of fuchsia pink, wild roses and the low-hanging trees that smell of apples after a summer rainfall.

'Beautiful, isn't it?' A voice interrupts my thoughts. I look around to find Matthew Tennant sitting there with a flask of tea and a paper. It is open at a half-completed crossword, and his pen is poised for another clue. I am a little startled but try to recover my composure without a blush appearing.

'Hi. I didn't see you there,' I say, shielding the sun from my eyes.

'You were somewhere else,' he says, and smiles. It is a nice smile. He is not drop-dead gorgeous like Greg but there is something about him that makes you want to look a little closer. He has a face that lights up when he smiles. His light brown, almost blond hair is cut close to his head, accentuating the cheekbones most women would die for. His lightly tanned arms are muscular but not big, with streaks of white, powdery building dust clinging to his skin.

'I am so sorry about the other day,' I say reluctantly. There is a part of me that doesn't want to bring it up, but it is not the sort of thing you can brush under the carpet, especially as far as first meetings go.

'It's not a problem. I never liked those trousers anyway. Oh, and I forgot to say, thanks for the Jaffa Cakes.' He laughs easily, like somebody who does it a lot and I like the laughter lines that appear at the side of his eyes. They are the lines of a man, not a boy; of someone who has experienced life, and I find it more than a little attractive. I smile with the thought.

'Are you any good with crosswords?' he asks.

I shake my head and confess that it's not one of my strong points. As much as I want to appear mega intelligent it is just not going to happen. He ignores my response and shows me the paper.

'Nine down: beginning with D. Remove most of the water from . . . ?'

With my curiosity pricked, I sit down and look at the crossword more closely. He smells of plaster and brick. I say the clue repeatedly in my mind but nothing springs to mind.

'Jaffa Cake?' he asks, producing a pack of mini ones from his jacket pocket. 'Did you know that sometimes there are seven in a packet instead of six?' he says, handing me the packet. I smile and open them.

'Only six,' I observe. 'I guess that means I'm not the princess.'

'Well, I won't waste any more on you, then,' he says, pouring some tea from his flask into a cup and handing it to me.

'How's it going in the tearoom?' he asks.

'Oh, not great. I think Dot is a little disappointed in me,' I reply, surprised at my honesty with someone I barely know.

'Don't worry about Dot, she's disappointed in everyone. Just don't take it personally.'

I look at my watch and realise I need to get back.

'It was nice to meet you again, Matthew, and thanks for the tea and Jaffa Cakes, it was just what I needed,' I say, because it was. I realise that for the last half-hour my mind has been free of the things I have been trying to forget all day.

'Call me Matt,' he calls after me.

Throughout the evening Lou, Mum and Moo phone to check that I am okay and Ben phones twice to talk about the business. I dial James's number but put the phone down again before it connects. Has he remembered? I guess not. He said at the time he didn't really feel involved, that it all seemed a little surreal and as if it was happening to someone else. That made two of us! Anyway, who could blame him for forgetting – I mean, why would you want to remember?

Arriving at the A & E department, I am ushered into a small room. My mind shuts down as I am examined, probed, hooked up to a drip and tests are done. Drugs take the edge off the pain and I lie on the most uncomfortable bed in the world, my mind empty, but perhaps that is the morphine, and I'm grateful for the numbness. I'm disconnected from the world that goes on around me, from the sounds of a busy department filtering through the curtain. Another patient accuses the nurses of kidnapping him and screams for his lawyer, his freedom, a fucking cigarette. In another lifetime, it would have been funny, but today I just feel sorry for him and worry that he, too, is as frightened as I am. I remain there, drifting in and out of the dark, numb place I have crawled into until a nurse comes in and tells me that they need the room and wheels me out to the corridor whilst my drip finishes its last half-hour. I float above my body and watch the bustling activity going on around me. Diane, the kind nurse with the smiley face, asks me if I am okay and I nod, afraid to open my mouth because I know that if I do, I will scream and never stop. Ben turns up and listens to the nurse's instructions about painkillers and aftercare, before leading me to the car and driving me home. A heavily pregnant Freya has remained at home and I can see he doesn't quite know what to say or do with me. James comes round but, tired from the pain, I reassure him that I'll be fine and he leaves me on the sofa with a blanket wrapped around me. I want it all to end and try to sleep, but my body has a different agenda and I lie awake praying for the pains to subside. I go to stay with Mum who talks when I want to and leaves me when I need to be alone, ensuring throughout that I am consuming over three thousand calories a day. She promises me it will get better and she is right, of course. Mums always are.

*

My black mood is not helped by another letter from the bank kindly reminding me that I still haven't attended to the issue of going over the agreed overdraft. The Pharmagenica accounts department tell me they are waiting for authorisation from the Vampire Queen and she still hasn't rung me back. I really should have known better and now it is only a matter of time before I have to give up and go back to the treadmill I so desperately wanted to escape. From feeling strong and ready to fight for my dream, the last week has plunged me back into feelings of uncertainty. That old devil called self-doubt is poking me in the ribs and, yet again, I want to cry. I sit in a quiet corner of the tearoom staring at the sandwich I have bought for my lunch.

'You looked sad sitting there, so I brought you a slice of carrot cake to cheer you up,' a voice says and I look up to see Matt standing there with two slices of cake. I don't really want any company, preferring instead to wallow in my misery alone, but I manage a weak smile and he sits down, pushing a plate towards me.

'Everything okay?' he asks, tucking into his cake with gusto. Despite its sticky frosting, I'm glad to see he doesn't use a fork.

'Yes, fine,' I lie, watching as his fingers become covered. He is clearly enjoying it and his eyes sparkle like a child with a treat.

'Oh, by the way, it was desiccate,' he says before taking another bite.

The blank space that is my thought process obviously registers on my face because he smiles indulgently at me.

'The crossword?'

'Aaah,' I reply, remembering. 'Of course, why didn't I get that?'

'So, come on, why the glum face?'

'It's a long story,' I say in an attempt to put him off.

'It must be bad. You haven't even touched your cake. It might help to talk about it, you know,' he suggests helpfully. I shake my head, hoping that he will give up and go away but he continues to eat, unfazed by my unwillingness to talk. We sit there for a few minutes and, much to my annoyance, I realise he has no intention of leaving. I look out of the window, feeling slightly uncomfortable for what seems like an eternity, and then, for reasons unknown, I find myself talking. Whether it's because he is a stranger, or because I have an urge to fill the silence, or maybe it's the genuine kindness in his eyes, I have no idea, but soon I am telling him everything. I talk about the business, of becoming frightened of the future again, the thought that I should just give up and go back to my old life, the miscarriage and how over the last few days I have wanted to cry all the time. He listens intently, and when I have finished he points to my uneaten cake.

'Are you going to eat that?' he asks. I shake my head as he pulls the plate towards him and for a moment, I'm not sure if he has heard a single word I have said.

'Sure?' he asks, before biting into it. 'Look, I'm not an expert but perhaps the memories of the miscarriage have sparked a chain-effect of emotions in you; a bit like a domino effect. They have taken you back to a time you don't want to remember and made you feel a little fragile about everything again, including the business. Obviously your current money worries haven't helped.'

'Mmmmm, I guess so,' I reply, relaxing into his voice.

'It's perfectly natural, a part of the grieving process. The thing is, you just have to go with it for a while, because to pretend it hasn't happened would be more harmful in the long term, and Maddy . . .'

I look down at the table because I can't look into his eyes. I'm afraid he will be able to see deep within my soul.

'There is no time limit on this sort of thing. You *should* remember something that had such a profound effect on you.'

I nod, twisting a napkin in my hands and swallowing hard.

'But don't make the mistake of getting it confused with the thought that you can't make the business work. Look at it as a positive, as a reminder of how far you have come in a year.' He scoops the last bit of cake on to a fork and offers it to me.

'That'll be fifty-seven pounds. I'm expensive but good,' he laughs.

'You do seem very wise,' I suggest, wondering how someone so young can possess the wisdom that usually comes with age. He can't be much older than me . . . thirty-six, thirty-seven?

'Mmmmm, not sure about wise, but sometimes it's easier to see things from the outside,' he replies, smiling at me. The smile reaches those blue eyes. Today they are the colour of my favourite jeans.

'This carrot cake was okay, but it would have been better without the creamy icing stuff on top,' he observes, turning his nose up.

'I have a recipe that doesn't have a frosting. I'll make you one,' I suggest, looking down at the napkin that is now in a thousand pieces. I suddenly feel exposed and shy with this person I hardly know, but who knows everything about me.

'Sounds great. I suppose I should get back to work,' he says, standing up. 'And don't worry, Maddy. Everything will be okay.'

I have been waiting for someone to tell me that all week and I smile from the inside as I watch him go.

Feeling much better after my talk with Matt, I resume my search for the perfect chocolate cake. This may have something to do with a text from Greg asking if I want to go out again. Hurray! He is coming round tonight and the excitement has taken my mind off things. Chocolate roulade with a filling of double cream? An indulgent chocolate sponge with that naughty double-calorie filling. Mmmmm.

I attempt to put all my worries about the business to the back of my mind as we spend the evening in All Bar One before heading back to mine with the promise of a late-night dessert. I'm not so sure about the chocolate roulade, but Greg loves it and I get the urge to lick the cream off his fingers. I reluctantly excuse myself as the urge to pee has become too much (probably the excitement of it all), and leave him to ponder on the wonder of my baking skills. I return to find him texting furiously on his mobile. He stops when he hears me approach, the look of guilt that passes over his face all too clear. I can hear bells ring and they are not the wedding variety.

'Greg, do you have a girlfriend?' I ask before I can stop myself. I'm not sure why I haven't asked before, but I just assumed he didn't. He looks at me sheepishly, like a little boy who has been caught shoplifting, before nodding yes.

'Why are you here, then?' I ask, suddenly feeling a little sick.

'Because I like you,' he says, as if it is the most obvious thing in the world. He gets up from the sofa and walks towards me.

My mind works overtime as it processes this new little piece of information that has just transformed the rose-tinted landscape I inhabited a moment ago to a shitty brown one. God, how stupid I've been. As he puts his hands either side of my face I look into his eyes for answers, but there is nothing there except the assumption he can kiss this little anomaly away. He pulls me towards him but I wriggle free before his lips meet mine.

'I think you had better leave,' I say quietly, making my way to the door.

'Are you sure?' he asks, and I nod yes.

He hovers by the door as if waiting for me to change my mind.

'You're angry with me,' he says, stating the obvious and I want to slap him hard.

'No, just disappointed,' I reply, wanting him away from me.

'My cake?' he asks, pointing to the roulade in the kitchen.

He wants the cake!!!

'Fuck the cake!' I say and close the door in his face.

The chocolate roulade is thrown into the bin and I go to bed struggling with the tears that threaten to fall. I've been so stupid. The first good-looking man who comes along and I act like a fool, blind to the obvious. No wonder his contact was sporadic. Bastard!

Bastard, Lou says.

Bastard, Moo agrees.

Not surprising, Mac tells me.

*

When Ben phones me in the morning I resist the urge to scream, 'Fuck chocolate cakes!' He wouldn't understand and I wonder if I should be considering Madeira cakes instead. Nobody can go wrong with a Madeira cake.

'Moo told me that you're having money problems and thinking of giving the business up?'

'Mmmmm. My old bitch of a boss hasn't been forthcoming in paying me for the big order and now the bank is getting upset. It's just made me realise that I'm no good at this business lark and that perhaps I should just give up before I get myself into a real mess.'

'You can't be good at everything, Maddy. That's why people have accountants and bookkeepers. You think you have to be good at everything but it's impossible. I can't make a cake to save my life but I can make a sound business decision,' Ben says and if he was here I would hug him.

'Look, why don't I lend you some money until they pay up, just to take the pressure off a little?' he suggests, his voice soft and reassuring.

'Thank you, but no. A temporary patch is not going to solve my problems. I need to think about what I'm going to do and it's not your job to sort it out for me,' I say, trying hard not to cry. The rollercoaster that is my life at the moment is taking its toll. One minute I'm up, the next minute I'm down. The women in *Red* magazine never said it would be so hard. I should sue them.

'It would be a real shame to give up now,' Ben says and I reply that it would; because it would, and I really don't want to.

*

I get a text: '8 letters beginning with N. Of little value?'

It's from Matt.

'Nugatory?' I text back.

'Wow,' he returns almost immediately. 'I'm impressed. U bake cakes & u know big words.'

When I find him, he is in the walled garden, crouched down by the old swimming pool. Now damaged, and tired-looking after years of neglect, the old mosaic tiles that cover the sides of the pool and the steps leading down to it are broken and discoloured. Once upon a time, women sat here with their glasses of lemonade fanning themselves, but now this part of the garden has been closed to the public for fear of someone tripping on the broken stones and falling in. As the person in charge of the lengthy restoration of the house and grounds, Matt and his team of two have a huge job on their hands. He is carefully scraping the effects of the weather from a statue of a nymphet, her skirts flying in the wind as she jumps over an imaginary lily pad. He is singing along to the Red Hot Chilli Peppers on the radio and practically jumps out of his skin when he realises I am there watching him. He smiles and I'm momentarily dazzled.

'Hello, beautiful. It's nice to see you smile again,' he says, getting up and brushing the debris off his T-shirt. Wow, beautiful? I don't think I have ever been called that before. Stop! He's just being nice to you because you're a sad muppet and he's a nice person.

'I feel much better, and I wanted to say thank you for being so kind to me the other day, listening to me ramble on, so I made you that carrot cake I promised.'

I hand him the cake box and he opens it excitedly, releasing the aromas of nutmeg, cinnamon and orange. It always reminds me of helping Mum stick cloves into oranges, tying red ribbon around cinnamon sticks for the large bowl of Christmas pot-pourri she would make, and of watching her make the Christmas cake with cherries the colour of her cheeks.

'There's no need to say thank you. Sometimes it's easier to talk to someone who isn't directly involved,' he says, sticking his face close to the cake. 'Mmmmm, this smells gorgeous. The girls will love it,' he says, and my heart skips a beat, just a little.

'Girls?' I ask.

'My daughters, Charlotte and Georgie,' he says almost self-consciously.

'I didn't know you had children,' I say, although there was no reason why I should. He must be married. Why did I assume he wasn't? Anyway, it doesn't matter.

'Charlotte is eight and Georgie is six,' he tells me proudly. As he talks about them I find myself thinking what a lovely person he is. See, not all men are like Greg. Some are honest, kind and good, and something tells me that I have made a friend.

'So, how is the business going?' he asks.

'Pretty much the same. I really don't want to admit defeat, but unless Pharmagenica pay me I haven't got any money to keep the business going,' I say sadly.

'Why don't you explain that to the bank? I can't imagine they will pull the rug from under your feet over this.'

'Mmmmm,' I respond, not entirely convinced.

'Hey, you don't strike me as a girl who gives up easily. Not many people would have the strength of character to set up a business. You should be really proud of what you've achieved so far.'

Yes! Yes! He's right, I should be. I am a strong, kick-ass

businesswoman. I'm thinking Uma Thurman in *Kill Bill*.
How could I forget! The Jessicas and Gregs of this world
are not going to beat me. Oh no, siree. I kiss him on the
cheek, causing him to blush, and skip off ready to fight
another day.

As soon as I get home I phone Ben.

'I'm going to see the bank to have a chat with them,' I
tell him.

'No need. The cheque is in the post,' he says
mysteriously.

'What do you mean?' I ask.

'I mean, I paid the Vampire Queen a visit today as your
business partner and threatened legal action if she didn't
get her arse in gear,' he says, and I can hear the triumph
in his voice.

'But . . . my business partner? Tell me . . . what did she
say?' I stammer, a million unanswered questions forming
in my brain.

'She's a bully, and in my experience bullies don't react
well when confronted. So I thought I would pay her a
little visit. I told her in no uncertain terms that I would
have the company solicitor on to her in the morning. It
helped that I dropped the name of a well-known city firm
who have a reputation for their ability to crush even the
largest of corporate names. She was like a baby lamb and
made the call to the accounts department whilst I was
standing there.'

I can just imagine Ben disarming her with his steely
gaze and six-foot-three frame clad in tailored Hugo Boss.
I would have loved to be a fly on the wall as she simpered
all over him. The relief floods through me, but so does
something else. Once again, Ben has been my knight in

shining armour but I can't help feeling a little cheated that I wasn't left to sort it out myself, that I didn't fight and win the war over the Vampire Queen, saving the world in the process; a world made better by cakes.

'Thank you. You didn't have to do that, but thank you,' I say, trying not to reveal the underlying feeling of disappointment. 'As always, you're my hero.'

'Somebody has to be.'

'Yep, I guess they have.'

When I'm sure the phone is safely back in its cradle I swear loudly at it. I could have done it on my own, for Christ's sake! I could have! I don't need a hero. Even if *he* turned up now I would tell him to sod off. You're too late, mate! Heroes are yesterday's story.

The relief is welcome and even Dot's bad temper can't rile me. I have three more orders and after another long day of delivering to the couriers in the morning and a day in the tearoom, I wander through the garden towards the swimming pool. Grateful for his kindness, I want to tell Matt the good news. As I approach he turns and smiles as if he is genuinely pleased to see me.

'Hey,' he says, motioning for me to sit on a bank of grass. 'Your carrot cake is gorgeous. In fact, I've brought some with me today,' he says, rummaging around in his rucksack to produce a tin foil parcel. He breaks off a piece and hands it to me.

I tell him about Ben and thankfully having another stay of execution for the company. He is genuinely pleased and we spend the next half-hour talking about the business and my family. He is understandably mystified about my makeover plans for Mum, fascinated by my relationship with Dad, understands the need for Ben to be a little overprotective – apparently it's a caveman thing – and laughs at my tales of The Bear and The Princess. I should be at home baking but I put off leaving and instead ask him about his work. He tells me of feeling utterly transfixed by architecture and sculpture on a school trip to Rome, of how he left school and trained for five years to be a stonemason after taking a degree in art history. His voice is full of passion and authority as he talks of light honey-coloured Helmdon stone and the way it catches the light, of his particular favourite, the dark Thornborough, with its beautiful streaks of cream and grey and I listen, fascinated as his voice washes over me. I feel slightly drunk as the heady perfume of old-fashioned roses fill my senses. There is the faint undertone of something else; like the spicy warmth of the carrot cake but more powerful. I cannot pinpoint it until just before I get up to go; it is the smell of dust and limestone; of citrus and warm skin. I breathe it in and feel a little light-headed. I look at Matt and make a silent wish that one day my chocolate cake will come (preferably next week) and he will be just like him.

I drive home to find three messages on the answer machine for orders. I put my apron on and set to work on two whisky cakes and an Earl Grey Tea cake, singing as I do so. The sunshine outside appears a little brighter; the fluffiness of my cakes a joy to behold. Even my singing voice is not half bad.

The next day, as I help Tilly make a batch of sultana cakes, the conversation turns to Matt.

'You two seem to get on well,' Tilly observes, smiling.

'He's a nice person,' I reply.

'Just nice? Not gorgeous?'

'Tilly! He's married.' I laugh, flicking flour at her.

'He isn't,' she says. 'His wife died a couple of years ago.'

'Oh God, that's so sad,' I reply. No wonder he was so kind and understanding, listening to me blurt out my woes. I immediately feel dreadful that I was making such a fuss over what seems such a minor thing in comparison to what he must have gone through.

'He thinks the world of his kids. I don't think he gets out much, which is a shame. He's so nice.'

'Mmmmm,' I reply. Now I'm in a dilemma. On the one hand, I feel real sadness that someone who must have been similar in age to me has died and left two children. On the other hand, I'm a little relieved that this means Matt is not married. Does that make me a bad person?

When I get home, for some unknown reason I get an urge to try another chocolate cake recipe.

As the cakes transform in the oven into what I hope will be irresistible indulgence of the sweetest kind, a text comes through on my mobile.

'Just tucking into the last piece of carrot cake. It's delicious. Thank u.'

CARROT CAKE

The majority of carrot cake recipes have a thick sour cream frosting but I like this one much better. It also uses sunflower oil and has raisins in it, which means it is also quite a healthy cake, if there is such a thing!

Ingredients

175g (6oz) dark brown soft sugar
175ml (6 fl.oz) sunflower oil
3 large eggs
140g (5oz) grated carrots
100g (4oz) raisins
grated zest of 1 large orange

175g (6oz) self-raising flour
1 teaspoon bicarbonate of
  soda
1 teaspoon ground cinnamon
½ teaspoon nutmeg

For the icing:
175g/6oz icing sugar
1–2 tablespoons orange juice

Method

Preheat the oven to 180°C/350°F/gas mark 4. Grease and line either a 20cm (8 inch) round tin or a 18cm (7 inch) square cake tin. Mix the sugar and oil together until blended. Add the eggs, and lightly mix. Stir in grated carrots, raisins and orange zest. Sift the flour, soda and spices into the mixture and lightly mix. Pour into the tin and bake for 40–45 minutes until cake feels firm and springy to the touch when you press it in the centre. Don't panic if it needs a little longer. Cool in the tin for 5 minutes before turning out on to a wire rack. Beat together the icing sugar and orange juice until smooth. Either drizzle or smooth over the top of the cake.

One kiss — add more if desired

'Good morning. How r u?' The text appears as I put on my apron. I'm surprised but pleased. It's nice to be asked. Another one comes soon after.

'7 down, ends in E. To delete or blot out?'

'Erase?' I suggest.

'That's 5?'

'And your point is?'

'The point is that the promise u showed earlier has disappeared and it would appear u are just as rubbish at this as I am. x'

Mmmmm . . . a kiss, that's nice. Don't read anything into it, Maddy; it's just a tiny friendly one. Okay, to delete or blot out?

'Expunge!'

'Wow, u r brilliant!'

'An apology would suffice.'

'Sorry.'

'Could do better . . .'

'Sorry, oh wise one?'

'Better . . .'

'Sorry, oh beautiful wise one who brightens my day.'

'Much better.' I am smiling as I put the thesaurus back into Dot's office. Thankfully, she is not in today and the atmosphere in the kitchen is relaxed, despite Amy's best efforts to keep some order in place. We spend the rest of the day texting each other and I feel like a sixteen year old.

I begin to look forward to my good-morning text messages and when one isn't forthcoming this morning I find I am more than a little bothered by it, which bothers me even more. The tearoom is busy and I don't have time to think about it too much, but I still manage to check my mobile on the hour every hour. Since when did a good morning from someone become so important? By 3.00 p.m., I'm feeling a little miserable and chide myself for being so pathetic.

'It's not as if I fancy him or anything, and even if I did, which I don't, it's just a passing crush because he was nice to me,' I mutter to myself, throwing eggs into a bowl.

'You need to get out more, talking to yourself like that,' a voice says and I look around to find Matt standing there smiling. I blush and smile back, wishing I looked a little more glamorous. With an unattractive stained apron, sensible shoes and hair scraped back I am hardly take-your-breath away material.

'What time do you finish today?' he asks.

'Four o'clock,' I say, trying to look as if his appearance is not that big a deal. He looks particularly lovely today in old Brownstone boots, battered Levi's covered in dust, and a faded blue, limestone-spattered T-shirt that has seen better days but shows off his long, lean body nicely. I find myself wondering what he would wear on a night out. I quite like him like this, though; he looks very sexy in a raw rip-my-clothes-off kind of way. God, I think the heat must be getting to me!

'I would have popped in earlier but I've been in an all-day project meeting about funding. Do you want to meet me by the pavilion just after four? I have something for you,' he says, looking a little uncomfortable, and I find myself nodding that yes I do. Very much, actually.

In a secluded area of the garden, shaded by lime trees, I find Matt waiting for me on the stone steps of the garden pavilion. He looks relaxed sitting there, leaning back slightly with his elbows resting on a step, one leg bent, the other stretched out in front of him. He always looks so comfortable in his body, not in a 'look at me, aren't I gorgeous?' way, but as if he has accepted who he is. There is a quiet confidence in everything he does. When he spots me he takes off his hard hat, and pushes his hand through his hair, causing the muscles in his arms to slightly flex. Steady! The pavilion resembles a tiny Greek temple but the scaffolding needed for the restoration obscures much of it. Matt tells me that it used to be a music and reading room used by the women who lived in the house nearly three hundred years ago and gives me a short history of the house and gardens. Mmmmm, I do like a man who tells me stuff.

I produce a couple of mince pies I had brought in for the girls to try as a possible for the Sugar and Spice Christmas range. It seems a strange thing to do in the middle of summer as the temperatures hover in the nineties, but I'm trying to plan ahead. I'm relying on Christmas being really busy. Matt takes the top off his mince pie and eats it first, before popping the rest into his mouth in one go. Ben would be impressed.

Matt makes lots of mmmmm noises when he eats and probably after twenty years together I would find this annoying, but, right now, I find it enchanting. He asks me if there are any more and I find myself admiring his very kissable lips as he devours another one. He is a Michelangelo drawing; charcoaled with care and precision, every muscle and sinew, the large hands, his slightly Romanesque nose, prominent cheekbones and full, sensual, almost feminine lips. I want to close my eyes and trace his features with my hands like a blind person. I shake the image from my mind. What is the matter with me? I must be coming down with something: Mills and Boonitis. When he has finished and licked his fingers of the sugar, he walks back into the pavilion where he's been working, and comes back with a piece of paper. He hands it to me with a shy grin.

'It's from the girls, to say thank you for the cake.' Matt stands there like a shy schoolboy, hopping from one foot to another and I realise that where his girls are concerned, his usual confidence disappears. I look at the picture of a funny-shaped fairy with a pink glittery dress, the girls' names and ages written across the bottom. I smile up at him as he runs a hand through his hair and looks at his feet self-consciously.

'You can throw it away if you like, but they insisted on doing something for you,' he says, sitting back down again.

'It's beautiful. I love it,' I reassure him and we sit there quietly for a moment.

'The girls were very impressed ... My wife, actually my ex-wife, died a couple of years ago and I'm not very good on the home-cooking front. I think they miss that,' he tells me, looking out towards the fields that surround the house. A shadow of sadness passes over his face and I want to touch it.

'It must have been hard for you all, losing your wife and then having to cope with the girls on your own,' I say tentatively.

'It's been a tough couple of years, I have to admit, but I don't mind being a single parent. It's so much better than how it was before. That was really hard. Lynnette left me for someone else a year before she died and I could only see the girls at the weekend. They would be so upset that it would take us a couple of hours to get back to normal, then just as we got used to each other again they would have to go back. I hated it.'

I think of my own childhood, spending every other Sunday with Dad and Susan, with Mum reluctantly letting us go, all dressed up in our best outfits. It was always a bit of a disaster, with Susan trying a little too hard, Dad treating us like we were aliens he didn't understand, and us trying to be on our best behaviour because Mum had told us to be. Sometimes we had to endure Susan's daughter Leanne, a horrid, spoilt girl who always had the latest Sindy Doll and was prone to lying and picking her nose and smearing the contents on my jumpers. The guilt at being there, knowing Mum was at home, upset and alone, weighed down heavily. We felt like little scabs that had crossed the picket line, sitting there at the golf club eating chips and beans, making polite conversation and remembering not to put our elbows on the table. The intimacy of our early childhood was lost, the cuddles and easy laughter were gone. Even the Knickerbocker Glories Dad always ordered didn't make up for it.

'So you and your wife weren't together when she died?' I ask, a little confused.

'No. Not long after we met, she fell pregnant with Charlotte. We got married, but if I'm honest, I don't think we would have done if she hadn't been pregnant. Don't get me wrong, it was good for a while but by the end, we were at each other's throats and didn't speak for about a year after she left. Then she was diagnosed with breast cancer. Apparently, she had ignored a lump and by the time they found it, the cancer had spread to her lymph nodes. It all happened very quickly. You hear of women who fight it for years but with Lynette it was a rare, aggressive form and within a year she was gone. It was a shock to all of us, especially the girls. They just didn't understand how someone could disappear, and then they had the whole upheaval of coming to live with me.' His voice cracks with emotion and I wonder how he has remained an upbeat person after such an awful time.

'Anyway, they are great now,' he says, and tells me of their swimming lessons with his mother-in law, Georgie's love of Barbie pink, and Charlotte discovering the delights of Girls Aloud. He makes me laugh with his anecdotes and I find myself wondering if they will ever know how much their father obviously adores them. Perhaps they already know from the way he makes their breakfast in the morning, the fact that he is there to kiss them goodnight. Did my own father ever talk about me in such a way? Did he adore me once upon a time and talk about me with the air of a man who has fallen in love? Can I be jealous of two other women under the age of ten?

*

Since the mad panic of the Pharmagenica order, juggling the business with my job at the tearoom is proving manageable. Although I would prefer a few more from the slow trickle of individual orders that are coming through, it's holiday time and my business plan had accounted for the dip in sales. Even Dot is being almost amiable and my questions about producing cakes in large quantities, the benefits of different wholesalers and the logistics of running a tearoom are being met with something resembling enthusiasm as she proudly demonstrates her years of experience in the trade. If I wasn't much mistaken I would think she was trying to help me and I could have sworn I saw a tiny smile cross her lips when she offered me copies of her Bible-like recipe file. Her advice and knowledge are worth their weight in gold and I buy her a bunch of flowers to say thank you, for which she gruffly tells me off and puts me on washing-up duty, just in case I make the mistake of thinking she actually likes me.

In my tea breaks I begin to scribble notes and form the outline of a business plan for my own imagined tearoom. I find myself thinking about it more and more; how everyone would wear flowery Cath Kidston aprons, of mismatched china teacups and fairy cakes in every colour and combination piled high on old-fashioned glass cake stands . . . Mmmmm. I also find myself looking forward to the phone calls and subsequent little walks with Matt. We flirt over the phone and laugh, but when we meet, there is wariness from both of us and we end up dancing around each other like two shy school kids. When I look at him and my stomach does that flippy somersault thing, I have to remind myself that we are just friends. I guess *he* will come along when he is ready and we will invite Matt to the wedding.

The subject of Matt comes up again as Tilly and I take a break. I refuse to be drawn on the subject, telling her that we are just friends.

'He makes me laugh, but lots of people make me laugh. End of story,' I remark, tucking into a slice of sub-standard chocolate cake. As I stuff a huge piece into my mouth, Matt appears and I choke. As I desperately try not to spray the contents all over the table, he pats my back and my mortification is complete. I wave him away and swallow furiously as my face turns red with the effort of not choking to death. He returns with a glass of water and I gratefully swallow some as he pulls a chair up to join us. Tilly initially looks worried at my obvious distress, but is soon chatting away with Matt and I am grateful for the opportunity to regain my composure. Why, oh why, can I not just once appear cool, composed and utterly gorgeous? Just once will do! Matt gently removes the fork that is still in my hand and the touch of his skin on mine is like a tiny electric shock.

'May I?' he asks and I nod mutely.

He takes a piece from my cake and puts it into his mouth, causing Tilly to raise her eyebrows and me to look away.

'It's okay,' he observes. 'Here,' he scoops up the last bit on the plate and offers it to me, 'the last piece is yours.'

I open my mouth obediently and take the piece of cake from the fork. To have someone share my cake and feed me is akin to undressing me in public; I know Tilly will now never believe me when I say there is nothing going on.

'Mmmmm, I do love a slice of chocolate cake, but something tells me yours would be a whole lot better.

Maybe I should place an order with Sugar and Spice,' he remarks, before getting up and leaving. I look at Tilly and blush, still reeling from the intimacy of the moment.

Thirty-bloody-two!!! God, it sounds so old. Anyway, no matter, it is my birthday and if there are two things I love in life it is Christmas and birthdays. Lou and I have a day of shopping planned and the delights of Top Shop are first on our list, followed by Whistles, Office, House of Fraser, Karen Millen ... As I lust over a particularly lovely summer dress, a text appears on my mobile: 'Hope u r having a nice day.'

The next ten minutes are spent texting and the lovely dress is soon forgotten as Matt makes me laugh, and I walk around grinning like an idiot. I feel like a teenager, not a thirty-whatever-year-old, and I like it. I like it a lot. Lou has wasted no time and whilst I have been mooning over my mobile she has managed to buy a pair of shoes and a top. Later, over a lunchtime glass of wine, she hands me my present: a Chanel nail varnish and some Elle Macpherson underwear.

'When somebody comes along, I want you to be prepared ... painted toenails and gorgeous knickers ... Anyway, I think I might have somebody at work ... he likes cake ... although he is a bit podgy around the midriff and ... well, it's worth you meeting him ... they're not things that can't be changed. Look at Carl when I met him ... those jumpers!' Lou shudders at the thought.

After treating myself to the dress, I leave Lou and make a quick dash back to fulfil an order for an Earl Grey Tea cake. Later I spend the evening at my favourite restaurant with Lou, Mac, Ben, Freya and Moo who arrives with a gorgeous-looking raspberry, blueberry and lime cake complete with a silver candle. Whilst we sit and chat, a message comes through on my mobile.

'Forgot this earlier. Your birthday kiss. X'

A kiss? I resist the urge to send a kiss back and instead text a demure thank you. I know I am blushing and I avoid looking at Moo, who has suddenly become very interested in what I am doing. Following copious amounts of wine and champagne Moo and I stagger back, giggling in the darkness. She sleeps in my bed and I am on the blow-up mattress again on the floor next to her, although this time I have made sure the stopper is securely in.

'So has *he* made an appearance yet?' Moo calls out into the darkness. I thought she had fallen asleep.

'Nope,' I respond, shifting position. I'm sure I'm losing air again and will be on the floor by morning, but I'm too drunk to bother getting up and checking the stopper.

'No one Scottish or swarthy?'

'Nope.'

'Two kids?'

At this point, I don't reply because I hadn't connected the prediction from Alice with the fact that Matt has two kids, until now. Surely it's just a coincidence, and if I remember rightly, she was a bit vague about the children part. Okay, so he is sexy, and wise, sensitive and funny, and yes, I look forward to seeing him, but he is not THE ONE!! *He* was supposed to sweep me off my feet with the big love thing and this is just a nice, flirty friendship. Thankfully, Moo doesn't notice my lack of response.

'I don't understand it. I was so sure he was near,' she

laments. 'By the way, I meant to say earlier, you are looking very radiant at the moment.'

'The wonders of Benefit Hollywood Glo,' I laugh.

'Are you sure *he* hasn't made an appearance?' Moo quizzes me, and I fully expect her to suddenly appear by my bedside, shining a torch into my eyes.

'I'm sure,' I reply. Moo snorts, and I laugh.

We wake up late and emerge bleary-eyed and hungover. As we sit quietly drinking our tea and munching our toast, waiting for signs of life to kick in, Moo looks as if she is trying to work something out in her mind. I wait, knowing that something is afoot, then, with an energy I thought we wouldn't see until at least lunchtime, she suddenly turns, and looks straight at me. I am trapped, like a bunny in headlights.

'So who exactly was that who texted you last night and made you blush like a schoolgirl?'

I find myself confessing all: about the sandwich order, the coffee incident, the good-morning texts, the way we have fallen into the habit of meeting up for walks, how he makes me laugh, but all the while confirming that he is not the one.

'We're just friends. I don't think anything will come of it and I don't want it to. He has too much baggage, Moo, and me as a step-mum? I can't see it myself. It's not really what I had in mind.'

'But it's doable,' Moo replies, smiling an 'I knew it all along' smile.

'Anyway, we haven't even kissed,' I say, and surprise myself at how disappointed I sound.

'But you want to!'

'No! . . . All right, yes!'

*

As I finish wrapping the previous day's baking, Matt texts me. 'It's beautiful here this morning. I have coffee?'

I calculate that if I get my skates on I can drop these off at the couriers, and still grab half an hour with him before I start work at the tearoom. It was a Sugar and Spice day yesterday and despite being really busy baking six cakes, trying to persuade the local farm shops and delis to think about taking our yet-to-be-decided Christmas range and catching up on my paperwork, I found myself missing our daily chat in the garden. I rush around in a frenzy, drive like a lunatic, spraying perfume and applying lipstick as I do so. Feeling flustered, I arrive but try desperately hard to act nonchalantly as I wander over and find him sitting on his coat underneath a tulip tree. He smiles and hands me a cup of steaming hot coffee. It tastes good and strong, with a touch of bitterness, and I hug my knees to my chest.

'You were right, it's beautiful this morning,' I observe, listening to the silence.

'It sure is.'

We sit quietly, gazing out over the early morning haze that has settled on the lake.

'Where's your favourite place to be?' he asks.

'By the sea. There is nothing better, no matter where you are in the world, than walking along a beach in the early morning with just the sound of the waves to accompany you.'

'Mmmmm, definitely,' Matt says, turning towards me, smiling. I smile back and, before I know it, he is kissing it away with the lightest of touches. His lips are warm and he tastes of toothpaste and coffee. When he pulls away, we look at each other and he looks as surprised as I imagine I do. We both laugh, suddenly embarrassed by what has just taken place. We look down at our shoes, at the grass, a dragonfly, at anything, anywhere, except at each other. My heart is pumping inside my chest and I think I will die in the ensuing silence.

'Would you like to go to the seaside for the day soon?' he eventually asks, turning to look at me.

'I would love to,' I reply, trying not to sound too eager as my heart sings. I'm sure the whole world can hear it.

'Great, I'll sort something out. In the meantime I have something for you,' he says, reaching into his rucksack and handing me a small box.

'A late birthday present.'

I open it to find it full of mini Jaffa Cakes.

'I think you'll find there are seven there,' he says, smiling at me.

I want to kiss him again but instead I mumble a thank you and offer him one. As we sit and munch away, I wonder if I imagined the kiss and, if I didn't, if he was now regretting it – or, more to the point, if I was.

I get up to leave, already late for work, as the morning sun begins to cover everything with its soft violet and gold gauze. I spend the rest of the day floating around the kitchen, getting on everyone's nerves by singing out of tune and forgetting to take the flapjacks out of the oven. Even Dot's fiery temper as she banishes me to clearing tables cannot touch me as I float on my own little cushion of lust, rewinding over and over in my mind the moment when Matthew Tennant kissed me.

The only thing that threatens to deflate my little cushion is the fact that said Mr Tennant is proving to be a little elusive and hasn't texted me at all since the Big Kiss. Potential reasons for his lack of communication are endless: he could be extraordinarily busy, or maybe he needs a little time to adapt to this new development in our relationship, or maybe he wishes it had never happened. By the end of the day the evil voices in my head are winning and have convinced me that all is not well, that it was all just a silly mistake and he is regretting the whole thing. With my mind going over every possible scenario I go to bed angry with myself for even getting into this predicament. It was just a kiss, for heaven's sake; he probably hasn't even thought anything of it. It was one of those silly moments that hopefully we can both pretend never happened. Yes, that's it. Tomorrow we will just carry on as normal and if he says anything I will say that I am just as embarrassed by all this as he is; that we should just forget it.

As I step out of the shower the next morning the door goes and in my panic to grab my dressing gown I stub my toe on the portable glass and chrome shelf unit that is home to a pile of carefully folded, colour coordinated towels. They are not there to be used, but to make me feel as if I am living a life straight from the pages of *Elle Décor*. The courier company is not meant to be here for at least another hour. I limp to the door with my hair dripping wet, my dressing gown on and carrying the four boxes that contain a lemon drizzle cake and three Victoria sandwiches. They took me until 11.30 p.m. to bake, and I was up at 5.00 a.m. to get them ready for their journey towards a firm of solicitors in the Big City. I hold the boxes steady with my chin, and open the door with my free hand. A voice says good morning. The voice, however, does not belong to Derek the delivery man, but to someone else. I peer around the boxes and have to stop myself from rushing back inside and shutting the door as Matt stands there grinning from ear to ear.

'Can I come in?' he asks and, unable to speak, I nod from behind the boxes. As I reverse and he steps inside, all I can think about is the fact that I have tangled wet hair, a scummy dressing gown on and no make-up. I decide to keep hold of the boxes in a bid to hide behind them, but he has other ideas.

'Here, let me help,' he says, removing them from my grasp to reveal the real me in all my glory. Life is just so bloody unfair sometimes.

'Would you like a cup of tea?' I ask weakly, unable to look him in the eye.

'No, thanks, I'm on my way to work,' he says, the smile evident in his voice. I look everywhere but at him, the urge to ask him why he is here at 7.00 a.m. hanging in the air. Say something, Maddy. Save him the trouble of doing it. Tell him that it was all a mistake, that you hope to remain friends. Tell him . . . my mouth becomes disconnected from my brain, and instead I talk about subjects that are not related to each other in double-quick time. I talk of delivery men, of cakes, of the weather, that the business takes up all of my time, that I have had to cancel a date tonight because I am so busy. Where did that little porky come from? Suddenly he is standing very close to me, causing the rapid fire of speech to increase tenfold and the inevitable blush to appear. I am surprised that it took so long.

'I wanted to call you yesterday but I had a bit of an emergency,' he interrupts, putting the boxes down, and I finally stop talking.

'Charlotte broke her collarbone at school and I had to rush home and take her to the hospital.'

'Gosh, is she all right?' I ask, shocked.

'Yeah, she's a brave little soldier, but it was all a bit hectic and scary for a while. Anyway, I couldn't have my phone on in the hospital and by the time we came out it was late, then it was a case of getting the girls fed, bathed and Charlotte took ages to get to sleep, bless her.'

'Poor thing,' I respond, wrapping my dressing gown so tightly around me that it threatens to break my ribs.

'I didn't stop until 11.00 p.m. and then I thought it would be too late to ring. I just wondered if you were okay and I didn't want you to think that I was . . .' Matt looks down at his feet with embarrassment before continuing almost inaudibly. 'That I didn't . . .'

There's an awkward silence whilst I wait for him to finish. This is not really going the way I had planned.

'You had a date?' he suddenly asks. Oh shit, I had forgotten about that.

'Oh, it wasn't really a date, more a favour really for a friend. You know how it is,' I say vaguely, waving my hands in the air as if brushing it all away.

'Can I kiss you again?'

'What?' I ask, because even though I heard him I convince myself that I didn't, that my imagination is playing tricks on me.

'Can I kiss you?'

Yep, he said it.

'Yes,' I say weakly. Yes???!!!

The next moment is one of true perfection: dark velvety melt in the mouth. My knees give way and he holds me up as I begin to sink down. When we finally break for air all I can say is, 'Wow!'

'Does that mean we are still on for the seaside?'

I nod and Matt smiles that gorgeous smile of his, the mischievous one that makes his eyes sparkle, and he kisses me again on the nose.

'Have a great day,' he says and moves towards the front door. Unable to move, I stay transfixed to the spot, thinking that I will surely faint as soon as he leaves. He turns to look at me.

'By the way, you look gorgeous,' he says and closes the door behind him, leaving me gasping for air.

When Derek eventually arrives to collect the cakes, I am still floating on air. I ramble on about how wonderful life is and hum. He frowns and looks at me from beneath bushy eyebrows as if I am on drugs. I smile as if I am and resume my humming.

The rest of the day is spent trying to concentrate on ingredient labels, ordering supplies, baking some fairy cakes for a hen party and two lemon drizzles, one for a new baby and one for an old dear's birthday. Every so often, my concentration dips and I find myself gazing out of the window, daydreaming disgustingly fabulous, dirty thoughts about Matt. The recipients of the cakes I bake today do not know it, but I have doubled the quantity of love and kisses added to each one. In fact, I am surprised that they do not fly out of the oven flanked by harp-playing cherubs, such is their lightness.

He loves the smell of the mincemeat I am making in readiness for Christmas and opens a jar to inhale the heady sweetness.

I love the smell of him. It's a natural earthy smell: limestone, soap and skin and I can feel my pheromones going into overdrive as he hugs me, lifting me off the ground.

'Ready for the seaside?' he asks, planting small kisses on my neck.

'Mmmmm,' I reply, wondering how this happened. One minute we are dancing around each other like shy school kids, and now? Now we can't tear ourselves apart. His kisses are melt-in-the-mouth meringues, piled high with tiny, sweet juicy strawberries, the lightest of rich, dark chocolate soufflé and the jammy bit in the middle of a doughnut you find with your tongue. Deliciously addictive, I find I can't get enough and soon we are ripping each other's clothes off. I thought I would worry about this part, and it surprises me that I'm not, although I do say a silent thank you to the god of fake tan and the fact that I have my sexiest undies on (well . . . it's always good to be prepared!). All I can think about is getting our clothes off as quickly as we can and feeling his skin on mine as we stumble upstairs. This feeling is short-lived, though, as I suddenly experience a little twang of nervousness and get the jitters.

'Hey, we don't have to do this if it doesn't feel right. There's no rush,' Matt says, gently brushing the hair away from my face.

No rush, what's he talking about? Of course there is; I have never wanted someone so much in my life. My nerves turn out to be a temporary blip simply remedied by one of his gorgeous smiles. Oh, how I love his smile . . . Again, please!

I feel a little drunk as we lie in my bed, limbs intertwined, gazing up at the ceiling.

'We can always go to the seaside another day,' I suggest, reluctant to tear myself away from the touch of his skin. It's hot outside and even hotter in my room; there are tiny beads of sweat glistening on what has turned out to be a rather gorgeous body. I can feel the hotness of his breath on my neck as he kisses it.

'Are you suggesting we spend all day in bed, Ms Brown?' Matt rests his head on his hand and looks down at me.

'I guess I was?' I answer, suddenly unsure if this was the right thing to say as I trace a finger along his stomach. It makes him shiver.

'I was hoping you were,' he laughs before kissing me again. The Sugar and Spice phone rings in the background and I consider ignoring it but I know I can't afford to.

'I'll still be here,' Matt confirms, sensing my dilemma, and I smile sheepishly before getting out of bed and making my way to my office. As I take an order for a whisky cake all I can think of is whether my bum wobbled too much as I ran to the phone.

Later, hunger gets the better of us and I spread a blanket on the small patch of grass in my garden and feed him some of the raspberry, blueberry and lime cake left over from my birthday.

'Pity it's not chocolate cake, but that was still delicious. Give your sister my compliments,' he says as we lie on our backs like cats languidly soaking up the sun.

'I promise I will make you a chocolate cake,' I tell him, not sure if I have found the perfect recipe yet. I look up at the light wisps of cloud that are smeared across an azure-blue sky as a plane flies across, weaving its own white trail. The smell of cut grass fills the air as bees buzz diligently around the fragrant honeysuckle and the sounds of a radio from next door become the soundtrack to our own romantic film set. Matt begins singing a tune I don't recognise. I like it when he sings. It means he is happy. I close my eyes as he traces the veins in my arm.

He suddenly jumps up. 'God, is that the time? Come on, Matthew Hamish Tennant, you can't just lie here enjoying yourself with a beautiful sex-crazed woman.'

'What did you say?' I ask, sitting up. A cloud passes over Matt's face as he looks at me.

'Beautiful sex-crazed woman?' he says sheepishly.

'No. Your name,' I say, unable to remove the concern in my voice.

'Matthew Hamish Tennant.'

'Hamish?' I repeat as if it is the name of a murderer.

'It's not *that* bad. Some of the coolest people have weird middle names. Kurt Cobain's middle name was Donald.' Matt bites his lip and runs a hand through his hair, which five minutes ago would have been enough to cause me to jump on him and rip his jeans off. Instead, all I can think of is the prediction from Alice. The words 'Scottish or Swarthy' swim in front of me, tantalising and shocking.

'You didn't tell me you were Scottish,' I accuse, causing his eyes to widen like a frightened little boy.

'I'm not. Apparently, Mum wanted it to be my first name but Dad refused, thank God. She loved to go hiking in the Scottish Highlands when she was a child. Personally, I think it was the name of her childhood sweetheart. Why else would you want to subject your child to a name like that?' He laughs, but I can see that I have worried him.

'Are you okay?' he asks, and realising that I must appear like some mad woman who has forgotten to take her medication, I smile and shake the image of Alice, wide-eyed in the candlelight, from my mind. I'm just being silly. It does not mean Matt is *him*. I kiss him and reassure him that I'm fine.

'Anyway, gotta go and pick the girls up,' he announces, getting up to leave. I had momentarily forgotten this part of his life and my thoughts of opening a bottle of wine and cuddling up on the sofa are swept away by the cool wind of reality. I am disappointed, but don't show it as he kisses me a thousand times on his way to the door.

'Talking of the girls, I forgot to ask you a favour. Can't think why, I guess I got diverted.' Matt smiles and hugs me tightly before kissing me again. I reluctantly pull away.

'Favour?' I ask.

'Oh, yes. See, I got carried away again. Mum and the girls are doing a fund-raising thing for Breast Cancer Awareness month in October. They do it every year and I thought it might be a nice idea if they had some cakes to sell at school. Can you give me the recipe for your fairy cakes?'

'I'll go one better. I'll make them,' I tell him, glad to be involved.

'That's what I was hoping you would say. I didn't realise I would have to sleep with you, though . . . I dread to think what you would make me do for a chocolate cake?'

'Just more of the same,' I confirm, hoping that there will be. What if this was a one-off?

He hesitates at the door and I want to drag him back in. 'See you tomorrow?'

'Mmm, definitely.'

'Bye then.'

'Bye.' I reluctantly close the door and lean against it, closing my eyes, letting the feelings and emotions of the last few hours wash over me. I shiver. What the hell am I doing? What happened to 'No, Matt, this isn't a good idea?' What happened to him not being my type and having too much baggage? A few kisses and I'm lost. Must try harder! I look around the kitchen feeling a little lost. A cup of tea, or something stronger? It may only be 4.30 p.m. but I remove a bottle of wine from the fridge and pour myself a glass.

Following the best night's sleep I have had in ages I arrive at the tearoom early next morning to a barrage of questions about my day at the seaside, including a snide one from Dot. The only person I had told about my day with Matt was Tilly; now it appears the whole of the tearoom knows. As I field the questions with as many ambiguous answers as I can manage I want to wring Tilly's neck, but I can't seem to find her anywhere. I set to work making some shortbread and find myself humming the mystery tune Matt was singing yesterday.

'So lovely to hear people happy in their work.' Lillian, the custodian of Carriage House, breaks through my daydreams.

'How is it going, my dear?' she asks and I confirm that everything is fine. She looks into the bowl of cake mixture I have just emptied into six cake tins and surprises me by wiping her finger around it. She sucks on it noisily.

'Lillian, I was wondering . . .' because it has only just occurred to me whilst she is standing there, that I have been.

'Yes, dear?' she asks expectantly. I don't have the heart to tell her she has some cake mixture on the white hairs above her lip. It looks like a creamy moustache.

'I've been thinking that it would be really nice if we held a little tea party in the pavilion.'

'Oh, how lovely. I adore tea parties,' she says excitedly, clapping her hands, and I suddenly get a vision of Tilly in fifty years' time.

'I thought we could do it in October – you know, Breast Cancer Awareness month. It could be pink themed. The Pink Tea Party.' I'm thinking of Matt and the girls. 'And we could invite all of the local ladies in the surrounding villages. It would mean they would get to see the house and gardens and then tell all of their friends about it. We could do it all for charity. For a breast cancer charity? I would supply all of the cakes. Pink, of course?' I talk quickly, amazed at where all of this is coming from, but the more I talk, the more I know it would be fabulous. We could wear pink and serve pink champagne . . . and . . .

'What a good idea. I shall investigate and let you know if it's okay,' she says, wiping her finger around the bowl again. 'So you like it here?'

'Yes, I do,' I reply.

'Well, you have a sparkle to your eyes. It obviously suits you,' she remarks and I find myself blushing. Is it written all over my face that I ripped my clothes off in a frenzy of unexpected passion on what was effectively a first date yesterday? I am saved from answering by the appearance of Tilly.

'I'm in love,' she sings out loudly, grabbing my hand and whirling me around the kitchen.

'Again,' Dot notes dryly as she hands Tilly an apron and tells her to get on with making the leek and potato soup.

As she absent-mindedly chops potatoes Tilly proceeds to tell me all about Tom, the new man in her life, before stopping mid-sentence, 'Listen to me rabbiting on! I forgot to ask, how was the seaside?' she asks.

'We didn't go,' I reveal, causing her to rush over in a bid to console me.

'Oh no, Maddy, what happened?' she asks, wrapping her arms around me. I feel a little guilty as I whisper the reason. The scream that emanates from her is deafening, and causes Amy to drop a bowl of salad, which in turn causes Dot to storm through the kitchen waving a spatula in her hand.

'Tilly, you will find yourself on permanent chopping duties if you do not have that soup ready in five minutes,' she shouts, and then turns to point the spatula in my direction. 'And you can stop mooning all over the place. You should be on your second batch of shortbread by now.'

When she has disappeared, Tilly insists I tell her all and I relent with a heavily edited version, which doesn't really leave out that much, but she sucks in each tiny morsel of information with enthusiasm.

'You mustn't tell anyone about this,' I tell her for the third time in as many minutes.

'I cross my heart. I promise I won't say a word,' she says, clapping her hands and hugging me. 'I'm so excited. We have both met "the one" at the same time.'

'Tilly, it's early days yet and I refuse to get carried away by a little passion.' My mobile beeps in my apron pocket. It's a text from Matt.

'Mmmmm . . . raspberry, blueberry and lime cake.'

It beeps again with another message.

'Mmmmm . . . kissing u.'

Then again, I am finding it hard to contain my excitement.

'Mmmmm . . . that lovely little freckle on your toe.'
Another message comes through immediately.
'Can't wait to do it all again xxx'
Breathe . . . OH MY GOD!

RASPBERRY, BLUEBERRY AND LIME CAKE (MOO'S CAKE)

Perfect for a summer afternoon, this is a beautiful-looking cake with the colours of the fruit bleeding through into golden sponge. It is also Moo's favourite.

Ingredients

225g (8oz) butter

225g (8oz) caster sugar

4 medium eggs

grated zest and juice of 2 limes

250g (9oz) self-raising flour
  sifted with a pinch of salt

25g (1oz) ground almonds

100g (4oz) each of blueberries
  and raspberries

For the syrup:

8 tablespoons lime juice (about 4 limes)

150g (6oz) caster sugar

grated zest of 1 lime

Method

Grease and line a 20cm (8 inch) cake tin and heat oven to 180°C/350°F/gas mark 4. Cream butter and sugar until light and fluffy. Gradually add beaten eggs. Beat in lime zest. With a metal spoon, fold in flour and almonds. Fold in enough lime juice (about 3 tablespoons) to give dropping consistency. Fold in three quarters of the blueberries and raspberries and spoon into tin. Smooth surface and scatter remaining fruit on top – it will sink as cake rises. Bake for 1 hour – cover with foil if browning too much. Whilst cake bakes begin making the syrup by placing the lime juice, sugar and zest in saucepan. Combine over gentle heat without allowing to bubble. As soon as cake comes out of oven, prick it all over with skewer and spoon syrup over. Ensure cake is completely cold before taking out of tin.

A sprinkling of jealousy

'Running late. See u at work later x.'

The text comes through and I try not to be too disappointed; I have my sexiest undies on, bought especially to tickle his fancy! My underwear drawer is going through something of a renaissance and is suddenly full of sexy, impractical creations with ribbons and the flimsiest of lace. Can't think why! Feeling a little lost, I decide to use the time to make the chocolate cake I have promised him, one full of hope, happiness and a smattering of lustful thoughts. As the rest of the world wakes on a beautiful, sunny, cloudless sky, I am singing at the top of my voice. As I search in vain for the seventy-five per cent minimum cocoa content chocolate, I suddenly remember the three chocolate cakes I made for orders yesterday. I will have to make him something else, but what? I look in the cupboard for ingredients and search for inspiration. Images of Matt lying in my bed fill my head. Wholesome, glorious and delicious: the warm overtones of citrus spice, skin the colour of pale gold and ground ginger, the taste of honey, cinnamon, salt and sugar. Ooooh . . . my mouth is watering in anticipation of another huge slice of that beautiful body.

Later, as I pop my apron on at the tearoom, I hear him singing before I see his face, and my stomach does a lurch. He pops his head around the back door, smiling, and looks around to check if anyone is around. I instinctively look around too, but the kitchen is strangely quiet.

'What are you doing here?' I ask, grinning from ear to ear like a crazed idiot.

'I missed my early morning kiss and couldn't wait till later,' he says, pushing me up against the storeroom cupboard, his strong, beautiful hands searching their way through my apron. The sound of Amy's voice causes me to pull away quickly, and I try to compose myself before she appears, but I am feeling decidedly flushed and breathless.

'So, Maddy, did you get all that?' Matt asks, putting on his best sensible voice.

'Mmmmm, I think so,' I reply, smoothing down my apron, aware that we are acting like something out of a bad seventies TV comedy.

'And you're clear about what I require later, or do you want me to go through it again?' he says, flashing a winning smile at Amy, who suspiciously smiles back as she pushes past me to get to the storeroom.

'And don't forget the Jaffa Cakes?' he adds mischievously.

'I've made you a cake,' I mouth to him.

'Perfect,' he mouths back, but the way his eyes roam over me I am not sure that he means the cake at all and I wonder when he became so blind. Not that I'm complaining, I like the rose-coloured glasses he appears to be wearing these days, they suit him.

'What time did you say?' I ask weakly, trying not to laugh.

'Did I tell you how much I love kissing you?' he whispers before saying in a loud voice, 'Let's say about three. Is that okay?'

I nod and try to regain some composure as he walks away grinning. I can hear him singing to himself as he goes. I quickly make my way to Dot's office before Amy appears again, to ask if I can work through my lunch break and leave an hour early.

The sunlight hurts my eyes as I make my way to the pavilion with my precious cargo and a skip in my step. I find him sitting on the steps, eyes closed, face upturned to the sun. I creep over and plant a light kiss on his lips; he opens his eyes and smiles.

'Hello, gorgeous. Now, where is this chocolate cake you promised me? I'm starving,' he says, pulling me towards him for another kiss, this time longer and a little more passionate. When we eventually pull away, I pass him the cake tin, sitting myself down next to him.

'Sorry, but I ran out of chocolate. I experimented instead and made you a sugar and spice cake. I may add it to the range and you're my gorgeous guinea pig.'

If he's disappointed, he doesn't let on. Opening the tin, he sticks his head in to inhale its hopefully seductive aroma before taking the slice I have already cut in preparation. Breaking a piece off, he pops it into my mouth before devouring the rest like a starving man.

'This is fantastic, Maddy. Really nice,' Matt says, and I glow with pride, thinking that I could not be happier. God, pass the sick bag. I reprimand myself for getting so carried away; it's just a bit of harmless lust and nothing more. I sit with my head leaning against his chest as we talk, his arm draped over me. I tell him all about Tilly and her latest man, whose name I cannot recall and he laughs when I tell him she is convinced that he is the one.

'You know, Moo predicted I would meet "the one" this year,' I blurt out, and immediately wish I hadn't.

'Well, she was right. Nice to meet you,' he laughs and I poke him playfully in the tummy.

'Assuming a little, I think, Mr Tennant. Listen, when *he* does arrive, I will be dropping you like a hot potato,' I tease back, thinking of my phone call to Moo last night.

'I knew it. I knew it!' she had proclaimed down the phone.

'What?' I'd asked, knowing perfectly well what she meant. I had just told her about our passion-filled afternoon and subsequent move into a relationship of sorts.

'I told you *he* was close by. It must be *him*!' she had almost shouted down the phone.

'It's not *him*,' I had replied, determined not to get carried away by all of this nonsense.

Moo's response had been a cynical 'Mmmmm . . .'

Matt gently traces his fingers along my neck and collarbone. His touch is soft and delicate, causing tiny shocks of electricity to shoot down into my arms and through to my fingertips. This is near to perfection. I say 'near' because the only thing that blights our otherwise dreamlike existence right now is the fact that he cannot spend the night or weekends with me because of his daughters. I push these thoughts aside and instead concentrate on his caressing.

'Okay, this man of your dreams. Tell me about him,' Matt asks, interrupting my dreamlike state.

'Still in the experimental stage,' I answer, and kiss him.

Early mornings, late nights baking and squeezing time to see Matt in between, means I'm running on pure adrenalin. He turns up on my doorstep every morning and tells me I am beautiful before I push him out of the door so that I can get on baking the previous day's orders. We spend hours on the phone and secretly meet in the garden to kiss like teenagers whenever we can, and sometimes, depending on whether he can get a babysitter or not, he comes round for a couple of hours in the evening. He makes me smile, sing and laugh out loud. I am deliriously happy, but also a little scared by the strength of my feelings; it has all happened so quickly and I haven't had time to catch my breath. I have to remind myself that it is purely casual, that he has made no noises to indicate anything different, and the fact that he has made no move to spend the night or weekends with me just proves that this is the case. I also have to remind myself that this is fine by me. I am far too busy with Sugar and Spice for anything more. When I'm not thinking about him, I'm thinking cake. From the moment I wake up, to the moment my head hits the pillow, recipes and ideas for the business fill my mind. It is exhausting, but exhilarating. I am doing it. I am actually, really, truly, doing it and Matt is the cherry on the top.

Lou arrives at our local Thai restaurant to find me already tucking into some spicy prawn crackers. With an impressive tan from a two-week holiday in the Bahamas and looking fabulous in the latest designer jeans, a chiffon summer top in a pretty jade colour, and matching sandals, encrusted with jade-coloured stones, she draws admiring glances from the other diners. The waitresses, who are all dressed in traditional Thai costume, bow and whisper 'Evening, Miss Lou' into the floor as she wafts past them in a cloud of Shalimar perfume. She gives me a hug before sitting down and I can see from the wide smile on her face that something extraordinary has happened.

'Guess what? I'm getting married!' she squeals.

'Oh my God,' I squeal back. 'Congratulations.'

As if blessed with a second sense, one of our waitresses glides over, her feet barely touching the floor. I order our favourite peach champagne cocktails and, realising I have eaten the whole bowl, some more crackers. Without pausing for breath Lou proceeds to tell me every detail of the night Carl proposed whilst they were on holiday.

'So where is it?' I demand, wondering how Carl managed to locate a diamond bigger than the one she already wears.

'I'm having it reset. Don't get me wrong, it's beautiful, but I really wanted something bigger.'

I smile because I wouldn't expect anything less from a woman who doesn't understand the word compromise. And why should she? When you are as gorgeous as Lou you don't have to, and that's exactly what we all love about her. Thank heavens Carl is confident enough in his own skin to take it all with a pinch of salt.

'I'm so pleased for you, Lou, I really am. In fact, I think I'm going to cry,' I tell her, trying to swallow the lump that has appeared in my throat. She looks so happy and it's all so lovely and romantic that I feel more than a touch emotional.

'Personally, I think it was the pole dancing that did it!' Lou raises her eyes cynically before laughing.

'A toast to pole dancing and huge diamonds,' I suggest. We clink glasses as she beams a smile whose brightness will only ever be surpassed by the diamond that will soon grace her finger.

'Now we just need to get you sorted out,' she remarks and I nod, grateful for the diversion of a red curry and pad Thai that is placed in front of us. I suck up a noodle but the end does a backflip and flicks up my nose, splashing red curry sauce over my face and top. I dab away at the red greasy stain that has ruined my mint-green top while Lou continues. She is used to my tendency towards clumsiness in public and now doesn't even acknowledge it when it happens, treating me instead like an indulgent mother who refuses to see the faults of her favourite child. She places a prawn delicately in her mouth. She has the art of eating seductively without ruining her lipstick down to perfection; something I clearly need to learn.

'We really do need to find you someone, Maddy,' Lou says, looking around the restaurant as if someone eligible might be sitting at one of the tables. I fill my glass up with wine, and take a deep breath.

'Actually, I've met someone,' I say cautiously, and the look of shock on her face is probably very similar to the one she wore when Carl proposed. I take advantage of the fact that she has been rendered temporarily speechless and tell her all about Matt. When I have finished, her perfectly plucked eyebrows are frowning slightly.

'Why didn't you tell me?'

'You were on holiday when it all happened. Before the

first kiss, I didn't think there was anything to tell. He was just a friend.'

'What's he like?' she asks and I tell her how perfect he is, smiling that irritating dreamy smile I seem to wear when I think or talk about him.

'But?' she asks, and I look at her as if I don't quite understand.

'I sense there is a but in there somewhere.' That's the trouble with having a friend who has known you for too long.

'Well ... I rarely see him at the weekends and he never stays the night. He says that's when he has to be with the girls. I sometimes feel like I'm having an affair with a married man.'

'Have you talked about it?' Lou asks.

'No. It's not serious enough to start talking about meeting the girls and I'm not going to push it.' I take another large gulp of wine. 'Do you think it's bad to be jealous of the time he spends with his girls?'

'No, I think it's only natural, but you have to respect he has to take it slowly for the sake of his kids. At some point, though, you are going to have to broach the subject. He can't keep you a secret for ever.'

Lou vocalises what I already know, but part of me thinks that eventually this initial attraction, passion or whatever you want to call it will fizzle out, and then I guess it won't be an issue. As we finish with some Jasmine tea, we talk of weddings. Would I do it all again? Of course I would: I am a romantic and believe in fairy-tale happy endings. Next time though, it will just be the two of us, not the whole relative thing and the big reception. I quite fancy New York, Paris, or a small village nestled in the hilltops of Italy, before escaping to a gorgeous boutique

hotel with a mini bar full of Jaffa Cakes, Maltesers
and champagne. There would also be a complimentary
chocolate cake, courtesy of a company called Sugar and
Spice.

OK! Interview

'So, congratulations are in order.'

'Thank you,' I gush.

'Tell us all about it.'

'It was all a bit of a whirlwind, really. We have just
returned from our honeymoon in the Tuscan hills and a
week in LA where we were guests of Elton and David.'

'And how did it happen?'

'Well, they do say the way to a man's heart is through
his stomach and my chocolate cake seemed to hit the
spot.'

'I hear Elton sang at the wedding?'

'Yes, he did a duet with my new husband. It was very
romantic.'

'I have to ask, did you make your own wedding cake?'

'No, my sister Moo made it. And yes, before you ask, it
was chocolate and covered in Maltesers.'

I ring Moo to wish her happy birthday. It is the weekend
but with orders to fulfil I have cancelled my planned trip
to see her and sent her a cake instead.

'Not as nice as my wife's cakes, you understand, but
pretty good,' Bob says in his unmistakable Stoke accent
before he hands the phone over to Moo.

'Thank you for my Benefit goodies, although I think
I'm going to need more than a dusting of gold powder to
disguise half a stone.' She laughs.

'Gok recommends big suck-it-in knickers but I didn't think you would appreciate it if I sent you those.'

'Got a pair, and I thought Bob was going to have a heart attack he laughed so much.'

'How are things? Are you okay?' I ask.

'Oh, still tired and running around like an idiot . . . told an indignant parent to bugger off the other day. Anyway, how is the business going?' Moo asks.

'Well, August was a pretty dismal month but I guess that's because everyone was on holiday. This month is a bit better, but it's still not enough to generate any real money,' I reply.

'It should pick up. Everyone loves a cake when the winter nights draw in and you have Christmas to look forward to which should hopefully be really busy,' Moo tries to reassure me.

'Let's hope so. But what do I do if it isn't? I can't keep ploughing money in to keep it afloat. Soon there won't be any left.'

'I don't know what to suggest, except to keep plodding on. Don't give up. You have to believe it will succeed, and nobody said that reaching for the stars was easy. If it was, everyone would be doing it.'

'I know,' I respond with a sigh.

'Are you enjoying it, though?' she asks, and I don't need to think about my answer.

'Yes, I am; it's hard but it's good.'

'Hurray!' Moo shouts. 'Sorry, The Bear has just got some baked beans on his spoon and they have reached his mouth. It's a momentous occasion.'

'Hurray,' I respond.

If The Bear can overcome the odds, then hell, so can I. A couple of baked beans, like a couple of cakes, are better than none. After talking for over an hour, we reluctantly end the phone call and I check my mobile. There are two text messages from Matt.

'On rollercoaster at Alton Towers. Georgie's been sick!'

I click open the second one.

'Wish u were here x.'

Well, you only had to ask, I want to text back, but I resist the temptation and decide not to text back at all. Am I punishing him and attempting to play hard to get? You bet I am!

I set to work on the two orders that came through yesterday and resign myself to spending the weekend on my own. James unexpectedly turns up with Frog in tow and makes us both a cup of tea. His visits have been few and far between lately and I'm surprised to see him. Tired, with red-rimmed eyes, hair all over the place and a top that needs a good iron, he looks as if he has just tumbled out of bed. I assume this has something to do with the blonde he has been preoccupied with of late. What was her name? Sarah?

'I'm worried about Frog. He seems to have got worse over the last few weeks,' James reveals, and there are tears in his eyes as he gives Frog an affectionate tap. Frog barely looks up and I agree that this is unusual.

'I know the vet said he was just old when you took him last time but this is different.'

'Do you want me to book another appointment?' I ask.

'No. I'm too scared of what he will say,' he confesses. 'I wake up in the middle of the night to check whether he's okay or not. I keep thinking he's going to be gone when I wake up.' His voice breaks and I put my arms around him.

'I'm not ready to lose him yet.' James shakes his head in denial and I nod in understanding. We both stand there in silence, feeling a little tearful at the thought of losing our little, hairy baby Frog.

'Stay for dinner. I'll cook you something nice,' I suggest, and James nods, blowing his nose noisily. As I busily prepare a roasted vegetable lasagne the phone rings, and thinking it is Moo, I ask James to pick it up for me. As I pop the lasagne in the oven, he hands me the phone and instead of Moo's, it's Matt's voice that greets me.

'Who was that?' he asks and I am momentarily taken aback by the suspicion in his voice.

'It was James,' I tell him.

'Your ex-husband?' Matt asks.

'Yes. Are you okay?' I ask. Why do I suddenly feel panic rising up in me? Matt knows about James. He knows that we still talk to each other. Okay, granted, it might seem a bit weird that James is answering my phone, but . . . but . . .

'You didn't answer my texts,' he says coldly and I can hear his mind working overtime as he adds two and two together and makes six.

'I thought you were busy with the girls,' I reply weakly. My stupid attempt at trying to make a point is, I can see, going to backfire on me.

'Well, you're obviously busy right now, so I'll leave you to it,' Matt says, and I can hear the anger in his voice. I have never experienced this side of him and his chilly tone scares me.

'Matt—' I attempt to explain but he cuts me off before I can.

'I've got to go, Charlotte is calling me,' he says flatly and the phone goes dead.

Bugger! Fuck! Shit!

'Who was that?' James calls out.

'No one in particular,' I say angrily, and proceed to noisily clean the kitchen of my cooking debris, banging and crashing as I go. As we sit down to eat, James turns to me.

'He'll phone back,' he says.

'Who?' I ask, playing dumb. It would feel kind of weird talking to James about Matt, as if I was doing something behind his back, which ironically is exactly what he thinks I am doing anyway.

'The no one, who just phoned,' James says, smiling at me. I give him an 'I don't give a damn' smile back as I swallow the tears away.

After dinner James leaves with a hug and a reassurance that he is feeling better (I'm glad to see someone is!). We agree to monitor the Frog situation and take it one day at a time; he also agrees with me that it's probably best to cancel his boys' weekend away. I watch them from the doorway. James tries to match the Frog's pace as he trots slowly alongside and I feel another lump in my throat. As I go to bed I check my mobile for the hundredth time in case I have missed a text from Matt, but there is nothing and my hurt turns to anger at the injustice of it all. I punch in the word 'Trust????' and press send before turning my phone off. If he phones now, I don't want to know.

The next morning I wake up angry. I drop the cakes I baked yesterday off at the courier, fuming. I drive to work livid. I stay angry throughout the day with a black cloud hovering above my head, ensuring everyone, including Tilly, keeps out of my way. With no return text or appearance from Matt, I consider just leaving it, but the urge to tell him a few home truths before I walk away is too compelling. At four o'clock, I storm over to the statue of the nymph but he isn't there. Next, I look in the small office he shares with Barbara Forsyth, the area art historian from the Heritage and Collections Trust, to find it empty. Feeling more angry and flustered at the thought he has already gone home, I storm out to search the gardens. With my vision blurred by anger, I don't see Lillian until I have nearly bowled her over. I apologise and try to force a bright smile.

'No matter, dear. You are just the person I wanted to see anyway,' she says brightly. 'The board has agreed to our little tea party.'

'That's fantastic news,' I reply but I don't feel it in my heart. I have no room in my head for anything else other than giving Matt a piece of my mind.

'Shall I find you tomorrow so that we can talk about it?' I suggest, but Lillian chooses not to hear me and instead begins to go through a list of women we should invite. As she seems to recite the complete female electoral register, I resist the urge to pick her up, put her under my arm and take her with me. Eventually she falters off.

'I can't seem to remember some of them. I'll have to find my list,' she says.

'I have to go, Lillian. Dental appointment.' I hurriedly begin to walk away.

'But that's the way to the gardens, dear,' she calls out in concern.

'Erh . . . I lost my hairgrip earlier. Just seeing if I can find it,' I reply before breaking into a run.

I eventually find him at the pavilion packing his things away. He looks surprised to see me and for a moment, I think he is going to smile but instead, he turns away and mumbles into his rucksack.

'What did you say?' I demand, knowing my face is red but not caring.

'I've got to go and pick up the girls.'

'Well, I won't take up much of your time, then,' I retort angrily and he turns to look at me. 'What exactly is your problem?' I ask, my arms folded in front of me.

'What do you mean?' he replies, his eyes suddenly flashing. There is a warning there but I choose to ignore it.

'You know about James,' I say.

'Yes, but I didn't know you were still quite so close,' Matt says quietly and there is a sarcasm in his voice I don't like.

'He was upset about Frog and I made him dinner. There was nothing untoward about it, and if you had given me the chance, I would have told you that before you abruptly ended the phone call.' I try really hard not to shout, but I feel as if I'm losing control.

'James gets dinner made for him. I don't even get a text message. I think it's understandable that I felt a little annoyed. I think most people would think it a little strange that you have your ex over for dinner when you're supposed to be seeing someone. Hey, how do I know he didn't stay the night as well?' Matt begins to angrily push things into his rucksack and I get the urge to grab it away from him. I want him to look at me. I will him to turn around, but my ability to move objects, levitate and change people's behaviour, seems to have deserted me.

'Oh, and you don't think those same people would think it was a little strange that you don't want to see me at the weekends? Even James sees me more than you do and I'm not, contrary to what you think, sleeping with him,' I retort angrily.

'James hasn't got two daughters to worry about!' he says, turning to face me, his features contorted with anger, and I wonder if I have gone too far. He looks as if he is about to strangle me. But no, even impending death does not stop me.

'Aah, yes, your other life. The one you won't share with me. Are you ashamed of introducing me to your daughters? Is that it?' I accuse, feeling the spiteful anger spewing out of my mouth.

'No, that's not it . . . I . . . how can you think that?' he stammers, as if I have taken the wind out of his sails. 'Look, I'm jealous of your relationship with James and I overreacted, but—'

'And I'm jealous of your daughters,' I interject. 'They get to have you every evening and every weekend. I'm clearly way down the priority scale. Great for the sex part but anything that means being part of your life is way off. How do you think that makes me feel?'

'Maddy . . .' Matt tries to stop me, but I haven't finished.

'Hell! I would be better off having a relationship with James. At least I could wake up to him on the occasional morning.'

'Well, maybe you should,' Matt spits back, and I resist the urge to slap him around the face. I take a deep breath and try not to cry. He takes a step towards me as if sensing the slight emotional shift but I hold my hand up to him, stopping him in his tracks.

'I don't know why I let this go on for so long. It was great for a while, sex with no strings, but let's leave it at that, shall we?' I shout, and storm off, the tears running down my face.

*

As I drive home a little too fast, the fields that are beginning to change from golden corn to fresh ploughed earth the colour of chocolate fudge brownies are a blur. My mobile phone rings but I ignore it and turn the radio up full volume. Once home I stamp around, moving boxes from one part of the house to another, not because I have to, but because if I don't I will surely crumble into a sobbing heap. How could I have been so stupid as to let myself get carried away? It's best that it ends now before I become too involved. Before? Before! Who am I trying to kid? It's too fucking late!

Muttering away, I drop a huge twelve kilo box of currants, and at least half of the contents spill out on to the floor. The little bastards get everywhere and as the tears fall and my nose runs, I attempt to scoop them all up, scrambling around on my hands and knees. There's a knock on the door and, still muttering, I get up from the floor and open it to find Matt standing there with a bunch of flowers and a bag of Maltesers. He is looking decidedly sheepish.

'Sorry, but these are all I could find at such short notice, so I got you some Maltesers to take your mind off the fact they are so hideous,' he says, handing me the dyed turquoise-blue and orange flowers that have obviously come from a garage forecourt. I take them and look deep into them as if they hold my soul. He is right, they are hideous and this should be enough reason to shut the door in his face.

'Are you going to let me in, then?' he asks, and for a brief moment I am not sure that I will. I look at the flowers again and reluctantly stand aside. I follow him in as he surveys the currants covering the floor.

'Accident?' he asks, turning to look at me, and instead

of shouting, 'Well, I am not counting how many there are in a box,' I nod forlornly. He moves towards me and takes the flowers and Maltesers from my hands, placing them carefully on the table. He takes my face in his hands and kisses me gently on the mouth.

'You taste salty,' he says, smiling, but I do not intend to be won over by some crap flowers, chocolate – although, granted, they are Maltesers – and a kiss. I pull away and attempt to lift the fallen box of currants, only for them to slip out of my hands again, spilling the rest of the contents on the floor. I sit on the floor and put my head in my hands.

'Just leave me alone, Matt,' I demand through the cracks in my fingers.

'No,' he replies and I feel his arms under mine, pulling me up. He hugs me but I remain rigid, my hands firmly by my sides like a petulant child. He lifts them and places them around his neck, and lifts my chin towards him. I reluctantly look up at his face; he is smiling at me and I want to poke him in the eyes. That would show him! But they are beautiful eyes, and so very blue.

'It's not just the sex, Maddy, is it?' he asks gently, and I find myself shaking my head, no. 'I'm sorry if I hurt you. Can we try and sort this out?'

'Yes,' I say in a small voice, because the fight inside me has disappeared and all I want to do is to stay here in his arms.

'You're kind of mean and scary when you want to be,' he tells me and I laugh, despite not wanting to. I want to stay mean and scary instead of the little pussy cat I have turned into in the last two minutes.

*

With the currants cleared away, I wave him off and agree to talk about it all tomorrow. Exhausted from the emotional turmoil, I have a bath, put on my sloppy pyjama bottoms and an old T-shirt that was once purple, but is now a mottled grey, and settle in front of the TV with a cup of hot chocolate. I watch *Waking the Dead*, which probably isn't a good idea as it's particularly scary tonight. I should turn over to something that won't give me nightmares. Instead I remain mesmerised by their investigations and my own theories on who did what to whom. The knock on the door makes me jump out of my skin and I look around in fear. It is dark except for the glow of the TV. I look at the clock. It is 11.00 p.m. and my hot chocolate is sitting untouched and congealed. I must have fallen asleep. Who on earth would be knocking on my door at this time? I am suddenly scared and sit silently, trying not to breathe, hoping they will go away. They knock again and my heart thumps noisily against my chest. I wait, and there is silence until my mobile rings. I jump out of my skin, then gingerly pick it up. It's my attacker, ringing to tell me how he is going to kill me.

'Maddy?'

'Who is this?' I ask, not wishing to give my identity away.

'It's Matt. Where are you?'

'At home. God, I'm so glad you called. Somebody is knocking at my door and it's freaking me out. What shall I do?' I whisper into the phone so that my attacker cannot hear me.

'Open the door.'

'What?' Has he lost his mind?

'It's me, numpty,' Matt says.

'What?' I ask again, thinking that there is only one numpty here and it isn't me!

'It's me! I'm outside, waiting to come in.'

'What are you doing here at this hour?' I ask, totally confused.

'Will you just answer the door before I am arrested for loitering?'

Matt is the last person I expected, although most people would be the last person I would expect on my doorstep at this time of night. I open the door feeling embarrassed by my appearance as he steps in. It's still that period in a new relationship when you want to look your best, when you want to hide the fact that sometimes you look like a bag lady, and pretend that your legs are always smooth and hair free, your eyelashes are always long and luscious, your skin is unblemished and glowing with health, not Benefit Hollywood Glo. Although, thinking about it, he has only seen me at my worst.

He grabs me around the waist and pulls me towards him. 'The girls are staying with my parents tonight,' he tells me, grinning from ear to ear. I try not to get my hopes up. 'Sooooo ... that means I can stay the night,' he declares triumphantly as he attempts to take my T-shirt off without pulling my head off.

'I'm not sure I want you to now,' I tease, as he leads me upstairs.

'Okay, I'll just stay for half an hour and then go home,' he says, smiling.

'Okay,' I reply, thinking the smile I am wearing now will be fixed on my face for ever.

'I like your jim-jams. Very sexy,' he says and I slap him hard on the arm.

'I mean it. You could be wearing a bin bag and I would

still think you were sexy,' he says, and I feel a big rush of something that means I have to remove his clothes very quickly.

There is something very special about waking up to someone in the morning, especially if you don't have dragon breath, your stomach is not bloated and there are no pillow marks entrenched in your face. Thankfully, this morning I had none of these things and after a quick dash to the bathroom to check he wasn't going to scream when he woke up, I enjoyed the couple of hours we had together before he left. I waved at him from the door as he drove off, feeling relaxed and a little dreamy. The morning seemed brighter than normal; the brickwork of the neighbouring houses glowed orange and red, the trees looked as if they were brushed with a dusting of gold in the warm glow of an early autumn sunshine, and the birds sang, sweet and melodic.

As I alternate the eggs and flour of the sugar and spice cake mixture I find my concentration keeps wandering to earlier on. We had taken our coffee outside into the garden and talked. Thinking back, though, I still didn't enter the equation. He had told me of the grief, the pain and the uncertainty of whether he would be able to get through it all and become a good single parent to the girls. Of how, after months of upheaval that included bed wetting, confusion and constant reassurance that he would never leave them, his daughters had eventually settled into a routine, accepting their mother's disappearance, if not totally understanding it.

'They have had so much to deal with over the last couple of years that I'm worried about upsetting their hard-earned confidence with any more drastic changes to their lives. I want you to meet them, but it has to be done in the right way, and at the right time,' he had said and I had nodded that I understood. How could I be so selfish, thinking of my own needs when there were two little girls who needed to know that their father loved them above all else; that someone wasn't going to come along and take him away from them?

'What if they got used to you and it didn't work out between us? It would be too much for their little minds to cope with. I mean, you've already told me you're going to dump me when your perfect man arrives.'

'I was teasing you,' I said, surprised that he had taken me literally.

He had kissed me then and changed the subject, but I was left with a feeling of uneasiness that still hasn't left me. I spoon the mixture into four cake tins and pop them in the oven before starting on a couple of Christmas cakes. So, if it's not just sex, what on earth is it? Are we officially a couple? Would he call me his girlfriend? How does he feel about me? How do I feel about him? I fold in the cinnamon and think of Christmas. Will we be together then?

I remove the sugar and spice cakes out of the oven to cool, and pop the Christmas ones in. Citrus and fragrant spices fill the house, making me feel ravenous and I tuck into some Jaffa Cakes because I don't have time to make anything decent. I know this is not good for my thighs but needs must, and boy, they hit the spot. Carrying my cup of tea upstairs I go to my office and check the to-do list. I have the Pink Tea Party to organise and I still plan to send the sugar and spice cakes to a few of the national glossy magazines in the hope that they will feature us. As I check my ingredients list, a text comes through and all thoughts of caster sugar are forgotten.

'Four letters beginning with L?'

I text back, 'Clue?'

'A rush of emotion.'

Now what do I do? Is this a loaded question and if so, how do I answer? Do I answer honestly? And if I do, what is my answer? Is it love? Am I in love with Matthew Tennant? Is he the one? Am I allowed to phone a friend?

'How do I know if it's love or lust?' I ask Moo.

'Maddy, you know the answer. You're just stalling,' Moo tells me. 'Bear, say hello to Auntie Maddy.'

There is a rummaging around at the other end and I say hello but all I can hear is heavy breathing.

'What do you mean, I'm stalling?' I ask.

'I mean, you're fighting it. Just go with it. I know you're scared of getting hurt but Matt might be *him* and you are going to live happily ever after,' she tells me.

I consider this: If I'm not thinking about cakes, I'm thinking about him and I find myself drifting off when I'm supposed to be concentrating on other things. My heart lifts whenever the phone rings and I spend too much time in card shops choosing the perfect one to give to him. It is a feeling that makes me want to sing out loud and sometimes I can't stop myself, much to the odd looks from everyone in the tearoom. I bounce around in a world that is brighter for his presence in it. I am trying really, really hard not to get too attached, but I am failing dismally. I can't even remember what it was like when he wasn't around.

Ask the audience?

'Okay, what does the spirit world say about it?' I ask Moo.

'On holiday.'

'On holiday?' I say, incredulous.

'Well, they seem very quiet at the moment so I can only assume they are on holiday or with someone who needs them more.'

'I need them!' I cry.

'Maddy, you need more than the spirit world to sort you out. You need a psychiatrist and lots of stabilising drugs.'

'Love you.'

'Oh, by the way, I need you to do me a cake. That sugar and spice cake you made for my birthday will be perfect,' she says.

'No problem. Can I ask what it's for?' I ask.

'It's for the guys at work. I gave in my notice yesterday.'

'Oh my God!' I scream down the phone. This is big. This is huge. This is bigger than my 'Is it love or not?' dilemma. I never thought Moo would do this.

'I've decided that I need to stop putting pressure on myself. I want to enjoy motherhood and, to be honest, Maddy, you have been the deciding factor,' Moo says but I am not sure what she means. Oh God, what have I done now?

'How?' I ask.

'The way you went for it with the business and made a massive change to your life has been a real inspiration. I know it hasn't been easy, but just look at how different your life is now. It made me think and question exactly what it is that I am scared of. Change? Making a mistake? Well, if I don't do it, I will never know and I may be missing out on something fantastic.'

Wow. I am stunned. Me, inspiring Moo? That can't be right; it's always been the other way around. To say that I am shocked is an understatement.

'I am going to throw myself into a world of gym babies, Music Tots and swimming. Hopefully it will also help me lose this post-baby weight,' she tells me and I can hear the happiness in her voice. Her tone seems lighter, as if a heavy weight has been lifted from her shoulders.

'I'm surprised, I have to admit, but really pleased for you. It will be great. Music Tots will not know what has hit them. You'll have them performing *Les Misérables* before they know it.' I laugh at the image of Moo getting frustrated at the lack of emotion and drama from a group of babies.

'I'll start them off easy with something like *The Lion King*,' Moo says seriously and we both start giggling because we know it's not too far from the truth.

'Anyway, back to you. Send that man of yours a text!'

'Okay, and Moo, I think it's really fantastic what you're doing. It's a whole new chapter in your life.' I try to reassure her because as much as she sounds positive, if the last few months are anything to go by, I suspect she is a little terrified by it all.

I put the phone down and send a text back to Matt.

'LUST.'

He texts back immediately.

'Wrong.'

'What is it, then?' I text back, my heart racing.

'LIKE.' He texts back and, despite myself, I find my bottom lip quivers just a little.

Bastard!

SUGAR AND SPICE CAKE

A fabulously easy cake to make, this is a lovely autumnal
cake with its warm, spicy overtones. Instead of the silver
balls, you could dry some orange slices and pop them on
the top for a special occasion.

Ingredients

225g (8oz) unsalted butter	225g (8oz) dark muscovado sugar
225g (8oz) self-raising flour	2 teaspoons baking powder
1 teaspoon ground ginger	1 teaspoon ground cinnamon
4 medium eggs	100ml (3½fl.oz) milk

For the icing:
150g (6oz) sifted icing sugar
2 tablespoons fresh orange juice
silver balls

Method

Grease and line a 20cm (8 inch) cake tin and preheat oven to
180°C/350°F/gas mark 4. Place all ingredients in food
processor and cream together.

Transfer mixture to tin, smoothing surface, and bake for
50–55 minutes or until skewer inserted into centre comes out
clean. Leave to cool in the tin. When the cake has cooled
blend icing sugar and orange juice together and spread over
the top of the cake. Do not worry if it drizzles over the sides,
as this is how it should look. Scatter silver balls over and
leave to set.

Gently fold in some hope

'Can we try that again, love, with a bit more animation this time if you can?' the chap from the local TV station instructs and I cringe. I am obviously no Nicole Kidman.

'Jeff, can we go again please,' he calls to his colleague who is currently showing Tilly his furry microphone and making her laugh. I am a vision of pink, with my pink apron, pink flower in my hair, pink lipstick and surrounded by cakes decorated in shades of – you guessed it – pink. Moo is dressed as a Pink Lady from *Grease*, complete with wig; Lou is dressed in a fabulous hip-hugging baby pink jacket with black pencil skirt; and Freya is looking pretty in a floral tea dress, keeping an eye on the two sugarplum fairies, Chloe and The Princess, who are peeling the icing off their fairy cakes. Even Mum looks radiant in a pale pink two-piece; in fact, she looks better than she has for ages. Has she had highlights put in her hair?

The ladies who lunch, who have responded to our invitation to our Pink Tea Party, surround the garden pavilion. It has been decorated with vases of pink flowers and the pretty floral bunting Mum has made although, personally, I think Tilly went a little overboard with the decorations and the pavilion looks like Barbie's bedroom. It is a little girl's dream come true and I wish Matt could have brought his daughters over, but don't get me started on that. It would have been the perfect time to meet them; a chance to do something together, something worthwhile. (Okay, it was an opportunity to promote Sugar and Spice as well – I am a businesswoman after all! And yes, it had crossed my mind that the girls would be more likely to see me in a good light if they met me at something like this.) Does that make me ruthless? Desperate? Or just a woman? Anyway, for all my good intentions, what happens? Matt decides that it's a good time to take them away for a few days. That's what happens!

We have been lucky with the weather; it's a beautiful early autumn day and the sun is shining. Tilly has done a sterling job of persuading local companies to donate prizes for the raffle, and everyone seems to be happy to put their hands in their pockets to buy items from our little pink stall. I have made a selection of iced fairy cakes, pink butterfly cakes with strawberries and butter-icing, meringues piled high with raspberries, and Victoria sandwich cakes topped with pink icing and sugared rose petals. The cakes seem to be popular and I'm ready to thrust my business card – which I just happen to have in my apron pocket – into their beautifully manicured hands at every opportunity.

'Okay, just smile and tell me all about what you're doing today. We can edit the bad bits out. Oh, and can we have you holding a cake, and maybe have a few ladies behind you?' the man with the camera says, trying to rearrange us. There's a lot of giggling from the women of a certain age who haven't seen so much excitement since Michael Aspel opened their village fête.

'What was your name?' he asks, and I tell him. 'Okay Maddy, if you want to start talking now, head up, that's it, smile, and go.'

It takes six attempts before he is happy and the sweat is running down my back. It's hard being a star.

I make my way over to Moo, Bob and The Bear. Bob has been made to wear a pink shirt and I can see he is not happy about it.

'People will think I'm an estate agent,' he grumbles.

'You look great,' I respond and then, turning to Moo, say, 'And so do you!'

'I'm ignoring Bob and trying those hip-hugging things. They are incredible but they take a bit of getting used to. There is no give in these babies. Every time I bend down I feel as if a buttock is going to pop out from too much pressure.'

The picture is not a pretty one, but whether it's the hip-huggers or life as a full-time mum, Moo looks better than I've seen her look for ages. She is looking positively radiant.

'So where is this man of yours?' she asks, taking me to one side.

'On holiday with his daughters,' I reply. 'One of them has broken her collarbone and is off school so he thought it would be nice to take them away for a few days.'

'Oh, I was dying to meet him.'

'Me too,' I say, feeling disappointed. At this rate, they are all going to think Matt is a figment of my imagination.

'So how's it going?' she whispers.

'He told me he was falling for me just before he left,' I admit, colouring at the thought of it.

'Oh my God!' Moo exclaims, dragging me further away to a corner of the pavilion. 'Tell me everything.'

I tell her of the trees, beautiful in their autumn colours of reds, burnished golds and copper, set against a bright blue sky. Of loving the feel of his arm around my shoulders as we walk along. Of snuggling into him, my face against his chest, or listening to the sound of his heartbeat as he kissed my forehead. Of him telling me that he would miss me.

'And, and . . . ?' Moo urges.

'And he asked if that was how I really felt when I answered his text message.'

'How did you answer?'

'Lust!'

'You didn't!' Moo says, shaking her head. 'Oh, Maddy! So then what did you say?'

'I asked him why he wanted to know.'

'And what did he say?'

'That it wasn't how it was for him, and I tried to make a joke of it by asking him if he was falling for me, and he said yes . . .'

'What did you say?' Moo can barely contain her excitement and I feel like we did as kids when I had my first-ever slow dance with Timothy Hart at the local disco.

'I didn't say anything. I just blushed.'

'Oh my God, Maddy. This is it!' Moo cries out, hugging me. 'He's your chocolate cake!'

'Do you think?' I ask, worried.

'Duh!' she responds and hands me The Bear.

*

The ladies who lunch and now eat cake leave, some a little worse for wear from drinking too much rosé wine with their slices of Christmas cake, courtesy of Sugar and Spice. We have raised four hundred and twenty pounds for breast cancer research and have had a thoroughly enjoyable day, although all of us are feeling a little tired because of it. The pavilion is cleared and crockery taken to the tearoom for washing up before we head home. Tilly waves goodbye, barely containing her excitement about an evening with some guy called Frank. What happened to the other one whose name I can't remember? I can't keep up.

Later, I make my way over to Ben and Freya's, where Mum is staying, to join them for dinner. As she has her pre-bed milk The Princess twiddles with her hair and I wonder if this is just one of the things we will have in common. Ben gazes down at her with the look of a man who has fallen in love and, as always, I find myself marvelling at the fact that my little brother is now a father. When she has gone to bed we talk of the business and my concerns about not making enough money to last until the end of the year. Ben tries to reassure me that this is normal.

'It's rare for a new business to make any profit in the first year, Maddy. You just have to try and keep going.'

'Have you thought any more about opening a tearoom?' Mum asks, barely able to keep her eyes open.

'Mmmmm, the more I think about it the more I think I would really like to do it. I figure that way there would be a daily income coming in and the mail-order part of the business can grow gradually as a sideline. I like the idea of a tearoom with a big kitchen much better than getting an industrial unit. It's just finding the right place, the money and having the guts to do it,' I confirm.

'When you were little you wanted a post office, then you wanted to be an air-hostess. Then that changed and you talked of being a fashion designer. You were always daydreaming of something,' Mum pipes up. I am not sure whether this is a positive or negative observation, and even less sure it warrants a response so, instead, I just smile indulgently.

'I do think it's the way to go. Look at the women who came today, they are crying out for somewhere outside London to have tea, cake and a gossip. Not everyone wants Starbucks,' Freya comments. She places tiny cups of strong coffee on the table followed by slices of warm Tarte aux Pommes because it's Mum's favourite. It looks as if it has come straight from the pages of a glossy magazine with its golden, caramelised apples set against crisp, white plates, and a little cream drizzled artfully over the top.

'And if word gets around that it's the place to be, then the world is your oyster,' she adds.

She looks just as gorgeous as always; even Mum looks different. Am I the only one feeling and looking like shit? I've felt so tired lately and my energy levels are at an all-time low. I really need to slow down a bit. All this rushing around, trying to cram everything in, is taking its toll; not that I'm going to get much chance with my hoped-for Christmas rush coming up.

Feeling exhausted, I decline more coffee and make my way home, knowing that I have to get up early tomorrow to bake a lemon drizzle and an Earl Grey Tea cake. When I get in, there is a message on the phone.

'Miss you, beautiful, and just in case you were wondering . . . yes, I do.'

I press play and sit on the stairs. I hug my knees into my chest and play it again, and then again.

My toast sticks in my throat and I am choking, but there is no one to help me and for a moment I think I am going to die. With tears streaming down my face and spluttering bits of toast all over the floor, I eventually recover and take a deep breath. The reason for my trauma is the appearance of a woman on breakfast TV who looks a little like me but . . . God, no!

It is short and sweet, but there I am, sandwiched in a little spot between Eamonn Holmes and Lorraine Kelly, arms waving, and talking as if someone has just wound me up from behind, and . . . pink is definitely not my colour. The phone goes and it is Ben, laughing loudly.

'I just saw you on TV.' He is laughing so much I think I might have to put the phone down on him.

'I know,' I say, embarrassed beyond belief. How many other people will have seen it? I can just picture it; everyone I went to school with is probably sitting around eating their breakfast saying things like, 'She hasn't aged very well, has she?' and 'Always was a bit weird,' before phoning the *Sun* to sell their story. What is it about me and the media? First the newspaper article, then this. Would I be this bad if I appeared on *Friday Night with Jonathan Ross*? Surely not . . .

'You looked like you were on acid or something.' Ben continues to laugh at my expense but I can't complain. If the shoe fits . . . I did look as if somebody had turned the fast-forward button on.

'The guy with the camera told me to be more animated,' I explain.

'I think you took him a little too literally.'

'Thanks,' I reply mournfully, wondering if I will ever live it down.

'Hey, it's good for business, and you know what they say, there's no such thing as bad publicity,' he says hopefully. God, I hope he's right. He begins to laugh again like a manic schoolboy.

'What?' I ask, slightly irritated.

'I'm sorry, Maddy, I can't stop thinking about it. You were so funny.'

His laughter soon turns to a choking sound, which serves him right.

'Are you okay?' I ask, after a while of listening to him coughing and spluttering down the phone.

'Choking on a custard cream,' he croaks.

'But it's eight-thirty in the morning! Surely that's not your breakfast?' I ask.

'Old habits die hard,' he admits, before giggling again.

No sooner do I put the phone down than it rings again but instead of someone else taking the mickey out of me it is a woman's voice I don't recognise. She introduces herself as the features editor of *Gorgeous* magazine, and I listen as she explains that the magazine is looking to do a piece on women who have had a drastic change of lifestyle and then tells me that they want to feature me. I think of all the times I have read about women who have followed their dreams and wanted it to be me. And now it is! How fabulous is that?

As I talk to her, though, I can't help feeling I don't really live up to the other people in the storyline. One is a former couch potato who is now climbing some massive mountain, the other is a woman who has sold up and is moving abroad to set up a donkey sanctuary, etc. etc. I hear myself, blah blah blah, and it doesn't sound very inspiring, so what do I do? I lie. Well, I tell a small fib that is loosely based on reality. I don't know why, but the words came out before I could stop them.

'Yes, we are planning to open a bakery/tearoom early next year. It's all very exciting,' and off I go, describing the tearoom that is in my imagination. When I put the phone down, I feel sick. Oh God, what have I done?

Jonathan Ross Interview

'Yes, you're right, Jonathan; I guess fame did come to me quite suddenly.'

'But I have to say, you've coped with the trappings remarkably well. You still manage to remain quite a private person.'

'I try to keep my life as normal as possible. The paparazzi will only chase the people who court it and I'm still the same girl from out in the sticks.'

'A bit like Jenny from the block?'

'I guess so, but I don't have a seventy-five-strong entourage.'

'But Madonna is a close friend?'

'This is true.'

'Wasn't she one of the first to visit your tearoom when you initially started?'

'Yes. It was quite remarkable. We couldn't quite believe it when she walked in and ordered a slice of Earl Grey Tea cake. A few days later, she returned with Gwyneth Paltrow and Stella McCartney for a girls' tea party and then we were featured in

Vogue's Top Ten British Treasures list and Stella was designing our waitress uniforms. The rest, as they say, is history.'

I take advantage of Matt being away and spend the rest of the week trying to plan for Christmas. I design and arrange the printing of our Christmas flyers then make more mincemeat and some Christmas cakes for the local farm shop. On top of this, I have had an order for ten chocolate cakes for a company that wants to reward its sales team, which has left me little time in between my days at the tearoom to do anything else. The fact that more orders are coming through is fantastic but I feel exhausted and I hope for a little reprieve over the weekend. Unfortunately, this is not going to happen as the doorbell goes early Saturday morning. I open it to find Ben standing there with The Princess in her buggy.

'I've picked up your flyers from the printers. Come on, get your coat on. Let's get out there and deliver these babies,' he urges me with an enthusiasm I am finding hard to match right now.

'I had planned to do it a little later,' I protest.

'No time like the present,' he demands, dragging me outside while I am still putting my coat on.

'I don't remember you always being this bossy,' I comment sulkily, feeling a bit put out that my day seems to have been already planned for me. I know Ben is trying to help, but it would have been nice if he had asked first; after all, it's *my* business and that means I am effectively the boss lady round here. Surely I should be telling him what needs doing? There is definitely something wrong here. I need to be more assertive with my helpers. But not today. Today I haven't the energy to argue.

We spend a couple of hours posting my Christmas leaflets as Ben talks to me about the business and what I should be doing next. He has a whole host of ideas and I want to remind him that it's just little old me in this business and I don't have the time, or the money, to do all of the wonderful things he comes up with. It's great when he can help me, but most of the time I feel as if there are not enough hours in the day, that my mind spins constantly with what hat I should be wearing at any given time: marketing, PR, accountant, baker, salesperson – oh, and not forgetting tearoom assistant. Let's hope these flyers generate some business and Christmas is a success, then I can employ a little helper. I limp home feeling cold with blisters on my feet and wonder what Matt is doing. I need a hug.

I open the door to an empty house that smells like a Christmas workshop and wish he was here waiting for me. After a batch of baking, I go to bed early feeling exhausted, but I can't sleep and I find myself gazing at the alarm clock wishing it said 11.00 p.m. and not 2.00 a.m. As I eventually begin to drift off a text message comes through from Matt.

'Are u awake?'

'No,' I reply.

'Just wanted u to know that I luv u x.' The words shine in the green light of the phone. Oh, God, what is happening? Somebody help me. I must be strong. I must be . . . I must . . . I . . . As I do battle with myself, another text comes through.

'Go on, say it. U know u want to xx.'

Smug bastard! But he is right and I have lost the struggle.

'Go to sleep! xxx' I text back.

'Not until you say it,' he replies. I lie there for ten minutes before taking a deep breath and picking the phone up again.

'OK, I luv u. But only a little bit.'

'That will do. For now! Night xx.'

'Goodnight x'

I go to sleep smiling.

Tomorrow! Tomorrow! Isn't that what the screeching child sang in *Annie*? Well, it appears she might have a point. I have just taken an order for thirty-five Christmas cakes from a company in the City! It transpires that the director's wife attended our pink tea party and suggested he might like to send them to his clients this year, instead of the usual bottle of whisky. So here I am, pacing in and out of the kitchen, picking things up and putting them down again, not actually sure where to start. I am panicking.

'AAAAAAAGGGGHHHH.'

'My God, Maddy. Are you okay?' Moo asks as I scream down the phone at her.

'Thirty-five cakes! I've just had an order for thirty-five cakes!'

'Hurray! Bear, shout Hurray . . . No, nothing, but he wants to. That's fantastic news, Maddy. So . . . what now?'

'Now, I have to buy a lot of sultanas,' I laugh, sounding like I feel: out of control and slightly hysterical. This could be it, the turning point that will bring Sugar and Spice into the lives of thirty-five potential customers, who will tell their friends and they will tell all their friends, and . . . oh my God, this is so exciting. I spend the next hour phoning everyone I know until I am practically hyperventilating with it all. Stay calm and breathe . . .

Rushing around like a headless chicken whilst on the phone is not a good idea. One minute I'm upright, the next I'm on my backside with a thud and making my way down the bottom four steps. Moo understandably panics on the other end and nearly calls an ambulance until I reassure her that I am fine, although, to be honest, for a moment I wasn't that sure. The big fluffy cloud of love that I have been floating around on did not soften the fall and when Matt phones later to tell me he is back from his holiday I can hardly move. When I tell him what has happened he sounds shocked and offers to drive over straight away. This pleases me immensely but I decline the offer, knowing that it will make it awkward for him with the girls.

'Are you sure you're okay?' he asks, sounding concerned. I like this someone caring about you stuff. It feels nice.

'Of course I am,' I reply with an ice pack stuffed down the back of my knickers.

'I'll kiss it better tomorrow,' he promises and I feel a tiny thrill of excitement at the thought.

By the next morning, a huge purple and black bruise covers my left buttock and I spend the morning moving stiffly around the tearoom, much to the amusement of the others. All I can think about though, is seeing Matt, who is back from his holiday today. I've missed him, and no sooner does Dot give me the go ahead for a break than I make my way to the pavilion, although my aching back and legs make the going a little slower than I would like.

I see him before he sees me, and my stomach does a little somersault when he looks up, and a huge smile spreads across his features. My aches and pains are briefly forgotten as I run over as quickly as I can and somehow manage to leap on to him, wrapping my legs around his waist. We kiss, and he tastes as good as I remember. We walk slowly through the garden. Shafts of sunlight stream through the gaps in the trees and the sound of swifts flying low, preparing for the journey to warmer climes, fills the air. This is my favourite time of year, when the summer has flown away, leaving her more beautiful sister to take her place. There is a chill in the air and we cuddle up for warmth. Cakes are pushed to the back of my mind as we kick the leaves that have begun to litter the ground. Some are falling around us, the light breeze carrying them down, twisting and turning in the air. I jump up and down, trying to catch one, but give up after a couple of attempts because it's just too bloody painful. Matt reaches out and with minimal effort, a leaf seems to fall directly into his hands and I excitedly urge him to make a wish, as, not one to be beaten, I attempt to try again. It's become a battle of wills; I'm determined to have my wish! Eventually I manage to grab one but it's a painful victory as my stiffening muscles cry out for mercy. I hold the yellow leaf in my hand and close my eyes. Let it be *him*. I turn to find him watching me, and I quickly make the wish again, in case the wishing fairies didn't get it the first time round.

'What did you wish for?' I ask, taking his hand.

'That we could stay like this for ever, here and now, without a care in the world,' he says, almost sadly.

'We can,' I reply, squeezing his hand tightly.

'Life isn't quite that simple, though, is it?' he replies, and I can feel a slight shift. I cannot put my finger on it, but I almost feel as if something has changed and like a subtle change in the temperature, it makes me shiver.

'It can be,' I reply, smiling brightly, but a sense of foreboding settles deep within me. He pulls me close and kisses the uneasiness away, pushing it to a place where I can't see it, then releases me with a playful tap on the behind, at which I cry out in pain.

'Sorry, hun, I forgot. How is that beautiful backside of yours?' he asks, smiling.

I check nobody is around before proudly showing him a glimpse of the huge purple and yellow bruise. Matt turns to me with a mischievous glint in his eyes.

'How do you fancy a quickie in the bushes?'

'I'd love to, but I've got to get back,' I reply, but he ignores this and takes my hand, leading me to a little secluded corner of the garden.

'Tell Dot you had to have emergency first aid for your bruises.'

Over the next few days, ingredients pile up in the kitchen and dining room, with boxes of sultanas, currants and raisins everywhere. Bowls of alcohol-soaked fruit cover every available surface and the house smells like a distillery. A phone call from another woman who attended our Pink Tea Party means I also have an order for six whisky cakes destined for a firework party in November and two hundred mince pies for a carol service she is organising for just before Christmas. I have gone from having almost no orders at all to an oh-my-God-how-am-I-going-to-do-it-all frenzy of activity. There are cakes constantly cooking in the oven, mincemeat bubbling away in huge saucepans, and a constant flow of people stopping by to help. I soon have Ben and Freya chopping ingredients, Lou doing anything that won't break her nails or mean she has to wear a hair net, and my usual passionate early mornings with Matt are spent making up boxes and wrapping cakes. My house now resembles Santa's workshop, and Ben and Freya's garage becomes Santa's store as the stockpile of Christmas cakes grow. They sit there in their boxes, young, and full of promise, all wrapped up in greaseproof paper and tin foil, soaking up the alcohol and maturing into delicious adults. It makes me feel like a James Bond villain of sorts, growing my secret population, ready to take over the world on Christmas Day.

I'm glad when it's the weekend and Moo arrives to lend a helping hand. She is staying with Ben and Freya and whilst The Bear spends some time playing kissing cousins, we begin baking. Moo and I work methodically, if a little messily, with Nat King Cole singing Christmas carols in the background.

'How's life being a full-time mum?' I ask, folding in a hundredweight of dark, syrupy, alcohol-soaked fruit.

'It's good, but boy, it's exhausting. What happened to just playing outside in the street? I thought my friends were all just drinking coffee and chatting in the kitchen whilst their kids played, but they have a scary schedule. We do gym babies on Monday, activity centre on Tuesday, swimming on Wednesday, Music Tots on Thursday and then it's Art Kids club on Friday. I need the weekend to recover,' she laughs, clearly enjoying this new aspect of her life. By the time she goes back to Ben's, we've managed to bake twelve cakes, which brings my total up to twenty-eight so far.

The next morning, before I start afresh, I wrap up warm and make my way over to Ben and Freya's to join them all for Sunday breakfast. I wish Matt was coming with me, but, as usual, he's playing perfect dad for the weekend, and can't make it. As I walk in the door there is much excitement as Moo drags me into the kitchen and pushes me on to a chair.

'Look at this,' Ben insists, pushing a piece of paper in front of me. There is a photo of a shop front, and a small description underneath; the words 'For Sale' spring out from the page. I look up at their expectant faces, feeling a touch uneasy by what they have up their sleeves.

'It's the baker's down in Silver Street. The old chap, you remember, George Hazelwood who ran it has died and his widow wants to sell,' Moo says excitedly.

'It has all the baking equipment included in the sale,' Ben adds. 'And it's got a flat on the top.'

'Leave your sister alone – she can have a look at it later,' Freya chips in, putting plates of scrambled eggs and piles of hot buttered toast on the table. I grab a slice of toast and pore over the details while everyone waits for my reaction.

'Eat up,' Freya insists, and I'm grateful for the reprieve as the attention is focused on the food instead of me. The details certainly sound good; it's in the right location, old interior, but nothing a lick of paint wouldn't change and room enough for a reasonable-sized tearoom. I try not to feel too excited by it, knowing that it will be too expensive. My fears are confirmed when I turn over the page.

'It's lovely, but out of my price range,' I say eventually, feeling a tad despondent.

'Why don't we take a look then, if you like it, we can work out how you could afford it,' Ben suggests with a mouth full of egg.

'It won't hurt to take a look,' Moo urges, and I nod, not really sure that it would be a good idea; it will only get my hopes up.

'We have an appointment at eleven,' Ben confirms, and I look up from my eggs at their smiling faces.

'Do I have a choice in this?' I ask, amazed.

'No!' they all chorus, and begin laughing. The Bear and The Princess think this is highly amusing and begin laughing too, which only makes us all laugh even more. Soon we are all laughing like madmen and the babies' Cheerios are flying everywhere in the excitement of it all. Freya produces coffee and warm croissants, but after a childhood of having them forced upon us, she is the only one who eats them. She shares them with The Princess and The Bear who greedily stuff them into their eager young mouths. Flakes of pastry hit the floor as they grin at us with matching jam and pastry beards.

I am dragged reluctantly out into the cold and, en masse, we make our way to Silver Street. People rush past, eager to get to their destinations, too cold to stop and linger for a while, and I shiver, wishing I had brought my hat and scarf with me. The estate agent, a fifty-something, tired-by-what-life-has-thrown-at-him sort of chap, looks a little shocked to see us all descend on him complete with two buggies. He is obviously as unsure as I am about how we are all going to fit in, but we manage and he looks around bemused as we chatter and Moo proceeds to fire questions at him. As she does so, I wander around, touching dusty surfaces, imagining the people that worked here for years, only to leave a couple of mouldy rolls in the corner and a rather tired-looking mop propped up against a door that is in need of a coat of paint. Empty of customers and people busily wrapping rolls and bread behind the counter, the place looks sad and neglected. The décor is like something out of the fifties and there are still crumbs littering the counter top; the mice have already packed up and gone, too. Queuing for my own loaf of bread barely six months ago I don't seem to remember it being so shabby and forlorn, but as the agent talks us through it, my imagination works overtime and I'm soon working out how many tables I could fit in and what colour to paint the walls.

'I would need to sell the house and get a loan from the bank,' I mutter to myself. See, I knew it would be a bad idea to come.

'It would be worth it, Maddy. I could do all the paperwork for you and phone the bank,' Ben urges me. I must have spoken aloud, or perhaps he was thinking the same thing.

'Whoa, slow down,' I say, not ready to start discussing the realities of it all. First, I have to sort it all out in my own mind and right now, it all seems a bit too scary to contemplate.

'I'll have a think about it,' I tell him, and I can see his shoulders droop just a little bit more.

'I'll ring you tomorrow,' I hear Ben say to him as we all begin to file out. Something snaps inside me and I suddenly feel really annoyed. I'm not the scared, frightened person I was before. I'm strong and this is my business, not Ben's. I know he has my best interests at heart but he needs to know his big sister is back! The protective cotton wool has to come off!

'No! I will think about it, and I will ring you,' I confirm to the agent in my sternest voice. Ben looks shocked, like a kid who has had his favourite toy taken away from him, but I smile brightly, determined not to falter in my new-found assertiveness.

*

Matt kisses the tips of my fingers, absent-mindedly listening as I talk about the tearoom. The girls are at his parents', and he is staying overnight. I can't help feeling like a thirteen year old who has just been given the chance to have her first sleepover. The ideas that are all flying around in my head come out of my mouth in a scrambled mess, and he laughs at me.

'So what do you think? Am I mad?' I ask.

'Yes, but I guess that's why I love you,' he says, looking up at me from his journey of kisses that is now making its way up my arm.

I can smell the sweet spiciness of cinnamon, nutmeg and brandy-soaked fruit as the last batch of Christmas cakes cool downstairs. The smell of childhood Christmases, and wishes coming true. Talking of which, I look at Matt and the blood rushes to my head. He is just sooooooo beautiful, and ... he is mine ... in my bed ... and ... naked! Forget about the Christmas cakes and the tearoom ...

Later, as I lie snuggled up against his back, feeling the soft warmth of his skin, I marvel that physically we fit together so perfectly. I also wonder how my family will take to him. Will they like him as much as I do? Will they ever meet him? Will I ever meet the girls?

'You could bring the girls in to the tearoom. They would love it. I thought it would be nice to have a children's cooking afternoon every so often. Charlotte and Georgie could be my little advisers,' I suggest cautiously. 'Don't you think it would be fabulous?' I ask when he doesn't respond.

'It would be great,' he says sleepily.

'Perhaps you could bring them over next week and we could show them around,' I suggest, the F word hovering like a bubble ready to burst. Not that F word; this is something a lot more explosive: F for Future! Again, Matt doesn't say anything.

'Matt?' I urge.

'Let's talk about it later.' He pats my thigh with his hand and I feel my heart drop. Foiled again.

My worries about Matt and the F word are briefly forgotten with another unexpected order for ten tins of mince pies and three Christmas cakes. Oh my God, how the hell am I going to cope with all of this? I should be pleased, and I am, honestly I am, especially when I type the numbers into the credit card machine, which has never seen so much activity, but I'm also just a little petrified by it all. There was a brief moment of triumph when I thought things were finally turning the corner, but this has changed lately to the nagging doubt that I might not be able to manage it all, especially in my small domestic kitchen. Again I find myself thinking about the tearoom . . . it has a big kitchen, it would solve the current problems with storage, and it would certainly make things easier for me using equipment designed to cope with baking in large quantities. It would be a huge commitment, though, and am I ready for such a big step? Where would I find the money? But it would be an investment for the future; the business can't grow in the current set up . . . and I could always sell the house and move into the flat above the tearoom. A little flurry of excitement rises in my belly. A Sugar and Spice tearoom? Could I do it?

Two hours later, with four cakes baking in the oven, I settle down with a much-needed cup of tea and absent-mindedly flick through an old magazine. Oh God, I had completely forgotten all about my interview with

Gorgeous magazine. I had meant to ring the journalist and set the record straight about my little fib about opening a tearoom. Well, that settles it. I've got to do it, haven't I? I pick up the phone and dial the estate agent's number.

BOOZY CHRISTMAS CAKE

October/November is a good time to make your Christmas cakes in order to give them enough time to mature. For those who don't like the traditional rich variety of Christmas cake, this is a lovely alternative. But, beware, with the fruit soaking for 3–5 days in quite a bit of cognac, this cake is strictly for grown-ups. This recipe will make two cakes; one for yourself and one which you can give away as a festive gift. How fabulous.

Ingredients

275g (10oz) each of sultanas, currants and raisins

100g (4oz) stem ginger, chopped

200g (8oz) natural-coloured glacé cherries, quartered

grated rind of 1 unwaxed lemon

2 teaspoons vanilla extract

150ml (5fl.oz) cognac

150ml (5fl.oz) ginger wine

350g (12oz) unsalted butter

350g (12oz) dark muscovado sugar

3 medium eggs

350g (12oz) self-raising flour

2 tablespoons ground mixed spice

1 teaspoon ground cinnamon

pinch of nutmeg

100g (4oz) mixed nuts, chopped

125g (5oz) glacé peel, chopped

1 teaspoon ground ginger

Put the sultanas, currants, raisins, stem ginger, glacé cherries, lemon rind and vanilla extract into a bowl and pour cognac and ginger wine over them, mixing well. Cover and leave for 3–5 days in a cool place.

Method

Preheat oven to 170°C/325°F/gas mark 3. Line two 20cm (8 inch) cake tins. Wrap brown paper around tins and secure with string. Cream together the butter and sugar until mixture is pale and fluffy. Beat in eggs gradually. Sift together flour and spices and fold in. Add nuts and glacé peel, then carefully fold in the pre-soaked fruits. Divide the mixture between the two tins and bake for 1½–2 hours or until a skewer comes out clean. Cool in the tins before removing and drizzling with 1 tablespoon of cognac. Wrap in greaseproof paper and foil. Then every three weeks insert a skewer into your cake, feed with a couple of tablespoons of cognac and rewrap until ready to decorate with a mixture of fruit and nuts.

To decorate:
Heat a mixture of 2 tablespoons of apricot jam and 1 tablespoon of brandy to make a glaze and brush the top of the cakes. Arrange fruit and nuts, e.g. Brazil nuts, walnuts, apricots, dates, glacé cherries, sliced figs, pecans, then brush with remaining glaze to finish.

Five heaped teaspoons of tears

Oh my God, it's nearly November and that means it's nearly Christmas! There are signs everywhere and people on TV telling me there are only fifty-three days, sixteen hours to go until Christmas or something equally as ludicrous. Thank you, but I don't want to know; I have a calendar, a diary and a house full of Christmas cakes and mincemeat. I KNOW IT'S NEARLY CHRISTMAS!

Matt makes me laugh briefly with a rendition of the Pogues' 'Fairytale of New York' at 5.30 a.m. this morning but it does little to abate the sheer terror I am now feeling and, after a sleepless night, I jump out of bed to begin baking my first batch of the mince pies I have orders for. Six hundred of them, to be precise. Bloody hell, how am I going to make six hundred mince pies? I look around at my once beautiful house with its carefully placed candles and coffee-table books that have now been pushed to one side. It is now looking as tired as I am, although this didn't stop the first couple to look around from putting an offer in. With my house sold so quickly everything is moving faster than I anticipated, and the thought of packing and increasing the number of boxes in the house makes me groan. Full of cake tins and ingredients, they cover every available surface, piled high, blocking out the light and giving me nightmares of being found buried alive by a hundred ton of mixed fruit. Every few days, I rearrange them in a futile bid to make it a little better on the eye or at the very least, a pathway for the Hoover to get through. I look around forlornly before shutting the door on it and heading out to the town centre. I have an appointment with the bank to sell my soul.

After not being able to find a parking space because of Christmas shoppers, I arrive at the bank ten minutes late, but I am still kept waiting another ten. Perhaps they are punishing me, or making me sweat so that I sign my possessions away as soon as I see someone. It's all been frighteningly easy so far; a few phone calls, a visit from a surveyor, and here I am, about to sign the agreement for a loan. My life is about to change yet again; I have sold my house and will live in the small flat above what will be my new business premises. If all goes well, The Sugar and Spice Tearoom will be open in the New Year. Did you hear that? I am about to own my own tearoom!

Maddy Brown: Entrepreneur.

Little ol'me is living the dream; making it happen . . . signing on the dotted line. I am not sure whether to be frightened half to death, or to jump up in the air with excitement.

As I sign, and then print my name, my hand begins to shake involuntarily.

'Are you okay, Miss Brown?' the business loans manager asks.

'Yes, I'm fine. Thank you,' I reply, and take a deep breath. I can do this.

'Okay, then, that's it, you're all set to proceed,' she says, smiling a cosmetically enhanced smile at me and I wonder if she is the woman they use on the advert. The one who sings and jumps over her desk to persuade you that taking out a mortgage with them is fun, fun, fun.

Oh my God, I've done it. It's going to be great; scary, but great.

I sit there, unable to move. Scary – great – scary – great – scary? Her earlier words come back to haunt me. 'You understand the risks fully. On non payment of the loan the bank will be forced to take action, which may result in taking possession of the business.' Or something like that. It was a lot more long-winded and spoken in financial speak that nobody really understands, but the sentiment was the same. What she meant was, if this fails, then you're fucked!

'Well, good luck, and make sure you tell us when the tearoom opens,' she says, getting up. I follow her lead and shake her hand. She has a strong handshake, presumably meant to reassure.

'What will you call it?' she asks, walking me to the door.

'Sugar and Spice,' I reply with a smile. I think I need some fresh air.

'Sugar and Spice, and all things nice . . .' she sings out to me, and I nod, wondering if I will be sick on her welcome mat.

Shock, then disappointment passes over Ben's face when I tell him. Although surprised that I hadn't told him about deciding to go for the tearoom, he is far more disappointed that I had gone to the bank and done everything myself.

'But I could have sorted all of that out for you,' he protests.

'I know you could have, but at some point I have got to stand on my own two feet without you constantly being there, ready to catch me when I fall,' I tell him, taking a huge swig of tea, and burning my mouth in the process.

'But it's only because I worry about you, and I want to help,' he says, the disappointment evident in his voice.

'I know, but you have to stop worrying about me. I'm a big girl and practically a grown-up.' I try to reassure him, but I can see I have upset him.

'And I have to try to do this on my own,' I say, and smile at his hurt-looking face.

The doubt I feel is pushed to one side. I have to believe I can be a brave, fear-nothing type who is sticking two fingers up at anyone who doubts me. Okay, I may be expecting a lot, but hey, aren't I nearly there? Oh, yes, baby. Do I not have my own business? Am I, or am I not, opening my own tearoom? So come on, world, bring it on.

I head home and I get the urge to jump up in the air and shout a loud yes. Unfortunately, I am taken by surprise by my early morning underpants-wearing neighbour Edmund who is putting his rubbish out. My jump turns into one of surprise and a high-pitched scream that causes him to drop his dustbin lid.

'Sorry ... sorry,' I mumble, my heart beating like a drum and I hurry away, eager to escape.

I get in with my brave new world feeling a little shaky as the kick-ass babe in me disappears and I recall my trip to the bank. The reality of what I'm about to embark on hits home and a feeling of terror envelops me. I pace the room trying to reassure myself that it will all be okay.

I need to calm down ... baking, that's what I need to do. I'll make some mince pies for Matt.

*

There is something very relaxing and immensely satisfying about making pastry. My hands knead into the soft texture and I can feel my mind clear: the calmness settle. As I spoon the delicious dark mixture into their little pastry beds, press their covers on and kiss them goodnight before popping them into the oven, life seems a little better. I have to fight the urge not to eat all forty-eight when they come out, beckoning me with their brandy-soaked fruit fillings, encased in melt-in-the-mouth pastry and sprinkled with icing sugar. It's so hard, and I succumb to one, but at times like this, I need carbohydrates and sugar and, like toast, they are the ideal comfort food. One more won't hurt.

Forty-six to go.

Can you eat forty-six mince pies in two hours?

Interview with Oprah

'I'd like to welcome our two guests this afternoon: the woman who brought cakes back into our lives, Maddy Brown, and actress Cameron Diaz.

'You seem to have taken the US by storm with your mince pies,' Oprah suggests, turning to me.

'It would seem so.' The audience cheers and claps.

'So what do you think it was that made us go crazy over them? A little birdie tells me that President Bush, Cameron Diaz, Tom Cruise and Jennifer Aniston have all pre-ordered them for their Christmas parties?'

'To be honest, Oprah, I am as surprised as you are. It's amazing, really. Jennifer and Courtney were spotted on the set of *Friends* with some, and now the whole country wants them.'

'I hear you're going to be making an appearance on *24* with the gorgeous Kiefer Sutherland?'

'Yes, I'm really excited about it.'

'So is this a new direction for you?'

'Oh no, Oprah, I love baking too much. It's just a bit of fun really.'

'So, Cameron, have you tried Maddy's mince pies yet?'

'I love them. I also love your Elizabeth sandwich. You know, the one with the jelly in the middle.'

'Victoria sandwich, and it's jam,' I correct her.

Matt watches me from my bed as I dress, and I like it that he is there. I don't want him to leave, but as always, we are heading in opposite directions and today I am going to Dad's sixtieth birthday dinner and he is heading home.

'I wish you were coming with me.' I look at him, mascara wand in hand, as he stretches like a cat.

'You still could, you know, it's not too late. Everyone is absolutely dying to meet you,' I suggest, hoping against hope that he will change his mind. 'It would be nice,' I add lamely.

'I've got to get back for the girls,' he reminds me gently and I turn away, ramming the wand back into my mascara more forcefully than is absolutely necessary. He reaches over, grabs my hand and pulls me towards him.

'Couldn't you phone your mum and ask her to have them for just a little while longer?' I plead, whine, beg. Please. Please.

'Please?'

· 'You know I don't like to take advantage of Mum. She has already done so much and Sunday is her golf day.'

Well, at least she would have something in common with Dad, if they ever meet! Matt attempts to kiss me but I am already pulling away. I told him weeks ago that it was Dad's birthday bash and I wanted him to come with me. I had hoped that he would take the initiative and arrange for the girls to stay at their grandparents' for the weekend, but it is the usual excuses and the 'no access at the weekend' sign goes up. I know I should be grateful that he stayed the night but I would have gladly traded it in for a couple of hours today. Am I being unreasonable wanting more? Obviously I am.

'I love you, Maddy. You know that, don't you?' he calls after me as I walk out of the room, mumbling that I have to get my things together.

I arrive at Dad's golf club wishing I had worn something warmer. The cold wind seems to go straight through the look-at-me-I'm-gorgeous, see-what-you're-missing-not-coming-with-me flimsy top I am wearing. By the time I arrive, everyone is already seated around a huge rectangular table with Dad at the top looking proud and happy. Susan is sitting beside him in a lace top that barely contains her breasts, much to the delight of the old codgers sitting opposite her. There are balloons with the number sixty on them attached to all of the chairs and a table full of presents. I look around for a space and inwardly groan as it becomes apparent that the only space left is between two of Dad's old golfing cronies. Oh, the pleasure of being on your own. I think of Matt doing fun things like watching a video with the girls and eating crumpets, or cycling through the fallen leaves until it's time to go home for a hot chocolate. Will I ever be a part of his life that involves the girls? Does he want me to be? I am beginning to think he doesn't.

I find myself having to make polite conversation with a man who has the personality of a dead fish. With his shirt stretched over a huge stomach that moves up and down with his laboured breathing, a perspiring top lip and ruddy complexion, I get the impression he is a heart attack waiting to happen. I pray to God he waits until he gets home because there is no way I will be giving him the kiss of life. On the other side of me is a man so tanned he would give Bob Monkhouse a run for his money. While telling me all about his time-share in Magaluf he leans so close that I am in danger of falling into Mr Heart Attack's soup in a bid to escape. I sit there eating the usual mediocre vegetarian option whilst Moo, Bob, Ben and Freya laugh and joke at the other end of the table. Matt should be here to save me from all of this, to make jokes about the letch and promise me a Thai takeaway when we get home. As Mr Heart Attack and Mr Tan drone on, the nagging concern at Matt's reluctance to let me be a part of his life gnaws away at me, chipping away at my big bubble of love. Perhaps he isn't 'the one'. I assumed that when *he* came along there would be no doubts, that we would sail away into the sunset, or at the very least, spend the odd weekend together. *He* would not have let me come on my own today. Would *he*? I disappear to the reception area to phone Matt, to hear the reassurance in his voice, but as if to confirm my worst fears his voice-mail tells me he is unavailable. I leave a message for him to say we need to talk and return for the speeches and cake-cutting. If I wasn't driving, I would also get horribly drunk but that will have to wait until I get home. I ignore

Mr Tan beckoning me over and pull up a chair next to Moo.

'Where is your man?' she whispers as some old fart tells his fifth not very funny golf story. We both laugh weakly in time with the others as the punch line is delivered.

'With the girls,' I whisper back. Moo frowns, and looks at me with a question in her eyes.

'It's Sunday, remember, and Sunday afternoons mean quality time with the girls. They go to the cinema, go swimming, that sort of thing. I think they were going bike riding today, but I'm not sure,' I explain, shaking my head to confirm that I don't understand why this doesn't seem to include me or why he is not here on one of the few occasions when I could really do with him making an exception.

'You need to talk to him,' she suggests and I nod again.

I should be driving home but instead I am travelling in the opposite direction. The anger and hurt that has been building inside me all afternoon is now at boiling point and I am blind to any alternative course of action that would be far more sensible. I arrive outside Matt's house. The lights are on, and I know as I switch the engine off that this is where I should hesitate, turn around and go home to a glass of wine and a good old cry. Now that I am here though, here where he doesn't want me to be, I am overtaken by something that is far from rational. At the back of my mind I know it is probably my time of the month and I am hormonal, but, as always, this is brushed aside in my bid to wreak destruction and cry as many tears as I can every twenty-eight days, because the world is surely against me. I knock on the door and wait. I could turn around now and if I run quickly, he would never know I was here. The door opens and Matt stands there, the shock on his face painfully obvious.

'Maddy?' he asks, as if I am a hallucination.

'Can I come in?' I ask, the brief uncertainty disappearing in a fog of anger that churns inside my stomach like a thousand poisonous snakes.

'Uh yes. Of course you can,' Matt answers, looking bemused. He moves to one side and I try not to look at his face as I step inside. Once in, I falter, suddenly not sure what I am doing here. In my anger, I forgot about the girls. If I continue, I will meet them, which is not the way I want it to be.

'Where are the girls?' I whisper.

'Watching television,' he answers, clearly confused by this sudden turn of events.

I turn around and retrace my steps.

'Maddy?' There are a thousand questions in his voice and I turn to look at him, smiling weakly.

'I'm sorry. I shouldn't have come, but I needed to talk to you. Can you come over in the morning?'

'Of course I can. Maddy, is everything all right?' he asks, touching my arm but tonight I don't want his touch because I feel ready to dissolve.

'I'm fine. I'll talk to you tomorrow,' I respond, and walk away, letting the tears fall as I do.

The next morning I am up and dressed by five, pacing the house, not knowing what to do. Instead of abating, the feeling that I must be honest with myself and say something only increased as I tossed and turned through the night. I cannot eat breakfast, instead I drink water; even my usual morning tea is making me want to throw up. I sit and wait for his knock at the door. It comes at 6.15 a.m. and another wave of sickness drifts over me as I open the door.

'Maddy, what's going on? Are you okay? I tried to ring you last night but you didn't answer the phone. I've been worried,' he says, looking confused.

'I'm okay. Really I am,' I reply, moving away.

'Did something awful happen at your Dad's party?'

'Only that I realised that I am tired of being on my own.'

'I don't understand,' Matt says, and I can see that he clearly doesn't. The snakes wriggle inside and I am angry and hurt all over again. Which part does he not understand?

'I sat there with a boring old fart on one side and a letch on the other, whilst everyone else played happy families. I was the only one there without a partner. Why? Because the man I am supposed to be having a relationship with, the man who says he loves me, is doing everything he can to avoid letting me into his life. He won't let me meet his kids, or make any gesture towards making me feel as if we have a future together.'

'Maddy . . .' he walks towards me but I hold up my hands in protest.

'How do you think that makes me feel, Matt?' My voice breaks with the effort of not crying, but I'm determined not to. I'm going to be strong.

'Maddy, I'm sorry.' We both stand there but I have nothing to say. Sorry doesn't explain or resolve anything.

'Look, we've discussed this and I have tried to explain. It's not black and white, and I have my children to consider.'

'Matt, the last thing I want to do is hurt the girls, but it would be nice to think that you wanted me to at least meet them, that you wanted us to spend the odd Sunday together. We are not sixteen year olds playing games of "don't let each other know how we really feel"; we are two people, who, supposedly, have fallen in love and that doesn't happen every day. Okay, it's happened quickly, but it's happened and I don't want a casual relationship, Matt, I want to be with you; not just today, but pretty much every day and that means I want to build a future where that can happen at some point.' I stop talking and feel relieved that I have at last articulated how I really feel.

Matt looks at me sadly and sits down. He looks at his feet and pushes his hands through his hair, something he always does when he feels uncomfortable, before looking up at me. 'Maddy, you and I are perfect as we are and I don't want that to change. If I'm honest, I'm not sure if our relationship would survive the pressure of you taking on my kids; there's a good chance you would hate it and leave. Then what happens, Maddy? We are left to pick up the pieces and I just don't know whether I can do that again.'

'There are no guarantees in life, Matt.' I am shouting now, hurt by what he has just said. 'Sometimes you have to take risks and go with it, because instead of assuming the worst will happen, it might just turn out to be the best decision you have ever made.'

'Why does it have to change between us?' he asks forlornly.

'Because I don't want this.' I throw my hands up in the air, and shake my head in protest as he looks at me with sad, puppy-dog eyes.

'I don't want to be the secret girlfriend who only gets to see you in stolen moments through the day and on the odd evening. Wow, if I am really lucky, I get to see you on a Saturday night, but I think if my memory serves me correctly, that has happened only once since we met. God, Matt, I might as well be having an affair with a married man and I don't want that. I want to be a part of your, and your children's, lives. Is that so much to ask?' I wait for a response but there isn't one. He stares at the floor as if waiting for it to open up and swallow him and I feel sick, knowing that I have lost the fight. The anger slips away, leaving a faint sense of desperation in its wake and I want to turn the clock back; back to the moment when Matt asked if I was okay, and I would let him kiss my worries away, but that is not going to happen; we have reached the point of no return.

'I love you, Matt, and I want to be with you. I thought you felt the same but as time goes by I'm less sure, which is why I need to feel that you can see an *us* in your future. Christ, I am not asking you to marry me or move in, I'm just asking you to let me into your world a bit more. I want to do the snuggled up and watching a DVD on a Saturday night, the bike ride with the girls. I want to share Sugar and Spice with someone.'

Matt sits there, avoiding my eyes, and doesn't say a thing.

'Matt, if you can't see that with me then you have to let me go and find it with someone else, someone who wants to be with me no matter what. Someone who is not scared of what ifs.'

I know the final blow is going to hurt, but the know-ledge that it is inevitable makes me believe I can cope with it. The tears are there; I can feel them, but they don't fall.

'I'm sorry,' he says to the floor, and I want to scream. LOOK AT ME! I AM STANDING HERE AND I LOVE YOU. I WANT TO BE WITH YOU. NOT

ANYONE ELSE. YOU! JUST GIVE ME SOMETHING, ANYTHING, TO HANG ON TO! I stand there, waiting for him to say something else, but he doesn't. I will him to speak with every fibre of my being; to prove me wrong; to say something that will make all of my fears disappear in a puff of smoke. I want the slipper to fit.

'Sorry for what?' I eventually ask.

'I'm just sorry, Maddy. Sorry I can't give you what you want. Perhaps you're right, I am scared of what ifs but I can't bear the thought of messing the kids' lives up again.'

Despite bracing myself for it, the last blow takes my breath away. A big part of me wants to persuade him that it will be okay, that I will never let him down, that our life would be good together, that I would never leave him . . . I could go on . . . Oh yes, I could fight as if my life depended on it and convince him of all these things, but then I see my father. No, I am done trying to persuade people I am worthy of their love and if he can't see it, if he is willing to lose me, then I have to walk away.

'I think you had better leave,' I say, feeling my whole body deflate, like a balloon at the end of the party. Matt looks at me, and I cannot read his face: anger, fear, hurt or relief? I want to ask him what it is that he feels right now as he stands there looking at me; I want to know. He turns and walks towards the door and it takes all of my strength not to stop him. Instead, I remain fixed to the spot, staring at the door as he closes it.

I sit in a coma-like state for over an hour, waiting for him to phone, but he doesn't and, reluctantly, I start on the orders I have to fill whether I am heartbroken or not. Thank heavens for baking. The hurt that has settled like a dull pain in the pit of my stomach is pushed aside as I focus all of my energy on producing the lightest sponge cake the recipient will have ever tasted. I want them to close their eyes and remember a moment in their lives when everything was good and uncomplicated. I want them to smile and feel the love and care I have folded in along with the flour, to feel what I want for myself more than anything else right now. A lot to ask from a cake? No, I don't think so, and right now, I need to believe.

Thankfully, I have quite a few orders to fill, which prevents me from spending the day just crying my eyes out. The added ingredient of salty tears would, I suspect, not be a good one. I check my mobile a thousand times throughout the day but each time the disappointment shoots painfully through me. That evening, when the tears finally come, I phone Moo.

'Perhaps he needs some space to think about things. He'll ring later,' she tries to reassure me, but I am not to be consoled.

'I thought he was the one,' I blub down the phone, wondering how something could hurt so much.

'Don't give up hope just yet,' she tells me, but I just cry even louder. I have held back all day and now I can't stop but, bless her, she stays and listens, making comforting noises every so often. With puffy eyes, I go to bed early, but the sanctuary of sleep eludes me.

I want to stay in bed and hide beneath the covers, but the tearoom beckons and I reluctantly go through the motions of getting ready. I cannot face breakfast and last approximately five minutes before I look at my mobile. There are no messages, no appearance of a little envelope and my heart sinks. The weather, grey and bleak, matches my mood as I drive to work in a daze, not caring that I am late. Dot can give me her worst and I won't care, but she does and I do, because I want someone to be nice to me, even Dot. Tilly arrives and hugs me when I tell her what has happened, but her reassurances and constant supply of Maltesers cannot lift the cloud of doom and gloom that has settled over me. The rest of the week goes by in a haze of working and baking done on automatic pilot. I don't cry again, but instead move around as if in a sleep walk, feeling numb, tired and sick. My mind replays every single word Matt said, every move of his body, and more than once I consider ringing him, but a little voice in my head stops me. As I hold the phone in my hand, I remember the promise I made myself and stop. If he thinks I'm worth it, he will phone, if not, he wasn't the one. Tired of jumping as the door goes and thinking every man who walks into the tearoom is going to be Matt, I am grateful when Thursday arrives. Tomorrow it is a Sugar and Spice day and then I have the weekend to hide away.

James phones and my planned weekend of healing via crap romantic comedy DVDs and chocolate ice cream is put on hold.

'It's Frog. He's taken a turn for the worse and I think it's time,' he says, his voice breaking.

'Okay, I'm coming over,' I say, and I get my coat. I arrive to find Frog barely there; he cannot get out of his bed to eat and doesn't even notice us. He may go on his own accord, but when? A week? Two weeks? A month? I reluctantly agree that we can't let him suffer any more and I feel strangely numb, unable to feel anything as James cries in my arms. I leave them both asleep on the sofa dreading what tomorrow will bring.

*

The next morning I arrive back at James's, and after stalling with three cups of tea we slowly make our way to the vet. James carries Frog in his arms and we talk in soothing tones as he drifts in and out of consciousness. So far I have been the strong one and have remained calm and pragmatic, but as soon as we get to the vet's door I crumble and I feel my heart break for the second time in a week. Losing Matt and now losing Frog suddenly becomes too much to bear and a strangled voice (it can't be mine) cries out that I can't do it. I begin to sob uncontrollably, my shoulders heaving with the effort of a week's worth of pent-up crying and James has to push me through the door. They say couples without children substitute with animals and Frog has been an integral part of our lives for nearly twelve years. From the time we came back early from holiday because we couldn't bear to think of him in the kennels, confused and frightened; to the weekends in Cornwall trying to persuade him that dogs loved the sea; to telling him he was outnumbered when he stood with his hackles up against thirty beagles from the local hunt. Everybody laughed at his howling when he heard the ice cream van, not stopping until he got a cornet of his very own, and we lost count of the times we rescued him from the local pond when he forgot he couldn't swim. For most of our married life, it was Frog and us against the world, and when I moved out he became a familiar face, sat in the local pub with James, his nose in a packet of crisps and adored by the locals.

We say goodbye to our first baby with soothing words but he barely acknowledges us, tired by what life has thrown at him over the last few months as he drifts away. It was, as the vet had promised us, dignified and calm but I still insist on grabbing his stethoscope to check that he really is gone. I cannot leave him unless I'm sure. It only upsets me more as I secretly hope to hear a heartbeat but instead listen to the sounds of his body giving up. James pulls me away and we wander back, huddled together with eyes swollen. Thankfully I am up to date with the orders, except for the mince pies, but they will have to wait and we spend the rest of the day slumped in front of the TV watching *Finding Nemo*, too exhausted from the tears to do anything else. As we sit there, not really taking it all in, I ask James where the blonde is.

'Bunny Boiler,' he replies.

'Oh,' I answer, as if this explains everything.

'Where's the builder?' he asks.

'Stonemason, actually,' I reply indignantly, quickly adding, 'he's gone.' James nods, as if I, too, have explained all. We are both too tired to enquire any further and gaze at the TV without watching it.

'I knew it would hurt losing him but I wasn't prepared for how much,' James admits into the silence, wiping his eyes of a fresh onset of tears. I hug him and we hold each other close. James is not an overemotional person; his laid-back character means that the small stuff generally goes over his head and the big stuff gets dealt with over a pint with his football buddies. Except for the odd tear at the end of a movie, I have never seen him really cry like this and it breaks my heart. I rub his back and stroke his hair like a mother would a child as he lets it all out.

'Thanks, Maddy. I'm sorry for losing it like this,' he says as I let him go to blow his nose.

'Hey, no need to say sorry. We have just lost our little baby Frog and your best buddy. You're bound to be upset,' I reassure him, wiping my own tears away.

'I'm sorry I wasn't there for you more when you lost

the baby,' he says in a quiet voice as if he isn't sure he should be saying it at all.

I am stunned. This is the first time he has mentioned it since it happened and I don't know what to say, but looking at his red-rimmed eyes and runny nose I realise it doesn't matter. We all deal with things differently and some things touch us more than others. Just because James managed to deal with it at the time and didn't carry the hurt, sadness and confusion around like a big, heavy lump of coal on his back like I did, it shouldn't make him feel guilty. It actually makes me feel sad that I have let it affect me so much, weighing me down so that I forgot to hold my head up high and see the things that were good in my life. It's part of my past, our past, but not of our future, and there I was lecturing Matt! A little ironic!

'As I said, no apologies needed. Now, how about I heat up some home-made butternut squash soup?' I suggest, smiling, and James nods his head forlornly.

Despite not feeling hungry, it tastes surprisingly good and brings some much-needed colour to our cheeks. Later, James falls asleep on the sofa and I cover him with a blanket before going to bed myself.

When James goes home I feel a little lost. Frog was the last fragile link in our weird relationship and I wonder how it will affect us both. At least I don't have to worry what Matt thinks about it any more. I have plenty to do; over four hundred mince pies to add to the three hundred and fifty-seven I have baked already, but any enthusiasm for the task in hand seems to be eluding me. The thirty-five Christmas cakes don't have to be delivered until the end of the month, which is a relief. I half-heartedly begin to make two batches of mince pies with the thought that if I keep myself busy it will stop me thinking about Matt, but it doesn't. I stop what I'm doing and instead gaze out of the window. The sky has no colour to it today; it's as if the blue has been sucked away, leaving a milky greyness in its place. Everything looks stark against it, even the birds that are left to the British winter look black. Although that could be because they are ravens and blackbirds. Not being a bird person, I wouldn't know.

I check my mobile again, just in case, but there is nothing. Face it, Maddy, he hasn't phoned because he doesn't believe in a future with you and as everyone knows, if you don't believe, dreams never come true. I tear myself away from the window and reluctantly get back to my mince pies.

I wonder what he is doing?

I don't care what he is doing.

I hope he is bloody miserable doing whatever he is doing.

With the rest of the afternoon gaping like an open wound in front of me I decide against my better judgement to go Christmas shopping, but it only makes me feel even worse. I am surrounded by hundreds of people: couples holding hands, families waiting to see Father Christmas, all doing normal Sunday things in the run-up to Christmas and I am jealous. God, what is the matter with me? I wouldn't even see him on a Sunday anyway. How can I miss what I have never had?

I miss his ability to make me smile. As another week limps slowly by I find myself getting stressed out about the small stuff. It is the end of the world when I flick the sieve accidentally and a layer of flour covers the kitchen. I am suicidal when I forget the two Christmas cakes in the oven until I smell burning; I scream when the credit card machine gets stuck, and I howl like a baby when I drop a tray of mince pies on the floor.

Working at the tearoom is no better as I constantly look out for him, dreading each time I have to walk through the gardens or take a lunch order to the house. Miraculously, I don't see him but perhaps he is doing his best to avoid me. I am relieved when Thursday comes and I don't have to worry about it for three days.

Following a hectic day of baking four Christmas cakes, decorating fifteen with glazed fruit and nuts, making a whisky cake and wrapping my order for thirty-five ready for the courier tomorrow, I phone Mum. I haven't heard from her for ages and feel guilty at my neglect. She sounds breathless.

'Oh, I've just got in from shopping,' she says when I ask what she's been up to. 'I went with Suzie and ended up spending a fortune in Marks and Spencer. They have a great range of separates now, you know.'

Hello, correct me if I'm wrong, but didn't I suggest this to her months ago and didn't she pooh pooh me? Who is this Suzie, and what has she got that I don't have?

'Suzie?' I ask. Suzie, it appears, bought a piece from the small gallery Mum works in part time, they got talking and, before long, had sparked up a friendship. Suzie is a divorced woman of a certain age and according to Mum looks a little like Marianne Faithfull.

'Suzie has so much energy. She has even persuaded me to start yoga. We're booked on a weekend away to explore our yogic sides in January.'

'Wow, that's great, Mum,' I say, pleased to hear the enthusiasm in her voice but also a little shocked. Mum exploring her yogic side?

'We've also been going to life-drawing lessons, which

is a bit of a giggle, although I haven't quite got the hang of drawing a man's . . . you know . . . his whatsit . . . his willy! I always feel I should overcompensate in case he wants to see what I have drawn.'

I am amazed that Mum has used the word willy. It doesn't sound right coming from the woman who told me on no account should I touch a man's 'bits' before he put a wedding ring on my finger, even if he begged me.

'Suzie really is a breath of fresh air,' Mum coos, and I don't quite know what to say. I'm pleased that she is experiencing a new lease of life, but if I'm totally honest, I'm also a little put out that it wasn't me who effected this change.

'Have you heard from your nice young man?'

'No,' I respond sulkily.

'Why don't you ring him?' she suggests gently.

'No, if he loves me and wants to work something out, then he will contact me,' I tell her vehemently.

'Aaah, *chérie*, have you considered that he might be too scared to? He has been through a rough time and you have to understand his reluctance to jump in with both feet.'

'I do understand, but Mum, I don't want to be with someone who is not one hundred per cent sure about being with me. That's like putting up with margarine instead of butter in your cake mix.' I feel angry at the thought of it all and can feel my heels digging in. This girl is not for turning.

After I finish speaking to Mum I phone Moo and tell her all about Suzie and the possibility that Mum has turned into a lesbian.

I arrive back at work to find Tilly wearing her Christmas fairy outfit under her apron. She has put mistletoe above the trade-entrance door, kissing everyone who comes through, much to the delight of the bread delivery man. As the door goes and Tilly squeals in delight at the next victim, I continue with a batch of fruit cakes and hum. I reason that, if I hum loud enough, it will drown out any thoughts and the less I think, the better. Above the sound of Tilly's excited voice is another, a voice I have replayed in my mind, over and over again, until the tape wore out and I forgot what it sounded like. I stop humming, and hold my breath, not daring to turn around. Perhaps he will go and I won't even have to look at him . . .

He is beside me, so close that I can smell him. He smells just as I remember – clean, of soap and fresh laundry brought in from the washing line. It makes me remember all that I want to forget. I try to concentrate on what I'm doing, but all my senses are reduced to one and I can't see or hear anything; everything is distorted. He stretches in that way I love, like a cat, his shirt lifting slightly to reveal his flat stomach. He has lost weight. My throat tightens and my stomach lurches.

'Hi,' he says.

'Hi,' I reply quietly.

Sensing the tension that has filled the room Tilly interjects and begins to tell him all about my plans for the tearoom as I try to remember what I was doing. Eggs, that's it, I need eggs. Concentrate on the eggs, Maddy.

'How's the business? Have you had the hoped-for Christmas rush?' He is talking to me again. I wish he would just go away and leave me to crumble.

'Good, thanks. I'm getting plenty of orders, which means it's been a bit manic of late but yes, it's good,' I respond, fiddling self-consciously with the tinsel Tilly insisted on putting in my hair.

'I'm glad,' he says, smiling. I wish he wouldn't smile.

He moves from one foot to the other as I continue with my cakes, trying desperately not to look at him but I last all of fifty-six seconds. I look up, we smile at each other and for a brief moment the connection is back. I always loved those little creases around his eyes when he smiled. There is a lump in my throat, constricting my air supply and, fearing I might cry, I turn away, breaking the spell.

'How are the girls?' I ask.

'They're great, thanks,' he answers.

Please go away. This polite conversation is killing me. He reaches over and pinches one of Dot's mince pies. As he does so, his arm brushes mine and the electric shock that jolts through me threatens to stop my heart.

Quick, page Dr Ross from the ER. We're losing her. Emergency CPR and 10mg of something with a long name needed ASAP. Her airways are blocked and she is having difficulty breathing. She needs the kiss of life and quick.

'Mmmmm. Not as good as your mince pies.'

Tell me you can't live without me and I will smother you in mincemeat. I will feed you mince pies for the rest of your life. I will lick the sugar from your lips.

'Well, for twenty-four pounds and ninety-five pence you can order a tin to be delivered in time for Christmas!' I respond and walk away without looking at him. I have no idea of where I am going but I keep on walking because there is a real possibility that I will promise a lifetime of mince pies in exchange for his heart.

MUM'S MINCEMEAT

Forget those horrid, sickly sweet, shop-bought varieties. If you really want to make yourself popular this Christmas then make your own mincemeat. The recipe is Mum's secret one, although I guess it isn't now. I also really like Delia Smith's recipe.

Ingredients

450g (1lb) raisins

450g (1lb) currants

450g (1lb) sultanas

225g (8oz) vegetable suet

450g (1lb) mixed peel – the unchopped version (it's more work but so much nicer)

450g (1lb) apples, cored and chopped

450g (1lb) dark brown sugar

1 grated nutmeg

zest and juice of 2 lemons

300ml (10fl.oz) stout (you can use rum or brandy if you prefer, even Guinness)

Method

Mince all of the ingredients together and spoon in the alcohol. Place in sterilised Kilner jars.

865 mince pies and two Christmas wishes

Eight hundred and sixty-five!! That's how many mince pies I have made so far. Perhaps I should say to hell with it and go for the one-thousand mark. I have also packed thirty tins of mince pies for delivery, decorated twenty-seven Christmas cakes, boxed up twenty ready for delivery on Monday – baked two chocolate cakes and taken orders for four more tins of mince pies and five more Christmas cakes. If that wasn't enough, I have also started to tackle my horrendously frightening but rather comforting to-do list for the tearoom. Staff and wages; then there's health and safety, a till, chairs, tables, baking equipment, wrapping and bags, pictures for the walls, toilets, toilet roll, a cleaner? I place a tick next to toilet rolls. I like to tick things off; it makes me feel in control. Moo has often told me I am a control freak and maybe she is right. She has also suggested that's probably what I found so hard about Matt, the giving over my destiny to someone else. Who knows? I don't need to now. I am good on my own and far, far too busy to think about anything else.

After some begging and reassurances that I still

needed him, Ben has helped me to find some chairs and baking equipment from an auction. He has also delivered some of the chairs to Susan who has agreed to re-upholster them for me. I have chosen some material for the aprons Mum is making, bought the paint, ordered a skip, and arranged for a team of builders to start the conversion from old dilapidated bakery to cosy, trendy, gorgeous tearoom as soon as I move in. With my move date only a couple of weeks away I am also attempting to pack and I feel like Dorothy in *The Wizard of Oz*, caught up in a tornado spinning round and round as boxes, mince pies, ever-increasing to-do lists and cakes whirl around me. Once again, nights out with Lou and Mac are cancelled, as I try to do as much as I can between the hours of six and midnight. I put another tick next to staff and give myself a silent pat on the back. Tilly has asked if she can come and work for me in the tearoom, which will make things easier and a lot more fun, although I'm not sure how Dot will take it so soon after I have handed in my notice. I finally plucked up the courage to do it yesterday but she didn't seem particularly bothered. I did hint at the prospect of me opening a tearoom to which she snorted with disgust, but then later asked me if I wanted the recipe for her special steak and kidney pie. I didn't have the heart to tell her that my fabulous little tearoom will be a place of beautiful, fragrant things and pots of brown lumps that smell of dog food was not really what I had in mind. Feelings of panic and excitement well up inside me as I think about it all, although right now it is the panic that has the edge.

Okay, enough of scary thoughts – I need to get back to my cosy, pastry-encased world and make another batch of mince pies.

Jonathan Ross Interview

'As it's the special Christmas Edition I've brought some mince pies for you tonight, Jonathan.' I hug him, careful not to crush my Armani sequinned sheath in the palest of pinks.

'A little bird tells me that you hold the Guinness World Record for baking mince pies,' he says.

'Yes, gosh, I had forgotten all about that.'

'That's quite impressive. Something else I'm impressed about, other than the obvious . . .'

He looks to the camera and raises his eyebrow. We laugh.

'I'm impressed, ladies and gentlemen, by the way this beautiful woman has continued to build Sugar and Spice into a successful company, despite setbacks and . . . and still finds the time to help others including the recent launch of her Pies for Poverty campaign in all of her tearooms.'

The audience applause makes me blush. Thankfully, it doesn't clash with my dress.

'Yes, all the profits from our mince pies will go towards helping those less fortunate than us. Chris Martin from Coldplay asked me to get involved and I thought this was a nice way of doing it.'

'So, how do you pick yourself up and keep going when things get tough and the tabloids are having a field day?'

'I am very lucky to have a very supportive and loving family behind me, and Jonathan, whatever happens, in the words of Gloria Gaynor, I will survive!'

'I've said it once, but I'll say it again, I'm a huge admirer. You never fail to impress me. What do you think, Mr Williams?'

'I think she's fantastic. I keep asking her for a date, but she keeps turning me down.'

I laugh coquettishly and blush ever so slightly before agreeing to sing 'White Christmas' with Robbie.

The dark, syrupy mixture falls easily from the spoon and I'm reminded of eating mince pies in the sunshine, of Matt popping them into that gorgeous mouth of his, of sugary kisses, of . . . Oh, bugger off! I shout loudly in a bid to drown the thoughts away but it doesn't work. Whoever said that time heals is a big fat liar because, whenever I hear 'Fairytale of New York' on the radio, I hear Matt's voice singing it instead, and I'm lost.

The sound of the door makes me jump and I open it to find Tilly standing there, beaming. She hugs me tightly and wanders in to survey the mountain of packing crates that now litter the floor. Wandering around, she picks things up and puts them down again as if she is looking for a gift in a shop. Quickly bored with the contents of my packing crates, Tilly settles herself down on the sofa and begins flicking through the *Heat* magazine she has brought with her.

'I saw Matt again the other day and he asked about you.'

'Oh,' I reply, trying desperately not to ask what he said. Yeah, like that's going to happen! 'So what did he say?' I ask as nonchalantly as I can.

'He wanted to know if you were okay. You don't have to worry, though. I said that you were.'

'Thanks, Tilly . . . So did he say anything else?' I can't help asking.

'No, not really,' she says and I'm disappointed. I try to concentrate on the mince pies I'm making but the little fork holes I've been making on the tops now look more like multiple stab wounds.

'So, changing the subject, how is your love life?' I ask her as I pop the pies into the oven and return to the task of wrapping all of my photo frames. I'm nearly all packed up and ready to go and the house looks empty and forlorn without my treasures around.

'Not good. Bobby and I split up but it doesn't matter, he wasn't the one . . . anyway, forget about Matt and Bobby. Where is your computer?' Tilly jumps up and, puzzled, I take her upstairs to the spare room. She settles herself down and my heart sinks as she logs on to a dating website.

'No, Tilly!' I say immediately.

'It will be great – we could have so much fun.'

'No!'

'Don't write it off just yet. Just take a look at some of the guys on here. Okay, there are couple of weirdos, but some of them sound really nice.'

I look at her as if she has lost her marbles but she is already flicking through a dubious gallery of photos and descriptions.

'Tilly, I'm not doing Internet dating. For one thing I'm far too busy, and secondly, I'm not desperate for a man. I am okay on my own.'

She looks at me like a puppy dog who has had her ball taken away.

I head back downstairs to check on the mince pies before I ram the keyboard down on her fingers. She follows me down and hovers around the still cooling mince pies.

'You can have one if you want.'

Tilly doesn't need telling twice. She removes the top and a little puff of steam pops out. The smell is gorgeous and I can't resist taking one for myself, and then we have another one each, just to check consistency of quality and taste.

When Tilly eventually leaves, I resume packing. In a couple of weeks' time, I shall be in the flat above the tearoom, trying to find places for all my possessions in the small living/kitchen area, tiny bedroom and even tinier bathroom. The thought of not fitting everything in makes me panic a little but doesn't dampen the excitement I feel. I picture myself as a Holly Golightly-type character living in a gorgeous eclectic mess of possessions, my little silver pots of herbs on the window sill, a fake crystal chandelier, books piled high on the floor, my sheepskin rug and a disgustingly expensive purple silk bedspread. Fabulous, daaaaaahling.

Packing, baking, tearoom ... baking, tearoom and packing ... this is my life now. I am too busy to think about anything else and have so far resisted Tilly's attempts at getting me to agree to a double date with some twin brothers. As I begin to pack the last bits and pieces, I come across my photo albums and begin to flick through them, reliving memories of me. There are no photos of Matt and me. Soon I will forget what he looks like and then I can move on.

The phone rings and I pick it up, trying to rub some life back into my right leg which has gone numb from sitting on the floor.

'Ms Brown, it's Geoffrey from Castle and Mays Estate Agents.'

'Oh, hello,' I answer brightly, 'I'm just packing the last of my stuff.'

'I'm sorry to have to tell you this, but we have a problem,' Geoffrey says in his peculiar nasally voice. My heart hits the floor before bouncing up again, causing my stomach to do a somersault.

'What sort of problem?' I ask slowly.

'The current owner of the tearoom, Mrs Hazelwood, has just contacted me. I'm afraid she has pulled out.'

'I don't understand. We were about to exchange.'

'I'm sorry, Ms Brown, but it appears she has had a change of heart at the last minute.'

'But why would she do that?' I ask, unable to comprehend what he has just told me. I look around the room at all of the boxes I have spent the last few weeks filling and panic sets in. 'She can't!'

'I'm afraid, Ms Brown, she can. I'll let your solicitors know and we can set about looking for other properties for you.'

'But I don't want somewhere else.'

'I'm sorry, there is nothing more I can do,' Geoffrey responds, his flat monotone voice revealing a lifetime of rolling on his back and giving up. He's sorry! That's not good enough. I want to storm over there and kick his sorry fat arse. Confused and angry, I put the phone down and sit on one of the boxes. There is a cracking sound as my weight hits something breakable but I don't care. I've lost my little tearoom. What the hell do I do now? I want to cry, scream, throw mince pies around the room, but instead I just sit there feeling utterly lost and helpless as I watch my dream float away. Ben would know what to do. I pick up the phone but then remember about standing on my own two feet and put it down again. I shout every obscenity known to man, kick a box and nearly break my toe before promptly bursting into tears. I blub, howl and weep for the loss of my bright shiny dream world where I was happy and successful, and then I blub, howl and weep a bit more for falling in love with someone who didn't want to inhabit that world with me. See what happens when you watch too many romantic comedies. I'm not Audrey Hepburn, Sarah Jessica Parker or Meg Ryan; I am stupid, naïve and have crap hair and I should have known better. Exhausted, and because I can't see out of my eyes because they are so swollen, I drink half a bottle of wine, three huge glasses of brandy and eat four mince pies before stumbling into bed. At 3.35 a.m., I have my head down the toilet bowl and am praying for mercy.

The next day even my trusted Clarins Beauty Flash Balm and Eye Revive Beauty Flash cannot hide the effects of yesterday. I look and feel dreadful. I park the van and check my reflection in the mirror, but the unforgiving natural light only magnifies the grey pallor of my skin and my eyes are slits peering out from swollen red lids. There is no way I can walk into the tearoom like this. Dot has some useful contacts for industrial mixers and I have arranged to pop in. Oh God, Dot hates it when people cancel. Okay, it may be the middle of December but there is only one thing for it: sunglasses, and if Kate Moss can get away with it, then so can I.

'Bob!' a voice calls out as a dog heads towards me. He enthusiastically jumps up, eager to be petted.

'Hey you,' I say, ruffling his head.

'Bob, come here. Sorry about that.' A man with a nasal voice and a donkey bray for a laugh appears. He grabs the dog and pulls him away.

'It's okay,' I say, and he smiles. If he thinks that I am

odd wearing sunglasses when the day is struggling for light, he doesn't let on. I turn, eager to get going, and the world stops mid axis. I lose the ability to breathe, to think, to run. When I was younger, I would have panic attacks before a maths test. Now, I am looking at the sum I will never have an answer to. Matt walks towards me and there is nowhere to hide. Oh my God. Please no. Not today.

Breathe. . .

Breathe.

'Are you okay?' the man asks me as the air kicks in and I begin to choke. For some reason known only to him, he decides to ignore the fact that I nod and wave my hand away, in what I assumed was the internationally recognised sign of 'Yes, I am okay, so just bugger off and leave me alone to attempt to recover in my own time'. Instead, he thinks it would be a good idea to play the hero and jumps behind me, wrapping his arms around my ribs. He nearly breaks them in the process as he squeezes hard and does a rather disturbing jerking action.

'What the . . .' I splutter.

'Heimlich manoeuvre. Learnt it in the territorial army,' he tells me proudly as I cough and spit on his shoes.

'Is everything okay, Maddy?' Matt is standing next to us and I'm not sure if it is amusement or real concern on his face.

'Yes, thanks,' I mutter, trying to banish the force-fifty blush. 'My friend here was demonstrating his army skills.' Matt nods and smiles at the man. He looks tired but lovely.

'You have a minder now? And the sunglasses? Presumably you're wearing them to fool the paparazzi?'

Bastard can still make me smile. Life is so unfair.

'Well, emergency successfully averted,' the man says through his nose, but both Matt and I ignore him. Matt is looking at me intently as if he is trying to burn his way through my glasses, straight into my soul. I look back at him defiantly.

'Well, it was nice to see you,' I say, making a move to walk away.

'Tilly tells me you are moving into the tearoom soon,' he says, with no intention of letting me go.

'Well, no, actually. The owner, Mrs Hazelwood, pulled out yesterday, so it's all off. I have no idea why she had second thoughts, but there you go,' I reply, not entirely sure why I'm telling him all of this.

'That's a real shame,' he replies. 'What are you going to do?'

'I've no idea, but I'm sure I will think of something,' I reply, agitated. I don't want to talk about this with him. 'Anyway, I have to go,' I say and begin to walk away without a backward glance.

As Dot talks about suppliers, my mind drifts off. It is full of Matt, and what has just happened: the way he spoke, the way he smiled, the way he ran his fingers through his hair, the way he made me so bloody angry, the way my stomach still lurched at the sight of him. When I emerge, it is already dark, which means I can take my sunglasses off. The roads are busy with people on their way home, or heading into town for some last-minute Christmas shopping and I accept that it's going to be a long journey home. My progress is slow, and as headlights flash past me, I find my concentration drifting off with thoughts of the past and the future. I remember the dreams I once harboured of Matt and the girls being part of the tearoom and Sugar and Spice. I have to let go of one part of that dream, but the tearoom? How can I let that go? I want it more than anything . . . Well, Maddy, do something about it, I say out loud. And slam my hand down on the steering wheel. Hell, I am now a strong, successful businesswoman and I should be fighting for what I want, not collapsing into a heap and crying about it.

When I get in, I ring Geoffrey from the estate agents and then Mrs Hazelwood. She agrees to see me tomorrow.

Mrs Hazelwood is smaller than I remember. She always looked larger than life behind the counter of the tearoom but now she looks as if someone has sucked the air out of her. With grey, short curly hair and eyes the colour of the large emerald she wears on her finger, her shoulders are stooped slightly and there is a slight tremor to her hands.

'I brought cake,' I say, carefully handing her a Christmas cake decorated with glazed cherries, almonds, pecans and apricot. It looks like a bejewelled crown.

She is charmingly gracious and serves tea in floral china cups and saucers with three slices of cake on a matching plate. So who has the third slice? Without prompting, she tells me all about her husband George. They ran the bakery for thirty-five years and had three children before he succumbed to lung cancer last year. She is clearly still devastated. She reminds me of a small child who has lost her way and I get the urge to hug her.

'I am so sorry, Mrs Hazelwood,' I say, knowing the words probably mean nothing to her.

'I presume you want to know why I pulled out of the sale?' she asks, taking a bite of her cake. 'Mmmmm, that's very nice, dear. Very nice.'

'Thank you,' I reply, taking a bite. Maybe a touch more alchohol? 'Mrs Hazelwood, I'm sure you have your reasons for making the decision you have, but I would be lying if I said I wasn't disappointed. The tearoom was my dream, as it was yours.'

We talk then of the highs and lows of her life in the bakery, of her children, of how she misses her husband and feels lost without the daily routine. I tell her about cooking with Mum as a child, of setting up the business and the plans I had, of fairy cakes, floral aprons and comfy chairs. It is a pleasant hour and I feel guilty for thinking that I could change her mind with a slice of cake.

'This really is lovely. I would love the recipe,' she says and I puff up with pride. From someone who has spent her life baking, it is a real compliment.

'I'll pop it round,' I tell her before getting up to leave, and then a thought occurs to me. 'I don't suppose you would be interested in helping me with the baking when I get busy?' I ask, and her face brightens.

'Of course I can, dear. I would love to. Just give me a ring when you need me.'

'That's great. Well, I had better get back to my mince pies. Thank you for the tea,' I say and wander back down the high street as she watches me from the door. I turn to wave and she waves back. Well, I tried, and I may have lost the tearoom but there will be another one, somewhere else, and I will make it fabulous. Anyway, I have gained someone who can help me in the future, which, if things keep going the way they are, is a godsend. Onwards and upwards, Maddy Brown.

I wander back home with the Christmas lights twinkling above me and I wonder if I will find a beloved George? Children rush past excitedly on their way to see

Father Christmas who is holding court in the market square and my thoughts turn to Matt and the girls. The wind bites at my face and gloveless hands and I shiver, increasing my step. Turning the corner, I can't help but hover in front of the tearoom. The sold sign is still there and I peer in through the dusty windows hoping for a Christmas miracle of little fairies and elves lining a shiny new counter with my cakes but it's too dark to see anything and I drag myself away. I wander past houses with their Christmas trees twinkling in the windows and the sadness overwhelms me as I imagine families gathered around choosing their favourite decorations. The fact that I miss Matt, the tearoom has fallen through and I may soon be homeless is suddenly nothing compared to the despair I feel at not having a Christmas tree. I break into a run towards Harry Willis, the florist who is just packing away for the evening.

'Is it too late to buy a tree?' I pant.

After ripping open numerous boxes I eventually find my Christmas decorations and set to work transforming my sad little world to one full of magic. Exhausted from the events of the last few days I am looking forward to a Saturday night of vegging in front of the TV and my now twinkling fairy lights. As I pour myself what can only be considered a jug of wine the phone rings and as always my heart does a leap, but it is Mac to check that I am still in the land of the living.

'I am unusually dateless tonight and I wondered if you fancied a drink?'

I decline, and confirm that I am slowly fading away; soon to be found buried under a thousand mince pies. Much to my delight, though, Mac arrives half an hour later with a huge bag of Maltesers and some Baileys miniatures, and we cuddle up on the sofa to watch *It's a Wonderful Life*.

'Did you think Matt was the one?' Mac asks me, and I nod forlornly.

'What about you, Mac? Do you think you will ever find the one?' I ask, and he smiles that gorgeous smile that gets all the girls in a tizzy.

'Eventually, yeah, but I'm quite enjoying the search at the moment.'

My bottom lip quivers with the thought of Matt going out with other girls in his search for the perfect one. Noticing that I am near to tears, Mac does what any male does in this kind of situation and panics. He looks around the room in uncomfortable desperation.

'Ice cream! We need ice cream,' he declares suddenly, and I clap my hands in agreement as he brings out the Ben and Jerry's Chocolate Fudge Ice Cream from my freezer and sprinkles Maltesers and the dregs of the Baileys on top. A thousand-calorie fix to mend a broken heart.

As we scrape the last bits from the tub, Mac receives a text promising a night of passion with a Latin lovely called Petra and I tell him to get his pert little arse out of here.

'Are you sure?' he asks, looking guilty.

'Of course; I'm shattered, and could do with going to bed early. Here,' I say, handing him his present of a Christmas cake. With a hug, he leaves me drunkenly hanging the empty Baileys miniatures on my tree before heading upstairs to bed, the fairy lights on my tree still twinkling in the corner of the room.

I open my bedroom window into a clear star-filled night.

'Father Christmas, if you are there and listening, I

know it's a little greedy, but there are two things I want this Christmas. If you do this, I promise, cross my heart, not to ask for anything next year!'

The phone call comes just as I am making, yes, you guessed it, some more mince pies and putting off making the phone call to Ben. The one where I say a pathetic, 'What am I going to do?' I pick it up with floury hands to the dulcet tones of Geoffrey the estate agent.

'Ms Brown, I've just had an unexpected phone call from Mrs Hazelwood. I am pleased to say that the tearoom is yours again if you want it?'

'Oh my God! Yes, of course I do. What? Wow! What happened to change her mind?' I ask, barely able to contain my excitement.

'Mrs Hazelwood was reticent about cutting the last links to her husband and hated the thought of the bakery being turned into a Starbucks of sorts. Now, though, it seems she has had a change of heart. She liked you and the plans you had for the tearoom.'

'That's fantastic.'

'So we are all set for an exchange of contracts early next week.'

'Thank you, Geoffrey,' I say and dance around the room, flicking flour as I go.

MINCE PIES

Ingredients for the pastry

200g (8oz) plain flour
140g (5oz) butter, chopped
  into small pieces

grated zest of an orange
50g (2oz) caster sugar
1 egg yolk

Method

Using a food processor, or your hands, combine the flour, butter, orange zest and sugar until they form crumbs. Add the egg yolk and a teaspoon of cold water and mix into a dough. Wrap in a plastic bag and chill in the fridge for 30 minutes.

For the mince pies

Preheat the oven to 200°C/400°F/gas mark 6. Grease pie tins. Roll out the dough and cut as many 7.5cm (3 inch) rounds as you need (this is approximate – you can gauge your own needs depending on the cutters and baking tins you are using). Put a heaped teaspoon of mincemeat in each pastry case. Cut out smaller rounds to form the tops or use a star-shaped pastry cutter instead. Cover the pies with the tops and brush with milk. Bake for approximately 20 minutes until the pastry is golden – remove to cool and sprinkle with icing sugar when ready to serve.

Mix all the ingredients together...

What hides in the bakery at Christmas?
Mince spies!

It's barely 9 a.m., Christmas Eve, but I still eat the mini bag of Maltesers that lies behind the picture of Santa flying through the air. With the last of my Christmas cakes winging their way to different parts of the UK, I spend the morning making last-minute deliveries of mince pies. Exhausted, I get home and pop a message on the Sugar and Spice answer machine and website to say no more orders will be processed until the third week of January. I breathe a huge sigh of relief. I got through it! Only just, but I did it, and it feels fantastic. I am off to Suffolk to spend Christmas with Moo, Bob and The Bear and I can't wait. The prospect of a Christmas without Matt has been depressing but I know The Bear will take my mind off things. I have half an hour before Mum picks me up and I take the opportunity of popping round to what will soon be the Sugar and Spice tearoom.

The builders and painters who made a start on things last week have finished for Christmas and there are still pots of paint everywhere, but the main walls are now painted in an old-fashioned cream, which has turned it from grubby and tired to clean and chic. One of the walls will soon be covered in a vintage-style wallpaper of cream, muted pale greens and rose pink, and after a thorough clean and a lick of paint the counter will be as good as new. I stand behind it, trying to imagine serving people, and it makes me laugh. The aromas of sugar, cinnamon, lemon, coffee and chocolate invade my imagination as I visualise the cakes lining the counter and the sound of a coffee machine in the background. I feel a rush of pride and excitement. I am going to have my very own tearoom. How fabulous is that?

My mobile goes. It's Mum, probably ringing to say she is going to be late, bless her. She has been here a million times but still manages to get lost.

'Are you okay?' I ask.

'You're not going to believe it, my darling, but this morning I strained my Achilles tendon which means I'm not able to drive. I've just got back from the hospital. I'm afraid I'm going to have to miss out on Christmas with you all. I've been trying to ring you all morning but you've been out.'

'Oh no! You poor thing. You can't spend Christmas on your own. I'll come to you. Moo won't mind,' I suggest, trying to banish the thought of her watching *Only Fools and Horses* on her own tomorrow.

'What a lovely thought, thank you, but Suzie and a couple of the girls are coming over with food and damson gin to console me. We're going to have a Christmas picnic, so no need to worry.'

Girls? These women are in their sixties, for heaven's

sake, and unless I'm very much mistaken, Mum doesn't sound disappointed at all at the prospect of missing Christmas with us.

'Darling, I would love to chat but I really must dash. I'm on my way out to an afternoon carol concert with Suzie. She has managed to find me some crutches from somewhere. You must meet her soon. You are going to absolutely adore her. Give my love to everyone. *Mwah mwah,*' she sings out, blowing kisses down the phone. My mother has not only turned into a lesbian but one that sounds like Joan Collins.

I arrive at Moo's tired from my unexpected drive and am immediately rushed into the living room for a restorative cuddle from The Bear. Moo runs around, refusing to let me lift a finger, despite my protests. Being a full-time mum obviously suits her and she looks fabulous, bringing in a constant supply of home-baked goodies. Whilst she sings along to Bing in the kitchen and Bob does some last-minute Christmas gift shopping, The Bear and I snuggle up on the sofa to watch *The Snowman.* I wonder if I will get what I want for Christmas? The big fat guy in the red suit did grant one of my wishes, and you never know, he might just come up trumps and grant the second one tomorrow.

We spend Christmas Day eating lots and doing very little, which unfortunately gives me too much time to wonder what Matt is doing. I check my mobile more times than I need to and each time my heart breaks just a little more. Is he missing me, or is he snuggled up with someone gorgeous with no expectations? As the day draws to a close I look out of the window and stick the V sign up at the sky, hoping Father Christmas will see it on his way home.

*

With Christmas over with there is plenty to keep me busy with the tearoom and getting ready for the party I am now hosting there on New Year's Eve. What in heaven's name prompted me to come up with that idea? Actually, come to think of it, the party wasn't my idea, it was Lou's, but she did it in such a way that I thought it was mine. James brings over the tea chests he has managed to find for people to sit on, Ben strings white fairy lights everywhere, and Freya helps me give the place a thorough clean. The glow that seems to surround her constantly like some kind of golden halo is a little dull at the edges and she looks as tired as I do. She even has a spot! Does it make me a bad person to feel pleased that she is human like the rest of us and for once doesn't look like Claudia Schiffer's twin sister?

The Princess helps by hoovering everywhere with her toy Hoover, and Lou wafts in and out most days threatening to help, but instead manages to divert my attention away with an on-the-spot manicure and a shopping trip for an outfit. With a massive checklist of things to do in the tearoom this could have been potentially annoying, but instead I find it a real tonic and allow myself to be turned from a miserable, tired-looking old bag into somebody who looks half decent, even if I do say so myself.

I am currently staying in Ben and Freya's spare room, living out of a suitcase with half my possessions in their garage and the other half here whilst I paint the flat. The builders are back next week and I have until the third week of January before I accept any more cake orders, which is not ideal, but until the tearoom kitchen is finished, I don't really have a choice. Freya has been a complete angel and has offered hers for baking in if things are not done in time. The next morning I can't help but overhear her being sick in the bathroom. I am not sure whether to say anything but over breakfast, as The Princess tucks into her yoghurt and watches a green and purple striped thing that looks like a cross between a hippo and an anteater on TV, I ask her if she is okay. I'm amazed to see there are tears in her eyes. I don't think I have ever seen Freya cry; displays of public emotion are just not her style and her pragmatic approach to the miscarriage I initially found hard to deal with. Later, though, I concluded that people deal with things differently and actually it's a godsend to have someone like that around. Three overemotional women in one family is more than enough.

'You're pregnant again, aren't you?' I ask, and she nods, a huge smile spreading across her face before she bursts into tears. Even her crying is delicate and restrained, not like my blubbing and wailing. I bet she doesn't even get a red nose.

'Is there a problem?' I ask, my heart missing a beat.

'No, no, I'm crying because I'm happy. Really I am. It's a girl.' She smiles, wiping her tears away and I give her a hug.

'Congratulations. That's wonderful news,' I say and smile, because it is. A few months ago it probably would have plunged me into despair, but today it doesn't, and I am reminded again of how different things are to how they were a year ago. It also crosses my mind that the new baby will be another female for Ben to look after, which means, hopefully, he will be far too busy to worry about me!

Later, as I head over for another day painting the flat, I can't help wondering if I will ever experience that wonderful moment when that little blue line shifts your world completely, turning it on its head and changing you for ever. Well, never say never. Anything can happen in the space of twenty-four hours as the past year has shown me and, who knows, tomorrow I may meet the man of my dreams who will adore me and my perfect chocolate cake. Talking of which, I think I may have found THE recipe and plan to make it for the New Year's Eve party tomorrow night. I open the tearoom door to a pile of redirected post. There is a copy of *Gorgeous* magazine with a compliments slip from the editor telling me the page to find the article on and I open the page entitled, 'The Day I Changed My Life'. As per usual, my photo is dreadful, but the website details are in there, which can't be bad. As I read it through, I cringe, wondering if I really did say all of those things:

'I got up one morning, and thought, what am I doing here? You only get one chance and instead of breathlessly trying to remain on the treadmill of life whilst somebody else increases the gradient, I should be out there making cakes. So I swapped my power suits for an apron and would encourage anyone to do the same. Well, not an apron, necessarily, but follow your heart and make a change in your life.'

Oh dear.

But hey! I'm in a magazine! A year on, and I am who I wanted to be!

The fairy lights twinkle nearly as brightly as my silver-sequinned scarf and my gorgeous silver hoovering shoes.

My hair has been carefully tonged into long, loose curls, and I am wearing a black chiffon black v-neck top that keeps threatening to show my cleavage. Feeling a little self-conscious about the push-up bra that threatens to launch my boobs into hyperspace, I keep hiking it up. As gorgeous as I feel tonight I am not the belle of the ball; that honour goes to Lou who is looking fabulous in a black dress that looks as if it has been sprayed on and gravity-defying black stilettos with silver-tipped heels. I smile as Carl winks at me and looks on proudly as she works the room and does that air-kissing thing that only she can get away with.

As everyone chats away noisily, drinking champagne from mismatched floral teacups and eating the fairy cakes decorated with white icing and edible silver dust, I think back to last year and how different things were. Soon I will be moving into the flat above and I have already treated myself to a satin bedspread the colour of damson jam that will go perfectly with my planned shabby chic Parisian-type décor. It will be the perfect single, successful girly pad. An image of Matt pops into my head but I hum loudly to banish it away. Surely he can't be the only man in the world who kisses like that, who has eyes I could melt into, who smells that good, who . . . Stop! It is the extra special something that makes a good cake: the quantity of fruit in the jam of a Victoria sandwich, the touch of Amaretto in a simnel cake or the insistence of seventy-five per cent dark chocolate in a chocolate cake. These are the things that set a cake apart from being just good to an absolutely delicious 'Oh, go on, one more slice then'. I have reached the conclusion that love is a bit like that too and one should never compromise in either. If Matt is happy to live without that essential ingredient in his life, then he clearly wasn't for me. It's over, but all is not lost, because at long last I have found the perfect chocolate cake recipe, which means *he* will not be far behind. That's the theory, anyway.

James walks over and kisses me on the cheek.

'I didn't think you could make it?' I ask, surprised to see him. Since Frog died, we haven't seen much of each other.

'I wanted to drop in and wish you a Happy New Year,' he says, and shyly waves to a girl standing by the door.

'Who is that gorgeous-looking lady?' I ask, intrigued.

'That's Caitlin,' he says, with a dreamy, faraway look in his eyes.

'But she's not a blonde,' I say, amazed.

'Mmmmm, I know . . .' he says almost bashfully. 'Anyway, gotta go, Happy New Year, babe,' James says, and plants another kiss on my cheek before disappearing with the beautiful Caitlin.

I wander around; chatting and making sure everyone has enough champagne as Frank Sinatra croons in the background. Moo and Freya are talking sleep routines and worrying about The Princess and The Bear who are being looked after by Freya's more-than-capable mother. Ben is trying to persuade Mac to swap his car for something a little more macho and less hairdresser whilst Bob prepares for the magic show he will perform later. The finale is a closely guarded secret, but I do know that there has been a lot of rehearsing over the last few weeks and it involves Moo in a box! Mum is flitting around the room as much as she can on crutches, looking lovely in an aubergine top, matching velvet scarf and black trousers. She is laughing and talking to everyone – including, much to our collective shock, Dad, although I suspect she is more than a little tipsy. Dad looks like a member of the Mafia, standing there nursing a large brandy in his black shirt and jacket and it makes me smile. I wander over and, standing on my tiptoes, reach up and plant a kiss on his cheek.

'What was that for?' he blusters as if I have just broken his arm instead. He touches his cheek and I want to reassure him my saliva is not acid based.

'Just because,' I say, because I am not sure myself. 'Because I love you,' I venture.

'Well . . . that's very nice. Thank you,' he replies and I can see by the way he takes a swig of his brandy that I have made him uncomfortable. I wait expectantly for him to reciprocate but there is just an awkward silence.

'Well done with the business. Ben tells me you're doing really well,' he eventually says and I nod, knowing that this is as near as I am going to get.

Ben appears and gives me a hug.

'All right, mate?'

'Yeah, I'm good. Still can't quite believe the tearoom is happening, though,' I admit.

'You've done good, Sis. You do know how proud I am of you, don't you?' he asks and I nod, hugging him close.

'Hey, you've lost weight,' I observe.

'Yes. It's those bloody horrible healthy muffins Freya is insisting I eat. She's banned biscuits from the house.'

'You look good on it.' I playfully tap him on the stomach. 'And I hear congratulations are in order.'

Ben beams a smile so wide I want to keep it as a snapshot for ever, to be taken out on rainy days. He nods and looks over at his wife with a proud smile, and she blows him a kiss. I squeeze him tight, because right now the love and happiness I feel for my little baby Battenberg brother is bringing a lump to my throat. Before I get the opportunity to become overemotional, Moo comes crashing in and pulls us apart.

'It's eleven forty-five. I think you should say a few words and make a toast,' she suggests and I surprise myself by agreeing.

'Looking good,' Ben comments and Moo does a little twirl. She looks beautiful tonight; her old flamboyance and chutzpah is still there but in a more understated, sexy way with a sparkly pale pink top, diamante drop earrings and jeans that hug her newly slim figure. Her hair has been styled in a complicated chignon thing at the back with strands that fall sexily around her face.

'How did you get your hair like that? It looks fantastic,' I ask as she drags me to the middle of the room. She taps the side of her nose and smiles enigmatically at me.

'You've been taking secret lessons from Freya, haven't you?' I accuse and she nods, causing us both to laugh aloud and everyone to look around. I try to regain my composure as she bangs a teaspoon on a cup and urges everyone to be quiet. I look at the smiling faces surrounding me and I smile back. For once I don't feel nervous and the expected blush is nowhere to be seen because this morning, when I looked in the mirror, I didn't need to tell myself that I was fabulous and gorgeous, I felt it.

Vogue cover and double-page spread

Maddy Brown of Sugar and Spice hosts a tea party with her friends: Kate Moss, the Arctic Monkeys, Lily Allen, Michael Buble, Sienna Miller, Ricky from the Kaiser Chiefs, Kanye West, Stella McCartney, Ray Winstone.'

Maddy Brown, the woman who brought us Sugar and Spice, is one of the most down-to-earth people we have met. Whilst others came with personal assistants for the photo shoot, Maddy came on her own. She is funny, intelligent and naturally beautiful, with perfect skin and glossy hair. We asked her if she thought she had found the perfect recipe for success.

'I don't think there is one, to be quite honest. One thing I have learnt, though, is that in any recipe, you can't go wrong with a generous helping of love and kisses, some non-stick cake tins . . . and always use good quality chocolate.'

As the chimes from Big Ben ring out from the radio, there is a knock on the door. Moo nudges me.

'You had better answer it. I think it might be *him*!'

I walk as if in slow motion to the door. Two little faces are pressed up against the glass, their eyes wide . . . and blue . . . just like their father's.

I open the door.

'What took you so long? I made a chocolate cake.'

THE BEST CHOCOLATE CAKE EVER

There are hundreds of chocolate cake recipes out there and, believe me, I have tried most of them. Depending on how you like your chocolate, you may disagree that this is the best ever, but all I can say is that it worked for me!

Ingredients

175g (6oz) butter

175g (6oz) caster sugar

2 large eggs

five heaped tablespoons of best quality cocoa powder (I always use Green & Black's)

175ml (6 fl.oz) milk

225g (8oz) plain flour and 1½ teaspoons bicarbonate of soda, sieved together

125g (5oz) good quality 75 per cent minimum plain chocolate, broken into chunks

Method

Line a 18cm (7 inch) tin and heat oven to 180°C/350°F/gas mark 4. Cream the butter and sugar until light and fluffy. Beat in eggs. In a separate bowl, mix the cocoa and half of the milk to create a smooth paste. Add the rest of the milk to form a runny liquid. Stir in half the flour then half cocoa mixture. Repeat. Sprinkle chocolate chunks on to the top of the cake. Bake in the oven for 1½ hours.

Pick up a *little black dress* – it's a girl thing.

978 0 7553 3746 0

IT MUST BE LOVE
Rachel Gibson
PB £4.99

Gabrielle Breedlove is the sexiest suspect that undercover cop Joe Shanahan has ever had the pleasure of tailing. But when he's assigned to pose as her boyfriend things start to get complicated.

She thinks he's stalking her. He thinks she's a crook. Surely, it must be love?

ONE NIGHT STAND
Julie Cohen
PB £4.99

When popular novelist Estelle Connor finds herself pregnant after an uncharacteristic one-night stand, she enlists the help of sexy neighbour Hugh to help look for the father. But will she find what she really needs?

One of the freshest and funniest voices in romantic fiction

978 0 7553 3483 4

Pick up a *little black dress* – it's a girl thing.

ACCIDENTALLY ENGAGED
Mary Carter
PB £4.99

Clair Ivars' flair for reading tarot cards deserts her when predicting her own future, and somehow she finds herself accidentally engaged to a stranger. What else have the cards forgotten to mention?

978 0 7553 3533 6

Mary Carter's crazily romantic novel will ensure you'll never dare doubt a fortune-teller again . . .

I TAKE THIS MAN
Valerie Frankel
PB £4.99

When Penny Bracket is jilted at the altar by Bram Shiraz, her mother decides to help out by locking him up in the attic. And Penny has some serious questions for her fugitive groom . . .

'Glib and funny, Frankel's always wickedly entertaining' *People* magazine

978 0 7553 3675 3

You can buy any of these other
Little Black Dress titles from your
bookshop or *direct from the publisher*.

FREE P&P AND UK DELIVERY
(Overseas and Ireland £3.50 per book)

TO ORDER SIMPLY CALL THIS NUMBER

01235 400 414

or visit our website: www.headline.co.uk

Prices and availability subject to change without notice.